NICE GIRL DOES NOIR
A Collection of Short Stories

by

Libby Fischer Hellmann

PRAISE FOR THE WORK OF LIBBY FISCHER HELLMANN

The Ellie Foreman Series

"Libby Fischer Hellmann has already joined an elite club: Chicago mystery writers who not only inhabit the environment but also give it a unique flavor... her series continues in fine style... (Ellie)... lights up the page with courage and energy."—*Chicago Tribune*

"Not only has Hellmann created a compelling group of believable characters, but the mystery she places them in is likewise plausible and engrossing. Highly recommended, even if you don't live in Illinois."—*David Montgomery, Chicago Sun-Times*

"A masterful blend of politics, history, and suspense... sharp humor and vivid language... Ellie is an engaging amateur sleuth." —*Publishers Weekly*

The Georgia Davis Series

"Hellmann brings to life the reality of hazing and bullying among teenage girls in a story with enough twists and turns to keep you reading to the end. Highly recommended."—*Library Journal* (starred review)

"There's a new no-nonsense female private detective in town: Georgia Davis, a former cop who is tough and smart enough to give even the legendary V.I. Warshawski a run for her money...Hellmann knows how to distill the essence of a character in a few unadorned but dead-right sentences."—*Chicago Tribune*

"Just what's needed in a mystery...Depth of characterization sets this new entry apart from a crowded field."—*Kirkus Reviews*

Chicago Blues

"This classy anthology of mostly original short stories from 21 renowned Windy City authors blends the blues, crime and Chicago, quite surpassing Akashic's recent *Chicago Noir*... This impressive volume has soul, grit and plenty of high notes." -- *Publishers Weekly*

"Twenty-one excellent reasons stay out of the Windy City..." *Kirkus Reviews*

"A monument in words to this funky, mysterious and eternal American city... a fine collection."-- Luis Alberto Urrea, *The Hummingbird's Daughter*

Nice Girl Does Noir

I don't usually like to read short stories, but these are terrific! I roared through them ... My highest recommendation here... absolutely a group of thoroughly satisfying reads!"—Molly Weston, *Meritorious Mysteries*

"[A] great place to get acquainted with Hellmann's talent... when Hellman explores the less sunlit areas of Chicago and times gone by, her canvas becomes not only more universal but has greater depth and emotional value. Aspiring short-story writers would do well to pay attention to how Hellmann creates both story and character arcs .."—Naomi Johnson, *The Drowning Machine* |

NICE GIRL DOES NOIR

Part ONE: The Ellie Foreman/Georgia Davis
Stories
Part TWO: Chicago Then and Now; Other
Places, Other Times

CONTENTS

PART ONE:
THE ELLIE FOREMAN/GEORGIA DAVIS STORIES

FOREWORD, PART ONE
By William Kent Krueger

Short stories are the poetry of prose. Mistakes, in a novel, can be buried. In a short story, they stand out like roaches on a sugar cookie. Short stories are precise, cut to the bone, every word a necessity. A novel may go far afield, but a great short story requires unbelievable restraint. Not many authors develop that control. Libby Fischer Hellmann has the hand of a master.

The stories that constitute this first volume of *Nice Girl Does Noir* have all been published previously in traditional venues. They're unified by the presence of two remarkable women: Ellie Foreman and Georgia Davis. Anyone familiar with Libby's novels knows these names. The two characters are different in history, family, appearance, and outlook, but they're alike in the ways that matter. They care about justice. They're fiercely protective of those they love. They can't let a mystery go uninvestigated nor a crime unsolved. And they're always struggling to be better than they fear they are.

Take it from a guy who knows her well: Libby is a nice girl. But she writes noir with a savvy edge honed on the hard, dark knowledge of the evil possible in us all. With each story she opens a door to a room that holds a demon—bigotry and politics in her award-winning debut effort "The Day Miriam Hirsch Disappeared", greed in "Common Scents", deadly desire in "A Winter's Tale"—and with prose too damn good to resist, she seduces us inside.

So you should probably interpret this introduction not only as an invitation but also as a warning. If you choose to read on, I can guarantee that Libby's stories will take you places nice people don't often go.

Kent Krueger is not only an award-winning novelist but also a prolific short story writer. Find out more about him at www.williamkentkrueger.com.

THE DAY MIRIAM HIRSCH DISAPPEARED

THE DAY MIRIAM HIRSCH DISAPPEARED was the first short story I wrote. My son had been given a book called "THE JEWS OF CHICAGO" for a Bar Mitzvah present, and when I thumbed through the photographs, they resonated -- especially the ones taken in 1930's Lawndale, at the time a prosperous Jewish community on Chicago's near west side. Little did I know then that the story I wrote about those photos would become the "prequel" to my Ellie Foreman series. Or that the Ellie Foreman series would be the prequel to the Georgia Davis series. The following story, which won the Bouchercon short story contest in 1999, was first published in the Bouchercon Program book. It was later published in ANTHOLOGY TODAY, where it also won a contest, and in the now defunct FUTURES MAGAZINE. You can also find it digitally on Amazon, and it is available on audio at www.sniplits.com.

The day Miriam Hirsch disappeared was so hot you could almost see the sidewalk blister and sweat. It was summer, 1938, and I'd been hanging around with Barney Teitelman in Lawndale, the Jewish neighborhood on Chicago's west side. Barney's parents owned a restaurant and rooming house near Roosevelt and Kedzie. Miriam rented a room on the third floor. She was a looker, as my father would say, although if he knew his only son was spending that much time with Barney he'd have kittens.

You see, we lived in Hyde Park, a few miles and a universe away from Lawndale. We were German Jews; the Teitelmans weren't. They were from Russia, or Lithuania, or one of those other countries with "ia" at the end of them, and what separated us wasn't just the Austro-Hungarian Empire. We were cultured, assimilated. They were rabble. We had come over before the Civil War; they poured in at the end of the last century. We were merchants, doctors, lawyers. They worked in factories, sweat shops, and, well, restaurants. In fact, when my father was being especially snooty, he'd ask which delicatessen their family owned. I, of course, disagreed with my parents. The Teitelmans talked louder and laughed more, and Mrs. T made a hell of a Shabbos brisket.

Barney and I had met by accident the previous May. We were waiting for the bus outside the College of Jewish Studies near the Loop, both of us in bowties and yarmulkes. My parents had sent me there to "enrich" my Jewish heritage. I guess Barney's did too. We stared warily at each other for a few minutes, like dogs sniffing each other out. Then I offered him a piece of Bazooka. He took it. We were best friends.

He only came to my house once. The frosty reception my mother gave him, after he told her where he lived, was enough. There wasn't much action in Hyde Park anyway. We tried to sucker the Weinstein girls into a game of strip poker behind the rocks at the Fifty-Seventh Street beach, but they gave us the brush off. We didn't care. They were ugly. By June I was taking the Cottage Grove streetcar to Roosevelt and transferring west to Lawndale as often as possible.   The first time I saw Miriam, Barney and I were wolfing down brisket sandwiches in the restaurant; I could feel gravy dribbling past my chin. I heard a rustle, turned around. She was walking past our table. No, more like gliding. Dressed in a pearly gown that swept to her feet, she was perfectly proportioned, with a waist so tiny that my hands ached to encircle it, and such a generously endowed bosom that my hands ached -- well, you get the idea. Her hair was gold, her lips red, and she had the most enormous gray eyes I'd ever seen. A guy could lose his way in them. Especially a fifteen year old. My mouth dropped to my chin; gravy stained my shirt. She was even carrying a parasol. I was in love.

There weren't many people in the restaurant that day, but you could feel the collective hush as she passed through. It was as if her presence had struck us dumb, and we were compelled to stare. As her skirt brushed our table, she cast a dazzling smile on Barney. He turned crimson. Then she was gone. The voltage in the air ebbed, and I heard the clink of silverware as people started to live, breathe, and eat again.

"So, who the hell was that?" I said, in my best tough guy tone.

Barney looked me over, knew I was bluffing. "Wouldn't you like to know?"

I leaned across the table and grabbed Barney's collar. "You don't tell me, Barney Teitelman, I'll tell your parents what you were trying to do to Dina Preis behind the shul last Saturday."

"You wouldn't." He didn't sound convinced.

I clutched his shirt tighter. "You got five seconds."

Barney's eyes narrowed. I guess he figured he'd better give me something. "All's I'll say is she's not for the likes of you, Jake Foreman."

I dropped my hold on Barney's neck and jumped up from the table. "Mrs. T? I have something to tell you." I headed toward the kitchen.

"All right already," Barney whined. "Don't go up the wall. She's Miriam Hirsch. She's an actress with the Yiddish theater."

"When did she show up?"

"Couple days ago."

Most of the actresses at the Yiddish theater were from Eastern Europe, but Hirsch was a German name. She and I had something in common already. Then I chastised myself for doing the same thing as my parents.

"I'm gonna be an actor," I said.

Barney balled his napkin up and threw it at me.

***

Apparently, I wasn't the only one Miriam impressed.

13

The next afternoon, as we were hanging out the window trying to blow cigarette smoke into the street instead of the Teitelman's living room, Miriam came out the front door. Sun-baked heat hung in the air like a blanket, and she opened her parasol to protect her head. Halfway up, it got stuck. I was about to run down and offer my assistance when Skull cut in front of her.

Ben Skulnick, or Skull, as we called him, hung out at Davy Miller's gym and pool hall. The Miller brothers were the closest things Lawndale had to gangsters. They'd moved over from Maxwell Street a few years earlier and built a restaurant and gambling casino next to the gym. Covering all the bases, I guess. Except the type of people who frequented the place weren't exactly high society.

Not that the Miller Boys didn't have their fans. It was Davy Miller's gang who fought the Uptown goyim in the 'Twenties so that Jews could use Clarendon Beach, and it was his gang who kept all the Yeshivah-buchers, religious students, safe from the Irish street gangs. The scuttlebutt these days was they were going after Nazi sympathizers on the north side. Whatever the truth, Davy Miller and his crew were proof that Jewish boys weren't sissies, a myth we were all eager to dispel.

"Look at that, Barney," I said, my eyes riveted on the scene below.

"I see."

Tall and dark, Skull cut a dashing figure. He was probably running numbers, greasing palms, and taking cuts off the locals in the area, but with his well-trimmed whiskers, neatly pressed shirt, and Italian suit, he looked like a successful businessman, not a thug. He wore a hat too, a snap-brimmed Fedora, and moved with a sinewy grace, like a cat stalking its prey. No one knew where he came from.

"He's gonna make a play for her." I wasn't sure if I was devastated or curious.

"Do you blame him?"

We watched as he struggled with Miriam's parasol, opened it, and presented it back to her with a flourish. Before

14

she disappeared underneath its shade, I saw the smile she gave him. And the lazy, appraising smile he gave back.

"You see that, Jake?"

I swallowed.

"Give it up, pal. You're way out of your league."

By the following week, Skull was dropping by the restaurant every afternoon. He'd order a glass of iced tea, which he tipped plenty for, but never drank. Sometimes he'd grab a game of gin rummy in the back room, but mostly he checked his watch every few minutes. Around two, he'd make sure to bump into Miriam and walk her to rehearsal. And back home again later.

One evening he walked her all the way up to the third floor. That was the last we saw of them all night. Of course, Barney and I snuck up to the third floor landing, but all we heard were strains of "Don't Be That Way" wafting down the hall from her radio. Benny Goodman. Barney dragged me back downstairs.

But I hadn't lost all hope. When Miriam's show opened, we started to hang around the stage door of Douglas Park Auditorium to catch a glimpse of her. Skull did too. When she came out, sometimes with her stage make-up still on, he would offer her his arm and they'd saunter down the street together. Sometimes they stopped for ice cream or a sandwich at Carl's Deli. On Sundays, they headed over to the roof of the Jewish People's Institute to dance. Even at a distance, you could feel the sparks fly between them. When they smiled at each other or danced the two-step, it broke my heart. I was jealous. I was in love -- with both of them. They were the epitome of glamour. They were swell. With bells on.

One night, though, was different.

"No, Skull, I won't do it." Miriam stared straight ahead as they stepped through the stage door. "Stop asking me."

There was a gleam in Skull's eye. "Oh come on, baby, it's only for a little while."

"No." Miriam walked three steps ahead of him.

"But you're the only one who can. You speak their

language."

"I don't care."

He stopped short. "How can you say that?"

"You have some chutzpah. How can you ask me to – well, to do something like that?" She whipped around to face him, her eyes flashing. Barney and I flattened ourselves against a building.

Skull backed off. His voice grew as soft as cotton. Wheedling. "You love me, don't you baby?"

She looked at him. She kept her mouth shut, but her eyes, as luminous as waves on the moonlit lake, said it all.

Skull moved in for the kill. He pushed a lock of hair off her forehead. "All I need is a little information. Then you can stop. Please. Do it for me." He paused. "For us."

Miriam pursed her lips, and I thought she was going to cry. Then, she sagged against Skull, as if he had somehow managed to squeeze all the air out of her.

Skull grinned and pulled her close, planted a victory kiss on her lips. "That's my baby."

She buried her head in his shoulder. We didn't hear her reply.

***

Whatever Miriam agreed to that night must not have lasted long, because we never saw them together again. Skull didn't come around to Teitelmans any more, and he didn't show up at the auditorium. Miriam came and went by herself. Occasionally, she hailed a cab and never came home at all. It was strange, and I was confused and angry. What had Skull asked her to do? It had to be something so evil that her only recourse was to break up with him.

A week later, on an afternoon so humid that nothing felt dry, Barney and I lugged groceries past the banks on the corner. Across the street we spotted Skull getting his shoes shined. He was reading a newspaper and scowling. When he saw us he tipped his hat. Barney and I glanced at each other. Did he really mean us?

As if to answer our question, he called over to us. "Hey, Teitelman."

Barney nodded tentatively.

Skull dropped a buck in the shoeshine guy's box, overtipping as usual, and crossed the street.

"You guys been following me for a while, haven't you?"

I swallowed. Here it comes. Our first real conversation, and he's gonna tell us to butt out.

"I'm glad I run into youse. I've been meaning to call. Are youse -- young gentlemen interested in a business proposition?"

My jaw dropped to my chest.

He squinted at us. "My business in other parts of the city has picked up recently and requires my -- my presence there. But I still need some --whadd'ya call it -- some representation here. You guys interested?" He yanked his thumb toward our bags of groceries. "Pays better than that."

I looked at Barney, then at Skull, trying to mask my excitement with a shrug. It didn't work. A soft yelp escaped my mouth.

"Good. Come around to Miller's at three." Skull turned on his heel, dropping the paper in the trash on the corner. I glanced at the headline -- something about hooligans throwing rocks at a group of German-American Bund members on the north side.

The long and the short of it was that Skull wanted us to do errands for him in the neighborhood. Nothing major, just running messages to Zookie the Bookie and picking up envelopes from some of the shops. At first he came with us to show us the ropes. Then we were on our own.

It was a fair trade off. We didn't have Miriam, but we did have Skull. In some ways, it was better. We were important. Even the guys in the pool hall nodded to us after a while. And we were making great money. Almost ten bucks a day. Barney and I made up new names for each other. I was Jake the Snake; he was Barney Bow-Tie.

On the days Skull was with us, I watched him operate. He was smooth. He'd flash one of his lazy smiles, and even the people he was bilking smiled back. Especially the ladies. The only time he lost his cool was the afternoon we passed Miriam. She was crossing the street to catch a cab. Their eyes met, and I thought I saw a look of infinite sadness, passion, and what-might-have-been pass between them. How could it be over, with looks like that?

***

I should have known it wouldn't last. One morning in late July my mother and father woke me up. Poised for attack, they stood at the foot of my bed.

"Jacob, you have some explaining to do." My mother's eyes were cold steel.

I tried to play dumb. "What's that, Ma?" I yawned. Slowly.

"Just exactly what have you been doing in Lawndale?"

"What do you mean?"

"Jacob, don't try to weasel your way out of this one." My father glared. "Henry Solomon saw you outside Davy Miller's the other day. How long have you been consorting with gangsters?"

"Gangsters? What gangsters?"

My father cut me off. "You want to play it that way? Fine. You're forbidden to go there anymore."

"But Barney's my best friend."

"He's a bad influence. They all are." My father wheeled around as if there was nothing more to say.

"But I've got a job. I'm making good money."

"Good money?" My father whipped back around. His face was purple. "That kind of money you don't need. You want a job, you work in Kahn's bakery. It was good enough for me -- it'll do for you."

I wanted to ask him why he figured Henry Solomon, one of our most respectable Hyde Park neighbors, was over in

Lawndale, but somehow I didn't think the time was right.

***

If the boredom didn't get me, the pretense did. Life in Hyde Park was intolerable. And hot. Not even a wisp of a breeze fluttered through the curtains of our wide-open windows. About a week later, it got so bad even my parents took off for the Michigan shore. I pled a toothache. As soon as they left, not without suspicious glances at the icepack clamped to my cheek, I hopped the streetcar over to Lawndale. Mrs. Teitelman was washing the floor of the restaurant.

"Where have you been, Jake? Barney's at a concert in Douglas Park. You just missed him."

"I'll wait." I looked around. The place was empty. I snuck a glance at the door leading to the stairs.

"How are things?"

Mrs. Teitelman followed my gaze. She shrugged, a grim set to her mouth.

"Did Skull come back?"

Another shrug.

I was just breaking out a bottle of seltzer when the door to the stairs opened, and a man crossed the restaurant. He had blond whiskers, a round red face, and an odd twitch in one eye. He didn't look Jewish. He hurried across the room, staring straight ahead, as if he knew he didn't belong and wanted to get out fast.

A few minutes later, Miriam skipped down the steps, her smile as bright as a box of new Shabbos candles. I froze. Who was this impostor? Where was Skull? I felt betrayed. She waved at me before gliding out the door.

Barney got back from the park around four.

"What's been going on around here?" I asked

"I don't know." He hung his head as if he were responsible for the turn of events.

"Didn't they get back together?"

"Nope. He hasn't been here at all. In fact --"

"What?" I was starting to feel panicky.

"I dunno, Jake. Sometimes she doesn't come home at night. And then one time, her eyes were all red rimmed like she'd been crying, and her dress was ripped. She didn't even have her key. My father had to let her in."

"Jesus, Barney."

He nodded. "And when she's here, she's 'entertaining' in her room. But it isn't Skull."

"The guy I saw earlier?"

"Yeah. I think he's goyim. Mother's ready to kick her out."

I turned to Mrs. T in desperation. "You can't do that. Where will she go?"

Mrs. T just looked at me. "Jacob, there are some things you're still too young to understand."

That afternoon we ran down to the pool hall and caught up with Skull at Miller's. We were sweating like pigs, but he was cool and dapper.

"Where ya bin, Snake?" He grinned.

"I was grounded, Skull. My parents." I rolled my eyes.

He looked at me speculatively. "Your parents must be real Nervous Nellies."

"They're German," I admitted.

"So are Miriam's," Skull said. "Crabbers. Stiff as sandpaper."

I took that as an opening and screwed up my courage. "How is Miriam these days?"

He ignored my question. "You know, it's a damn shame about you *Yeccas*." That was slang for German Jews. "One of the best guys I ever heard of was Arnold Rothstein. Practically started the Mafia. His family was German, but he was tops. You know what he did?"

I shook my head.

"Hustled the most famous pool shark in the country. Beat his tuckus off. And he hardly even played pool."

"How'd he do that?"

"Kept the guy up until he won. Forty hours with no

sleep." Skull winked at me. "Rothstein had style too. He ran a casino, moved a lot of booze, financed all sorts of capers. But he always wore a tux and he danced with the ladies every night." Skull's chin dipped. "He was -- whadda'ya call it -- a smooth operator."

I wanted to ask him more about Miriam, but I didn't have the guts.

***

Mrs. T never had the chance to evict Miriam. She never came back. Three days later they found her body in an alley off Lincoln Avenue. The German part of town. She'd been raped, beaten, strangled. The cops identified her by her purse.

A tough-looking Irish detective, Patrick O'Meara, came around to question us. Mrs. T told him everything she knew. About the theater. Skull. The man with the blond whiskers.

O'Meara hustled over to Davy Miller's to question Skull. We trailed behind. It was the first time we'd seen him ourselves in a couple of days. He looked bad. His shirt was wrinkled, he hadn't shaved, and his bloodshot eyes kept darting around the room. His mood seemed to shift from arrogance to desolation, and his answers were clipped and curt.

I began to think the worst. Miriam and Skull broke up. Miriam started up with other men. Skull must have been crazy with jealousy and he snapped. It looked that way to me. And to O'Meara. He wasn't nice to Skull. Told him not to go anywhere for a while.

Of course, the next morning Skull was gone, and no one knew where. Or they weren't telling. That was the only proof I needed. He killed Miriam. Maybe my parents were right after all. Lawndale people were different.

Barney and I were puzzling it over at the restaurant when O'Meara showed up. Mrs. T was upstairs getting dressed, so he nabbed Joey, the headwaiter.

"Ever seen this guy?" He showed him a picture.

Joey shook his head.

"You sure?" You could tell O'Meara didn't believe him. "Seen Skulnick recently?"

Joey kept wiping glasses with his towel. "Nope."

O'Meara turned around, saw us sitting at a table. We froze. His eyes narrowed, then he came over. I tried to look nonchalant.

"Your turn, boys. You ever seen this guy?"

He threw the picture down on our table.

I could hear Barney's sharp intake of breath. It was the man with the blond whiskers. I tried to be blasé.

But O'Meara was patient. Eventually, my eyes drifted back to the picture. O'Meara was waiting.

"So what's it gonna be, boys?"

"Who is he?" I croaked.

"You seen him?"

I met O'Meara's eyes and nodded.

"Name's Peter Schultz. They call him Twitch. Some kind of problem around his eye." O'Meara stared at me. I looked at the floor. I knew the name. Peter Schultz was the head of the German-American Bund in Chicago. They were Nazis.

"He was murdered last night," O'Meara said. "We found him in the same alley they found the girl."

Barney made a mewling sound in his throat. I felt old.

"He was stabbed about fifteen times, then strangled. They got him pretty good."

I didn't move.

O'Meara kept the pressure on. "You know, it's interesting. With him gone, their whole organization is up for grabs, you know?"

I didn't say anything, but the pieces were finally coming together. I knew who killed Miriam, and I knew who killed Schultz. I wondered if O'Meara knew too.

O'Meara went on. "Someone—someone close to him—knew the Kraut's habits so well they even knew what time he took a dump. They got him on his way to a Bund meeting. You have any idea who that might be?"

I kept my mouth shut.

He shook his head. ""Well, whoever it was, now there's one less Nazi in the world." O'Meara stood, put his hat on, threw us a world-weary glance. "They say all's fair in love and war. What do you think?"

What I thought was that I may have been wrong about Skull all along; that this was more about war than love. There may have been a reason why Miriam was dating Schultz; why Skull was pressuring Miriam to get information she didn't want to get. Skull used Miriam, but he was also her avenger.

"I'll be seeing you boys around," O'Meara said, then stepped through the door and left.

***

Skull never came back to Lawndale. At least we never heard from him again. I didn't hang around much either. School started, and I got busy with homework and sports. I met a girl at Hyde Park High, Barbara Steinberg. She was pretty nice. Barney called a couple of times, but neither of us pushed it. Other things were fast taking precedence. Hitler annexed Austria, and the news coming out of Europe was grim. No one seemed to remember the day Miriam Hirsch disappeared.

THE END

COMMON SCENTS

Georgia Davis made her first major appearance in my third novel, AN IMAGE OF DEATH which was published in 2004. However, she was also the protagonist in this story, which was written and published about the same time. In this story, Georgia, an officer on the Village police force, is anxious to move up to detective.

Officer Georgia Davis twisted her head toward her lapel mike. "Got it." She turned back to her partner. "Another Geezer call."

Robby Parker tossed his pop can in the trash. "Someone's fixin' to die?"

"No. Possible abuse. At Palatine Nursing Home." She balled up the wrapper her burger came in. "Just me, though. You're supposed to head back in."

Parker threw her a knowing look. "Sorry."

She shrugged as she zipped up her jacket. Juvies, Seniors, once in a while, a double D – the perks of the female cop in the suburbs. But it would end one day. She'd make detective. She had to.

Exiting the food court, they walked past the newest store in the mall, "Scensations", a luxury perfume shop where people designed their own fragrances. After customers chose a blend from over fifty oils and scents, the store poured it into a bottle, slapped on a label, and charged a hefty price for the privilege. The founder had to be a baby-boomer, Georgia thought, as she skirted the door. Who else would push the envelope of narcissism that far?

"Six months." Parker yanked his thumb at the window.

She shook her head. "It's a fresh gimmick. I give it a year."

After dropping Parker at the station, she headed to Palatine Nursing Home. A small, red-bricked building unrelieved by trim or shutters, it crouched behind a large tree whose branches were coated with glassy ice. Patches of dirty snow hugged the ground around it. Driving into a side lot, she parked next to an old Mercedes. The unremitting landscape, in desolate shades of gray, seemed to presage an endless year of Februarys. She pulled her collar up against the cold.

A cardboard sign on an empty desk inside directed visitors to the second floor. There hadn't been a receptionist in a while, Georgia recalled, as she mounted the steps.

She braced herself at the landing, but the smell, a combination of urine and old people, covered by antiseptic, thickened her throat. She peered down a hall with green-painted walls and a scuffed linoleum floor. A staffing station occupied the other end, and a head of brown hair occasionally bobbed up and down behind it.

Half way down the hall, a nurse emerged from a small storeroom, wheeling a cart with a water pitcher, tongue depressors, a jar of applesauce, and tiny cups filled with pills. Locking the door, she slipped a ring of keys into her pocket. Georgia approached her, the chatter from a radio muffling her footsteps. The nurse looked up with a harried expression, as if she were struggling to keep chaos at bay.

Georgia couldn't tell if her pale eyes, yellow hair, and washed out skin were the result of fluorescent lighting or her natural color. She checked her nameplate. Vivian Muldoon: Manager/Head Nurse.

"Officer." Muldoon stood straight and quiet, as if she was used to hearing bad news. "Is there a problem?"

Georgia cleared her throat. "I'm following up on an allegation of abuse."

The nurse stiffened. With her peripheral vision, Georgia saw the woman behind the counter look up, too.

"There must be some mistake."

Georgia pulled out her notebook. "Do you have a patient named Patricia Hanson?"

She dipped her head and led Georgia to a room at the end of the hall. The shades were drawn, and weak light spilled from a bedside lamp. Lying motionless on her side was a figure under a blanket. "Patricia, wake up, dear. You have a visitor."

Georgia recognized the cheery hospital voice most nurses used, somewhere between patronizing and irritating. Muldoon repeated herself. The figure stirred.

"Good girl, Patricia," the nurse said. "Can you roll over?"

Like an obedient dog, the woman began to push herself up, but when she saw the two women, her blank expression turned to horror, and she threw the bed-sheet over her head. "Don't hurt me." She shrieked.

Georgia and Muldoon exchanged glances.

"No one's going to hurt you," the nurse said soothingly.

"Where's Brandy? I need Brandy." The woman's voice spiked.

"Brandy's her daughter," Muldoon explained.

Georgia stepped forward. "Mrs. Hanson, I'm Officer Georgia Davis." She made her voice low and calm. "Brandy thinks you've been hurt. I'm here to investigate. But I promise not to touch you. I'll just look. Would that be okay?"

The woman didn't move, but Georgia could see her body relax. "Can you show me your face, Mrs. Hanson?"

The woman eased the sheet off her head, revealing sunken eyes, chapped lips, and a web of wrinkles on crepy skin. The woman lips began moving, but no sound came out.

Georgia leaned forward. "What's that?" Hanson's lips kept moving. "What's she trying to say?"

Muldoon shrugged. "I don't know. She has these – these moments."

Georgia nodded. "Mrs. Hanson, I'm going to come closer now."

The woman didn't reply, but her lips stopped moving. Georgia took a step forward. "Can you sit up for me?"

She pursed her lips as if considering the request, then drew back the covers and sat up. Georgia caught a glimpse of thin wasted legs freckled with brown age spots. But no bruising.

She nodded. "Good. Now can you lift your gown so we can check your stomach?"

She did. Georgia gasped. Several purple bruises were visible on her abdomen. The area around them was swollen and yellow.

"Let's see your back," she said quietly. Hanson swung her legs over the bed, and taking Georgia's hand, stood and turned around. There were more bruises on her buttocks. Georgia affected a calm she didn't feel. "You can get back to bed, Mrs. Hanson. Nurse Muldoon, let's talk outside."

In the hall her voice was sharp. "What the hell is going on?"

Muldoon spread her hands. "I don't know."

"Could some medical condition have caused these?"

"No. She's actually in pretty good shape for ninety-two."

"I'm taking her to the ER."

The nurse nodded her agreement. "Better to be safe. But bear in mind that bruising is common in older people. They're unsteady, and their skin is so thin. They bump into things, fall out of bed." She fixed her eyes on Georgia. "I'm sure there's an explanation. I've been head nurse and manager for sixteen years. We run a clean place."

"Where's her daughter? Didn't she call it in?"

Muldoon's eyes narrowed. "She was here this morning. But she left."

Georgia used the phone at the nurse's station. According to her nameplate, the young woman absorbed in paperwork was Louise Rooney, Nurse Administrator. Next to her near a stack of forms was a bottle of perfume, its amber liquid sparkling even in the flat overhead light. Georgia made out the word "Scensations" scrawled in loopy letters on the bottle.

"That yours?" She cradled the phone between her head and shoulder.

Rooney looked up. Georgia pointed to the perfume. The nurse nodded.

"The place sure hit the ground running." Georgia smiled. "What's yours called?"

"Tiger's Breath." Rooney reached for the bottle, unscrewed the cap, and waved it under Georgia's nose.

She breathed in a sweet, fruity fragrance with a slightly metallic overlay. "Not bad. Did you make it yourself?"

The nurse smiled coyly. "No. It was a thank-you gift."

"How's it smell when it's on?" Sometimes there was a difference.

"I haven't tried it." She looked longingly at the bottle. "I'm saving it for a special occasion."

With short brown hair, rimless glasses, and wide-spaced eyes that hardly blinked, Louise Rooney looked more like a field mouse than a tiger. But everyone deserved a special occasion. Even a field mouse.

***

A young doctor who reminded Georgia of the cocky resident on "ER" agreed the bruises were inconclusive. "Easy bruising, they call it. Very common. Happens from too much Heparin or Warfarin. Blood thinners." At Georgia's frown, he added, "The good news is that nothing's broken."

"But what if they were inflicted by someone? What might cause them? Or who?"

His faced emptied. "No way. I'm not going there."

She had the feeling that if she were a male cop, he'd be more forthcoming. "Come on, doc, help me out."

He looked at her, as if reading her mind. "Okay," he relented. "You've heard of cases where some overworked, underpaid aide snaps and goes nuts on a patient, right?"

Georgia nodded.

"Well, if you wiped asses all day, listened to non-stop complaints, and never heard a thank you..." He shrugged. "Working the wrinkle ranch can get to you."

"Have there been problems at Palatine?"

He hesitated. "Not that kind."

"What does that mean?"

He lowered his voice. "From what I hear, they're in a bad way. The owner can't sell the place – it's too small. Meanwhile, Medicare's down, there aren't enough nurses to go around, and he can't raise prices. It ain't the Taj Mahal." He glanced impatiently at his watch. "Look. Just count your blessings she's not seriously injured."

After she brought Mrs. Hanson back, Georgia called her watch commander.

"Should we get the States Attorneys' office involved?" He asked after she filled him in.

"I don't think so, sir. At least not yet." She fixed her eyes on Patricia's door. "Commander Green, I'm gonna stay with this a little longer. Try to get some answers, if you don't mind."

***

If the Palatine Nursing Home was running on empty, you couldn't tell from Gerald Decker's office. Done up in a Southwestern motif of pinks, blues, and oranges, it was the only splash of color she'd seen at the place. Behind his desk was a photo of a plump, bejeweled woman sporting a Jackie Kennedy hairdo. Mrs. Decker, Georgia figured. Probably the interior decorator.

A short man heading toward sixty with thinning hair and a thick mustache rose from his desk. Concern oozed from his eyes. "I was appalled to hear about Mrs. Hanson," he began. "We've never had any trouble like this before. I've told the staff to cooperate fully. And if there's anything I can do..." he offered a smile and sat down, his voice trailing off.

Georgia sat in a chair with a nubby beige fabric and pulled out her notepad. "What can you tell me about the daughter?"

"Mrs. Hanson's daughter?" Decker folded his hands in front of him. "I hardly know the woman." He paused. "No.

30

That's not entirely true. I do know there have been some problems with fees. And I gather that staff isn't that fond of her."

She noted the reference to "staff." "Is there bad blood between her and Muldoon?"

"I can't speak for Vivian, but apparently, the daughter's very demanding. Quick to find fault. Insists on special treatment." He rubbed a finger across his mustache. "When you're already overworked and underpaid, that can be upsetting."

"Your staff is overworked?"

"We're going through tough times, Georgia. The industry is consolidating, and we're one of the last independents. When my father-in-law built this place, it was a jewel, but now..." He stopped. "Sorry. You don't want to hear about my problems." His eyes roved her face. "Since when does the police force hire such attractive officers?"

She ignored him. And the patronizing way he called her "Georgia."

"Tell me about Nurse Muldoon."

Decker leaned back. "Vivian? She's the best thing that ever happened to this place. She runs everything."

"What about the rest of the staff?"

"I barely know them. They all seem to disappear after a few months. Though with what we pay, you can't really blame them." He shrugged. "Don't get me wrong. None of my people would ever put a patient in jeopardy." A pained expression slipped over his face. "Of course..."

"What?"

He laced his fingers again. "Well, I almost hate to bring this up."

"Bring what up?"

"Well, in some cases, it turns out that the abusers are actually family members."

"Are you saying Brandy Hanson battered her own mother?"

"I hope not." The lines on his face deepened. "Why would anyone hurt a defenseless old woman?"

She shifted. "I'd like to see her file."

He slid his tongue over his lips. "Patient files are confidential, but I think, under the circumstances, we can make an arrangement." He got up, left the room, and returned a moment later. "Sorry. It's not here. The girls must be working on it. Should I have it brought up?"

"No, that won't be necessary." She dug into her pocket for a card. "Why don't you call me when you get it back?"

He took the card, covering her outstretched hand with his. Georgia pulled back. "Now, Georgia, if there's anything else I can do, please don't hesitate to ask." She couldn't wait to take a shower.

On her way out she peeked into his Mercedes. On the front seat was a silver box tied with a blue ribbon. The unmistakable logo of "Scensations" was scrawled across the side. She straightened up. What the hell was going on? Was everyone on the North Shore trying to be Chanel?

***

"I've wanted my mother out ever since she moved in."

"Why is that?"

With heavy make-up and bottle-blonde hair, Brandy Hanson looked like a woman from the wrong side of the tracks still desperate to cross over. Her living room was spare but clean, with a couch, TV, and two chairs. She slouched in one of them. Her foot kept up a fast tap on the floor. An edgy aura suffused the air.

"The place is a hell hole. You've seen it. I don't want my mother to die there." She sniffed. "But what can I do? I'm just a waitress at Denny's."

Georgia searched for the right words. "It's got to be stressful."

"You don't know the half of it."

"How did you discover the bruises?"

"I saw them this morning, but no one would tell me a goddamn thing. And then that sanctimonious bitch --"

"Muldoon?"

She nodded. "She made it seem like I'd done it myself."

"How?"

Brandy grunted. "Sidelong looks. Shitty comments about ungrateful people. Things like that. I tell you, if I wasn't--"

The chirp of the phone interrupted her. Brandy went to answer it. "Yeah." Silence. Her features relaxed. "Good. That's what I hoped you'd say." She snuck a look at Georgia.

"Hey, I can't talk now. I'll call you back." She hung up the phone. Her foot had stopped tapping.

* * *

Two days later, a dense fog rose from the ground up. Swirls of mist hovered a few feet off the street, giving the sense of being lost in a bleak, mystical bog. Georgia chewed her lip as she drove to work. Her case was stalled. Maybe there had been no abuse. Just easy bruising. Maybe she should move on.

The word came in after roll call. Brandy Hanson had been found dead in her apartment. "No lacerations, wounds, or visible signs of trauma," dispatch said. "They'll figure it out on the table downtown."

Suddenly everyone was interested in her case. She ran it down for Detective Mike O'Malley, whose red hair and freckles clashed with his world-weary face.

"What's going to happen to her mother?" Georgia asked.

"Not our problem. Social services 'll sort it out. By the way, I need your help."

She tensed with anticipation. She had the background. Knew the people. Was he going to ask her to work the case with him?

"The techs are pretty much done with the place, but Health wants more paperwork on Hanson's mother.

33

Someone's gotta run interference at the daughter's apartment. Help search the place."

She blew out her breath. "Sure."

***

She found a thick file in Brandy's kitchen, but when she checked the bedroom, she froze. Resting on Brandy's bureau was a bottle of "Tiger's Breath" perfume. She stared at the bottle. Three people from Palatine Nursing Home had perfume from the same store. Two had the same scent. She started to pick it up, then stopped.

Did Decker give the same perfume to both women? He'd had a box of it in his car, and he'd come on like a randy goat. Maybe he'd been getting it on with Brandy, and Louise Rooney found out. So to keep her quiet, he – No. Decker accused Brandy of attacking her own mother. There was no love lost there. Georgia picked up the bottle. Maybe he was getting it on with Rooney and Brandy found out. No. Brandy wouldn't settle for perfume. She'd be chasing the mother lode

Maybe he was getting it on with both of them, and they found out about each other. Jealousy could lead to murder. She absently unscrewed the cap and breathed in the scent. Just like Rooney's. But then, where did the abuse fit in? Had Rooney done it out of revenge? Or did Decker, in a sadistic attempt to show Brandy who was boss? Georgia screwed the top back on and pulled out her cell. It was time to find out.

***

O'Malley let them both go twelve hours later. Decker had been at a poker game until two in the morning. The other players backed him up.

"What about the perfume in his car?" Georgia asked.

"Claimed it was a present for his wife," O'Malley said. "It was 'Love Potion", by the way. Not the same shit."

Georgia grimaced. "What about Rooney?"

O'Malley hesitated. "The woman's a dyke, Georgia. We talked to her companion. They went to dinner, then a movie. Plenty of witnesses."

Georgia slumped in the chair. "The autopsy?"

"Inconclusive. Looks like a heart attack." He flipped up his hands. "What can I tell you?"

She trudged out of the detectives' room, shoulders sagging. This had been her chance, and it turned out there wasn't even a crime. She'd be wearing a uniform forever.

***

The next day Georgia realized she still had the thick file from Brandy's apartment. Paging through it, she discovered it was filled with forms that authorized Medicare payments to the home. Explanation of benefit forms, they itemized scores of procedures performed on Patricia Hanson. Most were co-signed by a doctor and Louise Rooney. Georgia frowned; she hadn't known Brandy's mother was so ill.

Then it hit her. Patricia Hanson *wasn't* ill. Muldoon had said she was in pretty good shape for her age. She bent over the file.

An hour later, she had it. Decker was running a Medicare scam, using Rooney to submit bogus expenses. She didn't know all the details, but it seemed to involve doctors' signatures, whether real or forged, and invoices prepared by Rooney. Georgia added it up: they'd raked in almost ten grand on Brandy's mother in less than six months. Multiply that by fifty patients. Maybe Decker wasn't so anxious to sell the place after all.

She tapped her fist against her chin. Brandy must have seen her mother's file, caught onto the scam, and decided she wanted in. Decker and Louise Rooney could have tried to scare her off by attacking her mother, but when that didn't work, agreed to cut her in. That was the phone call Brandy got. Perhaps, they even sent over some "Tiger's Breath" as a gift to seal the deal.

And then she turned up dead.

***

A bitter wind raked across the parking lot as she pulled into the home. When she got upstairs, she learned Louise Rooney was gone.

"Haven't seen her in days." Muldoon rolled her cart down the hall. "After all the trouble you caused, she probably left town." She looked around. "You know, if Mr. Decker sees you here, after what you did, he's liable to-- "

"What happened to Patricia?"

Muldoon sighed. "Poor woman didn't have two cents to rub together. They took her to down to Champaign." Georgia blinked. Compared to the state institution, Palatine was a five-star hotel. "But two new patients came in this week. And we hired someone to replace Louise."

A fresh face peeked over the counter. "Vivian, could you check these charts? I want to make sure I'm doing them right. "

"Well, if there's nothing else," Muldoon smiled, "I need to get back to work."

Georgia was almost down the steps when O'Malley called.

Nurse Rooney was dead. They found her on the floor of her bedroom. Wearing evening clothes.

"That can't be. Muldoon said..." Georgia stopped. "How did she die?"

"Don't know yet. There were no visible wounds or trauma."

A chill edged up her spine. Muldoon was training the new girl. Just like she'd trained Rooney. Muldoon practically ran the place, she remembered Decker saying. Georgia thought back to the perfume on Rooney's desk. Maybe it wasn't from Decker. An image of Brandy's mother sprang into her mind; how terrified she was when Georgia first entered her room.

Muldoon had been with her. Georgia's hand moved to her holster.

"Mike, was there a bottle of 'Tiger's Breath' near the body?"

"How the hell did you know?" She heard his exhalation. "It was on her dresser."

Evening clothes. Rooney had been saving it for a special occasion. Georgia pulled out her cuffs. "Don't let anyone near it. I think I know what happened."

***

The lab discovered both perfumes were laced with DMSO, a popular skin care product with an interesting quality: by opening the pores, it transfers anything mixed with it -- in this case a lethal dose of ricin – directly into the bloodstream. Georgia found a container of DMSO in the storeroom. Ricin, an untraceable poison derived from ordinary castor beans, is easily made and requires only a minute amount to kill. And though DMSO does have a distinctive smell, it can be masked by perfume.

Muldoon's bank records revealed she'd amassed a small fortune. And when they put out a trace on ex-Palatine employees, they learned that two aides preceding Rooney also suffered sudden, unexpected deaths.

***

Brandy and Muldoon were a matched pair, Georgia thought as she drove back after the arraignment. The petty opportunist and the seasoned pro. One's death was the other's undoing. And poor Rooney was caught in the middle. But she'd been wrong about Decker. He might be a bottom feeder, but he wasn't part of the scam. He even bought his wife perfume.

Still, when she saw the silver box on her desk, she handled it carefully. She checked for a card. There was none.

She studied the box, then slipped on a pair of gloves to open it. The name of the perfume was "Chick Dick."

O'Malley said he heard her laugh from the other side of the building.

THE END

THE LAST RADICAL

In 1999 '70s radical Kathleen Soliah was arrested after spending 23 years under the alias of Sara Jane Olson. In 1975 she was charged with attempting to bomb police cars with the SLA, the group that kidnapped newspaper heiress Patty Hearst. But Olson vanished after she was charged and reinvented herself as a housewife - changing her name, marrying a doctor and becoming a mother of three in St. Paul, Minnesota. During that time she was active in the community and was known to be a progressive. I am old enough to remember her original crime, but what intrigued me was her life on the lam. Did she panic every time she saw a police car or heard a siren? How did she explain her youth to her husband and kids? How does someone with something to hide live? This story is the result of that curiosity. It was published in FUTURES Magazine in 2001.

Soft explosions of flame crackled and licked the side of the grill. The tang of charred meat filled the air. I edged closer, prepared to supervise, but when David, who had taken over chef's duties, spotted me, he raised his eyebrows and lowered his chin, his way of warning me to back off. I picked up the Merlot instead.

"I shouldn't, Ellie. I've had enough." Jamie covered her glass with her hand. My neighbors, Jamie and Ted Matheson, were over for dinner with their son Conrad.

"Nonsense," I said. "This is the last barbecue of the season. We'll be shoveling driveways soon. No. I'll be shoveling driveways. You'll be calling the snow plow service."

Jamie hesitated, then tipped her glass toward me. I poured.

Though the Matheson's lived only two houses away, the few hundred feet between us could have been the Berlin wall. I lived in a modest house with Rachel, my twelve-year-old daughter; the Matheson's had an estate with a cedar shake roof. Ted, an Internet security consultant, traveled a lot. So did David, who lived in Philadelphia but spent most of his weekends with me in Chicago.

Jamie and I, both workweek widows, had gravitated toward each other, though I was a little in awe of her. Not only was she president of the PTA, but she sang in the church choir, served on the village's Quality of Life committee, and used to be the soccer team Mom. She's also a gourmet cook. We used to take brisk three-mile walks around the village, but after hearing about her latest version of crème brulee or chicken in puff pastry, I'd get so ravenous I'd eat everything in the fridge.

Tonight I didn't try to compete. Just steak, salad, and plenty of wine. I was opening up another bottle when David said the meat was ready. I craned my neck. Black on the outside, pink in the middle. Perfect.

"Did 'ja see the new fence the Cavanaugh's put up?" Ted said between bites. It was a warm evening, and we were out on the deck. The sun had just dipped below the trees, and bursts of rosy light flickered across the yard.

"It looks nice," I said tentatively. Ted has his own take on things. I don't always agree with him.

"Are you kidding? It's an outrage." Ted sniffed. "They only did two sides. How cheap can you get?"

I swallowed. "Maybe that's all they could afford."

"I don't think so," Ted said in a singsong voice.

"Ted." Jamie's voice was sharp.

But the wine had evidently loosened Ted's tongue. "I saw their property tax bill a while back." His dark eyes glittered. "It's almost as high as ours." I almost asked how he'd managed to do that, but then I remembered he was an

Internet security expert. I glanced at David. We were thinking the same thing.

"People have different ways of doing things, honey," Jamie countered.

"Oh, Jamie, you're way too tolerant. You know -- "

"More salad anyone?" I cut in, brandishing a pair of tongs.

Jamie shook her head. I turned an imploring face to David.

"Got a funny story to tell you." He wiped his napkin across his mouth. I wanted to hug him for coming to the rescue. "Well, not funny, but interesting. A client came to see me the other day." David trades foreign currency for a large Philadelphia bank. "Guy's expanding his business and wanted to hedge some German marks."

Ted nodded.

"Anyway, I'm sitting across the table from this guy, and something about him looks familiar."

"What did he look like?" I asked.

"Just average. But it was driving me crazy. I was sure I knew this guy."

"Who was he?" Jamie gazed at David over the rim of her glass.

"I can't say. Client confidentiality. Let's call him 'Jack'".

Ted took a sip of wine.

"So. Jack keeps grinning, like he knows that I know him. Then, after we'd finished our business, he says, 'You're right, you know. You do know me.'"

Ted toyed with his fork.

"Turns out he was a Sixties radical. Part of a group called SHOUT."

"SHOUT?" I asked.

"Stop Human Oppression and Unrestrained Tyranny," David said.

Ted looked up. "Actually, it started out as the Society for Human Opportunity and Unlimited Trust."

"How'd you know that?"

Ted shifted. "I – I must have read it someplace. It's one of those things that sticks in your mind."

David went on. "SHOUT had their own commune in West Philly, not far from the Penn campus. They were way out there, like SDS and the Weathermen. Preaching about cleansing the system and the people's revolution."

A hazy memory jogged my brain. "Didn't they blow up a bank?"

"Two points." David raised his fingers. "They did, and a couple of people were killed. "

Jamie frowned. "So how come this guy's out walking around free?"

"They never proved he was part of the bombing. He claimed there was a 'gang of four'—two men and two women – who planned and executed the attack. He served a few years as an accessory, but the ones who actually did it are still underground."

"Scumbags." Ted grumbled. A conservative Republican and Vietnam vet, Ted's idea of a hero is Oliver North. He even resembles the colonel, with a razor-edge haircut and deep-set eyes.

"Rizzo got even, though." David said.

"Who?" Jamie asked.

"Frank Rizzo, former mayor and police chief of Philadelphia. A few years after the attack, the Philadelphia police stormed their commune and blew it up. Two SHOUT members were killed. The cops claimed they were armed to the teeth."

"I remember," I said.

"Everybody knew it was a lie," David said. "It was payback for the bank. The group fell apart after that."

"And your client?" I said.

"He stayed out of trouble, eventually started a business." David rubbed his nose. "Remember, this was thirty years ago."

"Strange story." I poured the last of the wine.

"The guy finally pulled his head out of his rear end," Ted said.

I pressed my lips together, curious about Jamie's opinion. Though she'd led a passionate fight against unnecessary development, helping to thwart a plan for a new village mall, she'd grown up in Connecticut on streets named "Elderberry" with lots of churches. She spent her life following the rules.

David rolled his wineglass between his palms. "So where were you during the sixties?" No one answered. "OK. I'll cop first. I dropped out of college and hitchhiked across Europe for a year."

I cleared my throat, emboldened by his confession. "I lived in a commune and sold underground newspapers."

"You didn't!" Jamie's eyes grew wide.

I nodded, remembering how convinced I was that life would never require a knowledge of furniture, china, or designer clothes. A crusader against a corrupt, repressive system, I wrote for the *Revolutionary Times* and read my "3M's": Mao, Marcuse, and Marx.

"What happened?" Jamie asked.

"It didn't last. They told me I was too bourgeois." I spread my hands. "The most I could aspire to was running a safe-house."

"A wannabee, huh?" Ted sneered.

My spine stiffened. "What about you, Ted? Where were you during the revolution?"

"ROTC then 'Nam. And damn proud of 'em both."

I suppressed a reply.

"Your turn, Jamie," David cut in.

"Well." She folded her hands in her lap. "I've never told anyone this." She looked at each of us.

"Go. You're with friends."

"Okay." She took a breath. "During our senior high school trip to Washington, we took a tour of the White House." She cast a sly look at us. "When we got to the Blue

Room, I stuck a piece of gum behind the door, right on the door jam."

I blinked. David stared. Ted snorted. "You what?"

She inspected her hands. "And you know what? When we went back a few years ago on one of those tours your Congressman sets up, I felt behind the door of the Blue Room. You're not going to believe it, but the gum was still there."

My mouth dropped open. No one said anything. I started to applaud. "You win, Jamie. You really stuck it to the system."

***

Rachel and I stopped by Jamie's a couple of weeks later. Halloween was close, and Rachel wanted to be a hippie. I wondered if she and Conrad had eavesdropped on us the night we had dinner. Or maybe it was Conrad's idea. With his faded army jacket, pierced ear, and attitude, the fourteen-year-old was the antithesis of his parents.

I'd managed to scrounge up a pair of old bell-bottoms and a peasant blouse, but we still needed beads and peace symbol. I didn't think Jamie would have anything, but Rachel insisted we try.

Jamie opened the door before we knocked. "Hi. I saw you coming down the street."

She led us into the kitchen, a swirl of red quarry tile, gleaming white appliances, and lemon accents. I sat down at a glossy cedar table with a vase of mums on top. A minute later, two glasses of lemonade and a plate of homemade cookies appeared. The cookies were warm.

"I'm not sure I have anything," Jamie said after Rachel explained why we were there, "but let's take a look. Come on."

"Is Conrad here?" Rachel asked as they mounted the stairs.

"No, he's at..." Jamie's voice faded, and I couldn't quite make out where Conrad was supposed to be.

I munched cookies, idly scanning some papers on the table. Notes from the village's Quality of Life meeting. Whether to fund a proposed historical society. And how to organize the next Fourth of July celebration.

The trill of the phone interrupted my eavesdropping. It rang twice. Maybe Jamie couldn't hear it upstairs. After the fourth ring, Ted's voice boomed out. "This is 555-9876. Leave a message." That was Ted. Nothing cute. Barely polite.

A man's voice followed. "It's been a long time, my friend." I stared at the phone. "We're anxious to talk and smell the jasmine. We have a lot of catching up to do. We'll expect to hear from you soon." The caller disconnected. An uneasy feeling skittered around inside. Talk and smell the jasmine?

When they came back, Rachel was clutching a string of blue beads. I inspected them. "These are too good."

"Mom!" Rachel cried in dismay.

"What are they?"

Jamie shrugged. "Lapis lazuli, maybe."

Rachel's eyes were shooting darts, but I shook my head. "We can't, Jamie. What if something happens to them?"

"I'll be careful." Rachel whined.

"Come on Ellie," Jamie said. "I trust her."

I looked at Jamie, then Rachel, standing next to each other in solidarity. "Okay. I don't have a prayer against both of you." Rachel threw her arms around me. "By the way, Jamie, someone left you a strange message. Something about talking and smelling the jasmine."

She replayed the tape on the machine, her face blank. "Must be a wrong number. I'll erase it." She started to hit delete.

"What if it's for Ted?"

"He talks to everyone on his cell phone."

"Still, shouldn't you save it for him?"

She took her finger off the button. "You're probably right."

Just then Conrad pushed through the door. Rachel's face grew crimson, and she seemed to forget how to move. Conrad brushed by her, if he expected nothing less than adoration. I bit my lip.

***

David and I entered the house after dinner Saturday night, warm and languid from too much food and wine. Inside an unnatural stillness greeted us. Blue light from the TV spilled into the hall. The springs of the couch squeaked, and I heard rustles. I peered into the family room.

Conrad was on one end of the couch, Rachel the other. Their faces were flushed, and the air felt steamy. The coffee table was littered with a videocassette sleeve, the remote, and a couple of glasses. Rachel tried to flash me a guileless smile. I stomped into the room. Rachel was only twelve years old.

"Do your parents know you're here, Conrad?"

He shrugged, seemingly fascinated by something on the wall. I picked up the phone. By the time I'd punched in four digits, he had a change of heart. "My mother's out of town, Mrs. Foreman. At my grandma's. I don't know where my father is."

I paused, then punched in the last digits. This was my daughter.

Ted picked up right away. "Hi, Ted. This is Ellie." I explained the situation as dispassionately as I could. He stormed in minutes later and dragged Conrad out. We heard him through the closed door. "You idiot. You know the rules. What the hell were you thinking?"

I told Rachel we'd talk about it in the morning. She slunk off to bed. David helped me straighten up.

"It's all my fault," I said, plumping the cushions on the couch.

"How can you say that?" he said.

"She sees us. We're not married."

"Ellie. We're adults. She's not."

"She thinks she is."

"Oh come on. Every kid experiments with sex."

"David. She's only twelve. Conrad's fourteen. There's a big difference."

"You're the one who lived in a commune." He teased. "And don't tell me you never played Spin the Bottle."

"Rachel and Conrad weren't playing Spin the Bottle." I took the glasses into the kitchen. "She might as well be Lindsay Dellinger."

David followed me in. "Who?"

"Lindsay Dellinger. She was one of *those* girls. You remember, don't you?"

He offered me a slow smile.

"See?" I waggled my finger.

"I don't know Lindsay Dellinger."

"Doesn't matter. Here it is almost forty years later and the only thing I remember about the girl is her reputation. Which, when I mention it, immediately prompts you to leer. What if Rachel ends up like her?"

I sprinkled soap in the dishwasher, expecting one of David's calm, rational replies that would reveal the flaws in my logic. That would convince me Rachel was in no danger of being branded. It didn't come. I straightened up. He was looking past me. "David?"

"Sorry. I was just thinking. Remember the guy I told you about the night Ted and Jamie were over?"

"The guy who wanted to expand his business?"

"Yeah. Well, he backed out of the deal."

"Really." I wiped my hands on a towel.

He nodded. "What you said about reputations reminded me."

"You're not surprised, are you?" We started back to the family room. "People can't paper over their pasts with money."

David sat down on the couch. "But he'd come so far. Remade his life. Why would he throw away this opportunity?"

I dropped down next to him. "Maybe he wasn't sure he wanted it anymore. Maybe he couldn't reconcile the image of what he was becoming with what he used to be. Some people never escape their past."

"You did."

"I was just a wannabee, remember? And in my own way, I paid a price."

"But what you did wasn't intrinsically wrong."

I kissed his fingers. "You still believe that people act out of principle, not self-interest."

"Is that what Jack did?"

"I have no idea." I settled in the crook of his arm. "I guess I'm just jealous."

"Of what?"

"Your moral certainty."

"Don't be. I didn't expect Jack to pull out. We'd just talked a week before."

"Oh?"

"We were going over some hedging procedures. When we were done, I asked him whether the acronym for SHOUT had changed at some point. You remember what Ted said at dinner."

"Right."

"Well, Jack was so quiet I thought we'd been disconnected. Then he asked me how I knew."

"What'd you say?"

David shrugged. "That my girlfriend's neighbor told us."

***

The next morning I told Rachel she was too young for the kind of behavior I'd seen the night before and that I didn't want her seeing Conrad any more. She barely spoke to me afterwards. I counted the days until she turned twenty.

I debated whether to tell Jamie. Ted had probably filled her in, and I didn't want her to think I'd gone ballistic. But I didn't want her to think it had gone unnoticed either. As it happened, the only time I saw her was in passing. She was preoccupied with her mother, who'd suffered a sudden stroke. She was going back to Connecticut.

***

When I was young Halloween used to be my favorite holiday. But now that horror has gone mainstream, I hate it. Even so, I stayed home to "ooo" and "ah" over the headless monsters, blood-soaked vampires, and fearsome witches that roamed our block. Rachel baby-sits a lot of them, and I felt obligated to help grease the wheels of her burgeoning enterprise. What they call in marketing "extending good will".

Between doling out candy and appropriating more for ourselves, we tried to watch a movie. We were barely past the credits when a thump sounded at the door. I asked Rachel to open it.

Rachel was whimpering, one hand clasped across her mouth. I peered out the door. A dead raccoon lay sprawled on the mat. Some of its ribs protruded through its torso, and pieces of entrails with shiny white gristle gleamed in the light. Road kill.

***

David didn't come out that weekend. It was just as well. Rachel and I stayed home to watch videos. Afterwards, I flipped on CNN. The anchor reported that a former Sixties radical had been killed in a fire out East. Jack Halsey, according to the newscaster, had been associated with SHOUT, a Philadelphia group responsible for blowing up a bank thirty years ago. I called David. Jack Halsey had been his client.

***

The explosion woke me from a dead sleep. Glass shattered. Alarms blared. I tore out of bed, screaming at Rachel to wake up. A pungent smell wafted through the air, and it was chilly inside. I understood why when, instead of windows, I saw gaping holes framed with shards of glass. We stumbled down the stairs and raced out of the house.

The smell was stronger outside. I ran toward it. Toward the Matheson's'.

The blast had thrown most of the house up in the air, snapping walls and furniture into giant pick-up sticks. Three of the walls had collapsed, leaving a mass of fiery debris. A cloud of dust hovered above, a pale fog against the dark sky.

As I drew closer, I heard the sounds of disaster. Sirens cut through the air. Neighbors shouted. Doors slammed. Police and firemen converged on the scene. Hoses were uncoiled and jets of water flooded the house. More people arrived, including the fire marshal and his dog. He promptly walked the German shepherd around the perimeter of the property. The dog kept his head down, snuffling everything in its path. That's how they found Jamie, in the woods behind the house. She was alive, but her leg was broken.

***

I didn't get much sleep that night. Neither, apparently, did village detective Mike O'Malley. He was at my door by eight the next morning, with Special Agent Reese Brightman. I knew O'Malley, a tall, freckled, no-nonsense cop, and he raised an eyebrow in greeting. Despite the blustery morning, Brightman wore regulation sunglasses.

O'Malley stepped inside. "I hear you know the Matheson's.

I nodded. "Have you found Conrad and Ted?"

"We found the kid. He was spending the night at a friend's."

"Thank god."

"But we can't locate the husband. You have any idea where he might be?"

I shook my head.

O'Malley shifted. "Tell me, Ms. Foreman," he said, "Did the Matheson's have a strong marriage?"

I twisted one hand in the other. "It had its ups and downs."

"Any infidelity? Affairs?"

"Not that I know of." I scanned both their faces. "Why?"

O'Malley and Brightman exchanged glances. The FBI agent nodded. "We found a body in the house," O'Malley said. "Female. Pretty well charred." I swallowed. "She was stabbed before the bomb went off. A kitchen knife."

My hand flew to my throat. "And you think—"

Brightman cut me off. "We don't know what we think. What about Mrs. Matheson? Wasn't she supposed to be out of town?"

An edgy feeling spread through my gut. "She was in Connecticut for a few days, taking care of her mother."

"What do you know about Mrs. Matheson's youth?" Brightman interrupted.

"Her youth?"

"Was she involved in any political activities?"

"Jamie?" I said. "She's about as political as Martha Stewart."

***

The victim inside the Matheson house was Pamela Winger, who'd been implicated in the Philadelphia bank explosion thirty years ago. She'd been missing, but according to a source, she and Jack Halsey had stayed in touch. Winger apparently figured that Jamie killed Halsey and flew to Chicago confront her. The source -- who had to be Agent Brightman -- theorized that Jamie killed Winger, then planted the bomb to destroy the evidence.

They took Jamie to the Federal lock-up. A few days later I got a message she wanted to see me. I didn't want to go, but they said I was the only person besides Conrad she'd listed on her visitor request form. I drove downtown, showed my ID, and was escorted to a small room. I slid into a chair. Jamie hobbled in on crutches. Purple smudges ringed her eyes, and the orange prison jump suit hung on her slender frame. But she maneuvered gracefully and sat down as if we were at the Ritz Carlton for tea.

"How's Conrad?"

"Martha said he could stay with them as long as he wanted."

Her face relaxed. "She's a friend, Ellie. So are you."

I felt my stomach twist. "Not any more."

She reeled back as if I'd slapped her.

"How could you deceive me like this?" She gave me a blank look. "PTA, church choir, soccer mom. The gum story really had me going."

"What do you mean?"

"You were one of the SHOUT people who blew up that bank, and you've been living a white-bread life ever since." I shook my head. "And I thought you wouldn't step on a crack in the sidewalk."

"Ellie, you're wrong."

"I guess so." I leaned forward. "You knew who 'Jack' was from the start, didn't you? When you got that cryptic phone message about jasmine, you realized he'd tracked you down. The trips to your mother's were a lie. You went to Philadelphia to make sure he wouldn't expose you."

"No. You don't understand."

"But Jack wouldn't cooperate, would he? He'd already taken the rap for you once. So when he threatened to turn you in, you killed him. Pamela Winger too."

Jamie squirmed in her seat.

"How did you learn explosives, Jamie? Did SHOUT teach you? Or did you teach them?"

Jamie raised her hands, as if warding me off.

"What I don't understand is why you came back to your house. Why didn't you disappear like you did thirty years ago?"

She blinked. "Ellie, go away. This visit is over."

"I know. It was motherly love. You just had to see Conrad."

She pressed her palms together so hard that her nails whitened. "Ted called at my mother's. He said Conrad was sick and I had to come home. I caught the first flight back.

When I walked in, the body of that-- that woman was on the kitchen floor. I was running out to get help when the blast went off."

I stared at her for a minute, then stood up. "Nice try, Jamie. Or whoever you are."

***

I waited for Ted to surface, but after a month I realized he never would. I was surfing the net one night, and just for fun, I ran a search on SHOUT. The results produced several articles that traced the group's history, but none of them mentioned how the group changed its name. I checked again. Ted had seemed so sure.

That's when I knew.

Ted. Always on the move. The Ollie North persona. It was the perfect cover. It was Ted who went to Philadelphia. Ted who killed Halsey and Pamela Winger. Ted who lured Jamie home, intending to destroy her too.

I called Brightman the next morning, but he wasn't convinced. Ever since Kathleen Soliah was arrested, the Bureau's wanted to close out the Sixties, and he maintained that Jamie was part of SHOUT. David found her a lawyer, and according to him, she has a good chance.

We never did find out why Jack Halsey backed out of the currency deal. Maybe he wanted to keep his money liquid. Maybe he thought he'd need it to "manage" Ted. Maybe he decided he didn't want to be a capitalist after all.

***

I was shoveling the walk one winter day when Conrad showed up. The mound of debris that had been his house was now covered with snow. Conrad studied the property then strolled over to my house.

I leaned on the shovel. "How are you Conrad?"

"Okay." An olive green bundle was under his arm.

"I'm glad." My anger at his behavior had long ago faded. He had his own problems; he'd carry his father's burden forever.

"I – I came by to apologize for something," he said. "Last Halloween. The raccoon on your porch? It was me. I was mad. I hope you forgive me."

I looked at him. The earring was gone, and he'd cut his hair. "It's forgotten," I said. "Another life. But thank you for owning up."

"I'd like Rachel to have this." He handed me the green bundle. It was his army jacket. "It's the real thing. My mother got it at an Army-Navy store in Philadelphia."

I corrected him. "You mean your father."

He shook his head. "No." He took the jacket back. "It was my mom's." He held it up. Just above the breast pocket was a tiny embroidered white flower.

"It's supposed to be jasmine," he said. "I thought Rachel would like it." He handed it back and started to walk away.

I stared after him. Jasmine. Talk and smell the jasmine. Jamie was Jasmine. Jamie and Ted were in SHOUT together. I clutched the jacket to my chest. I had been wrong. Ted didn't blow up his own house, abandon his family, vanish without a trace. It *was* Jamie. Tired of thirty years of subterfuge and lies, she'd taken matters into her own hands. My eyes drifted to the woods at the back of the lot where they found her. Ted had never been found. Could there be other charred remains-- besides Pamela Winger's -- somewhere on the property?

"Conrad?"

He turned around and gazed at me, his shoulders hunched.

"Why are you giving this away?"

"I'm getting rid of some stuff. We're moving."

"Moving?"

"As soon as my mom gets back."

"Your mother's gone?"

He stiffened. "It's only for a few days. She'll be back. She said so."

I bit back a reply. He turned away. I watched him trudge through the snow, fourteen but already stooped like an old man.

THE END

Libby Fischer Hellmann

A WINTER'S TALE

This Ellie story was published in 2005 in the TECHNO NOIR anthology, edited by Eva Batonne and Jeffrey Marks. Bear in mind that the anthology was released pre-Facebook and Twitter.

Edward Kaiser was a cold fish. Richer than God, as my friend Susan would say her lip curled, but a cold fish nonetheless. He made his millions in high tech – something to do with floppy discs -- bought a huge estate on the outskirts of the village, and proceeded to behave like royalty. You never saw him around town, he didn't return calls, and he rarely mixed with us "commoners."

So when he was found dead at his keyboard on a blustery January morning, his screen saver winking over his lifeless form, no one seemed distressed.

Except his wife, Lisa, who reportedly was so devastated that Lew, our village pharmacist, hand-delivered a prescription of Xanax to the house.

"With three refills," Susan said as we power-walked down Happ Road that afternoon.

Snow crunched under our boots. Though the roads up here are always clear, except for mounds of dirty snow on the curbs that last until April, people neglect their sidewalks. Probably because there aren't that many to begin with. Sidewalks, that is. People, too.

"Three? How do you know?"

Susan flashed me her Cheshire Cat smile. I've never figured out how she knows exactly what's going on in our tiny community, but I'm happy she does. I'm even happier she tells me about it.

"She found his body, didn't she?"

Susan nodded. "She came home from a tennis match, went into his office to tell him she'd won, and there he was."

"So you think she needs the Xanax because she found him or because her tennis schedule is up for grabs?"

Susan shot me a look.

I hiked up my sweatpants; the elastic was coming loose. "I'm sorry, but I can't summon up too much sympathy for her."

If women are built for either speed or comfort, Lisa Kaiser was an Indy 500 contender. Young, slim, and athletic, she had long glossy hair and enormous brown eyes—I remember when I met her thinking a person could get lost in them for days. She and her son, Sam, stood to inherit a bundle; Edward's first wife had died years ago.

"Edward wasn't much to write home about, I grant you," Susan said, "but Lisa's different. I've never seen her without a smile, and she always stops to chat. I can't tell you how many times she asks about Dara."

"That's because Sam's in her class," I said. Along with Rachel, my thirteen year old.

"Maybe. But *she* drives Sam to school every morning. Not the chauffeur. And she took her shift at the Book Fair just like everybody else."

"So she pulls her weight. Still, how can you feel sorry for someone who's going to inherit a gazillion dollars?"

"Fifty gazillion."

I sucked in a breath.

As we passed the Catholic Church, a ray of weak sun broke through the overcast and struck the stained glass window. "Heart attack, huh?"

"Don't even think about it, Ellie. Everybody knows a bad heart runs in the Kaiser family. Plus, most of the money is going to the kids from his first marriage."

"Really?"

"Lisa signed a pre-nup. She won't be destitute, of course. She's in for a few million."

"How old are his kids?"

"They're both over twenty-one. Left home a long time ago."

"And Lisa's barely thirty."

"Thirty-two last week."

"Happy Birthday."

***

Two weeks later, I was in the supermarket frowning at a bin of imported, waxy tomatoes, wondering how I could stand five more months of them, when a cart bumped me from behind. I spun around. Lisa Kaiser struggled to steer hers away.

"Oh, Ellie. I'm sorry." A flush crept across her face. "I'm so clumsy."

"Don't worry about it." I angled my cart a safe distance away. "How are you doing, Lisa?"

She eyed the tomatoes and gave a little shrug. "You know how it is."

"I know what a shock you've been through. Please let me express my --"

"Don't." She brushed my arm with her fingers. "I got your lovely note. I haven't gotten around to responding, but I ..."

"You just did."

She smiled tentatively. "Thanks."

I turned back to the tomatoes, picked out four, and slid them in a plastic bag. "How's Sam?"

She tore off a bag from the roll above the bin. "He's been so brave. He adored Edward, you know. He's trying so hard to be ..." She bit her lip. "By the way, Rachel's been really sweet. Sam told me they've been e-mailing every day. You should know what a compassionate daughter you have."

I smiled, my insides growing all soft and warm the way they do when someone says something nice about my daughter. I closed my bag with a twist-tie and looked back at Lisa. She stood there, her bag in hand, looking small and lost.

I cast about for something to say. "Lisa.. is – is there something – I mean, would you—"

Her eyes filled, and she lowered her head. Her shoulders started to heave. "I'm sorry." I sensed she was trying hard to control herself. "I'm not – I just -- it's been so—so hard." She looked up with an anguished face.

I remember how overwhelmed and isolated I felt when my marriage ended, though Barry is very much alive. And will undoubtedly remain so just to be a thorn in my side. But Lisa looked vulnerable. Impulsively I burst out, "Would you like to get coffee?"

"I'd love to."

We pushed our carts over to the coffee bar, a recent addition to the store. I bought lattes and carried them over to a small, planked table.

"It's just all so overwhelming." She sat and wiped her nose with the sleeve of her jacket. "I really loved him. And now, well, Sam and I, well, we're just rolling around that monster of a house."

I rummaged in my bag, pulled out a pack of tissues, and pushed it over.

She dabbed at her eyes. "I guess I'm going to have to get used to change."

I nodded. Anything I said would sound trivial.

"A lot of change." She pried off the lid of her coffee. "The house, for starters."

"What do you mean?"

"I called a realtor. She's going to list it -- privately, of course -- next week."

"You're selling?" I'd never been inside, but it was supposed to be quite a showplace. It had won several awards and was featured in a decorating magazine.

She gave me a sad little smile. "Life has a funny way of punching you in the gut." She paused. "The truth is, Edward was practically broke when he died."

Despite my hot drink, the muscles in my face froze.

"I know. But it's true." She blew on her coffee.

I didn't know what to say. This was huge news. And Susan didn't know it. I didn't want to pry, but I sure wanted to know more. My face must have registered how torn I was, because she gave me another half-smile.

"I never paid much attention to Edward's business affairs. I'm just a 'trophy wife', you know."

I started to cut in, but she overrode me. "No, it's okay. I know what people say. But his lawyers sat me down the other day, and, boy, did I get an education." She unfolded the tissue and started punching her plastic stirrer through it. "You know that piece of metal – the metal spring that's on a floppy disc?"

"Sure."

"Well, Edward invented it."

"You're kidding."

"He was smart enough to patent it. Sold licenses to all the floppy disc manufacturers, quit work, and collected all the royalties –"

"Hold on. Are you saying he – you – get paid for every single floppy disc that's sold?"

She dipped her head imperceptibly.

I almost whistled. If that was true, fifty million was a pittance. I could be drinking coffee with the next Melinda Gates.

Except that she'd just said Edward was broke.

She went on. "There are really only two or three disc manufacturers of any size. The biggest is Riteway. That's where most of Edward's royalties came from. But recently their payments dried up. Practically disappeared."

I frowned. "Why?"

"They claim they've been hit hard by competition. And the economy."

"But they're the biggest disc maker in the world."

"Right. And discs are a commodity product. So I'm told." She added hastily. "Not dependent on economic conditions."

"What do the lawyers say?"

"They're trying to figure it all out. But Riteway isn't being very helpful. In the meantime, there are the legal fees, the accountants' fees, and no money coming in." She punched another hole in her tissue. "And of course there's the house. You'd be surprised at how fast it all goes."

"I'm sorry, Lisa. I had no idea."

"No one does." She gave me another sad little smile. "I'm glad I never took it all seriously, you know?"

"What will you do?"

"I don't know. Go back to work, I guess."

I wondered what a trophy wife does when her medal tarnishes.

"You know, I can't help thinking that maybe the stress of it all got to Edward. He was suing Riteway for the money."

"You don't think he --"

"Suicide? No. Edward was a fighter." She looked over. "I know people around here didn't like him. But they didn't know him. He was very shy and gentle. Almost afraid of people. But strong. That's why I fell in love with him." Her eyes locked onto mine. "And he'd just had a check-up. Everything was fine. Except for his ear."

"His ear?"

"He has Meniere's Disease. Gets spells of dizziness. Ringing in the ears. But besides that, he was fine. Cholesterol. Blood pressure. Everything."

"They say that's when it can happen."

"Maybe." She clamped her lips together.

"What?"

"Well," She hesitated. "I do know he was pretty angry that morning."

"Angry?"

"Someone came to see him. Right after I took Sam to school. When I came home, I saw the car out front. They were in Edward's den, but I could hear them arguing."

"Who was it?"

"I don't know. I couldn't hear the words. Just the shouting."

"You think it had something to do with the—the situation?"

"I don't know. I went out for tennis – I didn't even say goodbye..." She blinked several times. "And when I came home...."

I leaned forward. "Lisa...did you tell the police about this?"

"Of course."

"What did they say?"

"Well, since I couldn't identify who was here, and no one else in the house saw him, they didn't do much. And then when the autopsy came back with the heart attack, well, they basically said there was nothing they could do." She balled up the tissue and pitched it into the trash.

***

When I got home, I went online and checked out Riteway. It was part of Comron, a huge conglomerate that apparently had made the transition from bricks and mortar to high tech. In addition to Riteway, Comron owned a gallery of businesses, including network servers, ethernet cards, even a pharmaceutical division.

I also did a search on Edward, which bore out everything Lisa said. Edward had been a geek who studied at MIT, then did research at Xerox Parc with the Alan Kay crowd. He'd been working on his own when he came up with the disc drive spring. His first wife was from Lake Forest, and after the wedding, they moved from Silicon Valley back to the Midwest. They had two children, a boy and a girl, but a few years later, his wife died of cancer.

Just out of curiosity, I did a search on Lisa. I was surprised by the results. Twelve years ago, under the name of Dorset, Sam's middle name, she bylined a couple of articles that appeared in something called "The Grapevine." When I clicked on the URL, I discovered that "The Grapevine" was the company newsletter for Riteway Corporation.

Company newsletters are generally authored by the company's PR or communications department. Which meant that Lisa Dorsett Kaiser – at some point -- must have worked for Riteway.

***

A week later I was doing paperwork upstairs, longing for jonquils to poke through the snow when a white Mercedes SUV pulled to the curb. I watched through the window as Lisa Kaiser opened the door and climbed out. A skimpy tennis skirt hung below her down jacket, but her long legs, tan even in winter, were bare.

"Hi, Ellie," she said when I answered the door. "I'm sorry to bother you, but something strange is going on."

I looked at her legs.

"I didn't change – I jumped in the car as soon this came," she said. "I was spooked."

"Why? Was it an article in the Riteway company newsletter?" I hoped my voice sounded as irritated as I felt.

Her eyes widened. "You did a search on me."

"You said you didn't know anything about Edward's business dealings. But you worked for the company that bought his invention."

"I-- I didn't think it was important. Yes, I worked there. That's how I met Edward."

"Is that so?"

"Yes. I wrote the press release about the license agreement. I interviewed him, and it just kind of took off from there."

"You said you didn't know anything about his business dealings."

"That's true. Once we got serious, I quit my job." She licked her lips. "Ellie, if I thought it would bother you, I would have told you. But you were just so wonderful when we had coffee, and I was so -- " Her voice trailed off. "I'd been doing a lot better, you know. In large part because of you." She pulled something out of her bag. "I was hoping you'd take a look at his. But – if you don't want to, I understand."

I stood there. I didn't know what to do.

She must have taken that as a rejection and turned away from the door. "It's okay. Just forget about it." She started back toward her car, her shoulders slumped.

I waited until she was almost at the curb. "Hold on, Lisa."

***

I opened the clasp of the envelope she handed me and drew out a small photo. Turning it over, I saw a black and white image of a farmhouse in the center of a grassy field. The house had clapboard siding and a wraparound porch in front. Prairie grass on both sides of the house stretched to a line of trees in the back. It was a wide angle shot, but very grainy, and I couldn't pick out any details. Something about it felt old – like it had been snapped with a Brownie camera and stuck into an album with those white corner holders.

"What is this?" I asked.

Lisa shrugged. "I don't know. That's why I'm spooked. It came in the mail."

I turned over the envelope. Lisa's name and address were typed on the front. The cancellation stamp indicated it had been mailed from downtown. But that was it. There were no other markings on the envelope. No return address.

"Was there a note?"

"Nothing."

I studied the picture again. "Why bring it to me?"

She looked down, as if suddenly shy. "I – I know you've had some experience with things like this. And, like I said, well...." Her voice trailed off.

"The quality of the shot is lousy. What do you think I can do?"

"I'm not sure, but you're a video producer..."

"Lisa, this is a still. It's a different technology."

65

She looked at me steadily.

"Why don't you just forget about it? Throw it away? You know how screwed up the post office is these days."

"No." Her voice was sharp. "It was addressed to me. I—I can't. And after what happened to Edward, I'm scared." She wrapped her arms across her chest. "Ellie, I understand if you don't want to help. But is there anyone you know who would?"

I looked at her. Her face was pale and drawn. Dark circles ringed her eyes. I thought about the loss she and Sam had suffered. How, after a tragedy like that you analyze, rework, and second-guess everything, wondering whether there could have been something, anything you might have done to prevent it. I'd done that when my mother died.

I sighed. "Leave it with me."

Denny Horton was a commercial photographer who escaped to the country after burglars made off with the equipment from his Chicago studio. I hadn't seen him in over a year, but after I dropped Rachel at school the next morning, I called and headed out to Kenosha.

"Ellie." He wrapped me in a bear hug when I arrived. "Great to see you. Come on in."

He'd grown a full beard, probably to compensate for the expanding area of shiny pink skin on his head. But he still had the same twinkle in his eye, as if he'd just heard the funniest joke in the world and couldn't wait to pass it along.

Heavy furniture and faded raglan rugs gave his living room a timeless feel. The smoky aroma of bacon hung in the air. I tried to ignore how much my mouth watered.

"You've done well for yourself."

Denny's eyes crinkled at the corners. "You ain't seen nothin'. Come on up"

Upstairs, several doors led off a hall that was hung with a gallery of poster-sized black and white photos, landscapes and portraits. Behind one door was a traditional photography studio with a Macintosh, an art stand, and a mounted camera. The second door opened into a video-editing suite with banks of monitors, switches, and an Avid.

I whistled, suitably impressed. "If you build it, they will come."

"And to think I owe it all to those punks who ripped me off." He led me back into the first room. "So what's shakin'?"

I pulled out the photo of the farmhouse. "You mind taking a look at this?"

He inspected the shot. "What am I looking for?"

"I don't know. Anything that tells us where it is." I explained the situation. "I promised someone I'd check it out."

Denny sat down at his Mac, booted up Photoshop, and placed the photo in his scanner. After a few clicks of the mouse, the farmhouse appeared on the monitor.

"Okay." He laced his fingers together and stretched them out backwards. "Let's roll."

He pulled down a menu, and a group of icons appeared on the screen. He clicked on a graphic that looked like a hand and began to move it slowly over the image. When he reached a small dark area just to the left of the farmhouse's door, he dragged an icon that looked like a magnifying glass over it.

The area grew larger and blurrier. He clicked on more icons, tinkering with the contrast, brightness, and resolution. After a few moments, something materialized.

I leaned forward. "What is that? "

"Let's see." He pulled down another menu and clicked.

"What are you doing now?"

"Creating more contrast. If something is blurry, we can sharpen it up, maybe figure out what it is. I'll try five hundred per cent. You lose detail, though."

He clicked again and suddenly three numbers appeared in a black box on the side of the door.

I stared at the screen. "Two five seven?"

"Probably the number of the house." He clicked on the image he'd initially scanned in. "See where we started?" He grinned. The un-retouched original showed nothing but a dark mass.

I stared at the monitor. "Two-five-seven... but where? It could be anywhere."

"That's true." He turned back to the monitor.

"Let's see. It's farm country. Maybe if we could figure out what crops they were growing in the field—Hey, wait a minute!"

"What?"

"Look at this." He pointed to a long, skinny object about twenty feet away from the house on the edge of the frame.

I squinted. I hadn't noticed it until now. "What is it?"

He didn't answer but began to work again, this time more slowly, panning icons across the object, then backing up the other way. After a while, something that resembled a telephone pole appeared.

"Lemme rescan this."

"Why? It's just a telephone pole."

"Maybe not."

I watched as he magnified the image, pasted it into a new file, and played with the sharpness and contrast. "Take a look."

I did and saw a post that looked like it stood eight feet above the ground. On the top was a white sign with black markings. As Denny continued to sharpen the image, letters and numbers came into focus.

"What is it?" My breath came more quickly. "What does it say?"

"It's a road sign," Denny said. "It says CR Ninety Three."

***

County Road Ninety-three cuts through the western edge of Joliet, I learned that night, so after dropping Rachel at school the next day, I printed out directions and headed south. It took over an hour, but finally, I turned onto a road where frame houses and weathered barns shared space with new colonials and offices. I couldn't tell if the neighborhood was supposed to be rural farmland or suburban sprawl. Apparently, the developers couldn't either.

The mantle of snow on the ground skewed my perspective, making everything appear cleaner, bigger, and sharper. I passed the house before I recognized the wrap-around porch and clapboard siding.

I backtracked and parked at the end of a driveway that either wasn't visible in the photo or hadn't been built when the shot was taken. A blue Dodge Ram was parked at the end.

As I walked up to the front door, I realized I hadn't recognized the house because it was in much better shape than in the snapshot. It sported a fresh paint job, new shutters, and new windows. White curtains fluttered at the windows.

A female voice answered my knock. "Just a sec."

I wiggled my fingers through my gloves. There was no lake breeze this far away, and the bright sun did nothing to warm the frigid air.

The door was opened by a young woman with a baby in her arms. "Hello." She smiled. "Can I help you?"

I watched the baby grab a fistful of long, brown hair. She gently disentangled his fingers.

"I—I'm sorry to bother you. My name is Ellie Foreman. I'm from Chicago."

"Annie Caruso. You're a long way from home."

***

After I explained why I was there, Annie took me to visit her neighbor, Gwen Teasdale. The Teasdale's had farmed these parts for generations, she said, and like Annie, Gwen lived on one of the few farms left.

The woman, now in her eighties, set out tea and a plate of home baked cookies.

"That house has an interesting history, child," she said.

"How so, Mrs. Teasdale?"

"Call me Gwen, honey. Everyone does. Old maid Gwen." She winked at Annie. "You young people think I don't know that."

Annie colored from the neck up.

I smiled.

"That used to be owned by the Whitney family."

"Whitney?"

"Yes ma'am. Thomas Whitney was the first warden of the state prison."

Of course. "I didn't realize we were that close."

"It's just over the rise." Gwen looked at my face and laughed. "Don't worry. It's mostly closed now. Anyway, they moved out a long time ago. His wife ran off with one of the guards."

"Who moved in?"

"No one. It just sat here. For a long while, I reckon. The place was a dump, in fact, until the Mansteads took it over. They grew soybeans and corn. But their kids – they had two sons – didn't want any part of the farm. It went through a couple more families before Annie and her husband bought it."

"What happened to the Mansteads?"

"They passed on. One of the boys was killed in Vietnam. The other boy—well, now let's see. I think he went on to college. Did real well, I recall Virginia saying. Got himself a fine and fancy job at some big company."

"You know which company?"

"Sorry." She touched her forehead. "It's clear out of my mind."

"What was his name?"

"Let's see. The brother who died was Pete. But the other one's name was Harvey. That's right. Harvey Manstead."

***

When I got home, I went online and did some research on

all the names Gwen Teasdale had given me. After I found what I was looking for, I grabbed my keys, threw on my coat, and called up to Rachel.

"I'll be back in a few minutes, honey. Why don't you boil water for pasta?"

"When I'm done on IM."

"Who are you chatting with?"

"Sam Kaiser. Hey, did you know they're moving?"

"I heard."

"He says it's soon. His mom told him to start packing."

"Oh, I'm sure it's not that soon. The house just went on the market."

"Whatever."

I wound around the long drive to the Kaiser home. There were no sidewalks in this part of the village, just wide expanses of snow-covered lawn. I parked and trudged up a shoveled path to the house, a Tudor with steeply pitched gables, massive chimney, and half-timbered exteriors. Tall, diamond-paned windows stared out from the stone facing. Though it was almost dark, I could make out a sign on the lawn that said "Under Contract."

Maybe Rachel was right.

Lisa answered the door in a blood red designer pants suit. Her face was carefully made up, and silver flashed at her ears. She looked as if she was going out. It took her a moment to focus.

"Ellie. What are – I didn't expect you."

I motioned toward the sign. "That didn't take long."

"We were lucky." She smiled. "At least something's going right."

"Well, I have news, too."

She shot me an expectant look. "The picture?"

"I traced it."

She pressed the palms of her hands together. "What did you find?"

"The farmhouse used to belong to Harvey Manstead." I watched for a reaction.

She brought her hands to her chin, and her brows drew together. "Harvey Manstead? That name sounds familiar."

"He's the Vice-president of Finance at Riteway Corporation."

"Of course." She dropped her hands. "He was involved in setting up Edward's royalty payments." Her frown deepened. "But I don't understand. Why would someone send me a picture of a house that belonged to him?" "Good question. The only thing I can think of is that someone wanted to send you a message."

"What kind of message?"

I stamped my feet in the cold, wondering why she didn't invite me in. "Well, given all the corporate accounting scandals, you might want to take a closer look at those royalty payments."

"What are you saying?"

"That there could be a whistle-blower inside the company."

"Ellie, do you think Harvey Manstead is behind Edward's problems?"

"I'm just saying that it wouldn't hurt to take a closer look."

Lisa shook her head, as if she were in shock. "I can't believe it."

"Lisa, what did Edward tell you about the royalty payments?"

"Not much. They started out fine, but then they became irregular. And when he tried to investigate, they brushed him off."

"What about that argument he had the morning he died? What can you tell me about that?"

"Like I said, I don't know who it was."

I rubbed my hands together to ward off the cold. "But you saw the car. What kind of car was it?"

Her eyes narrowed, as if she were concentrating on her memory. "I think it was red."

"A red what?"

"Something big. Four doors. Red. That's all I know." She laid her hand on my arm. "Ellie, do you think he—Harvey Manstead was here that morning? Arguing with Edward?"

"Like I said, I'm not saying anything. I'll get back to you."

"Oh, god. What if Harvey turns out to have a red car, Ellie? What do I do then?"

"You go back to the police."

***

Village Detective Dan O'Malley was at my door two days later. "We have to talk, Ellie."

"Why do I have a feeling I'm not going to like this?" I led him into the kitchen and poured him a cup of coffee.

He dropped his tall frame into a chair and dumped three teaspoons of sugar in his mug. "We paid Harvey Manstead a visit this morning."

"And?"

"How well do you know Lisa Kaiser?"

"I knew I wasn't going to like this." I poured myself coffee and sat down. "Our kids are in the same class. She asked me to look into that picture for her. Why?"

"She's gone. Took her son and skipped."

My jaw dropped. "When?"

"Sometime over the past twenty-four hours."

I flashed back on her red pants suit. The slightly unfocused expression. Had she been getting ready to run when I showed up? No. She'd waited for me to call her back with the report that Harvey Manstead did indeed have a red Lincoln Continental -- I'd talked to the manager of his garage. And she'd obviously called the police after that.

"Where'd she go?"

"We don't know. But Manstead has an interesting story." He sipped his coffee. "When we asked him what he knew about the royalty payments, he was evasive. Wouldn't say a thing. Even had his lawyer show up. Meanwhile, a uniform called from Kaiser's house to say it was all shut up."

I bit my lip.

"Manstead didn't believe us. Thought we were playing him. So we took him over there. Thought maybe it would loosen his tongue." O'Malley smiled. "Once he realized she was gone, he flipped like a pancake."

"He was embezzling the royalty payments?"

"Yes and no."

I cocked my head. O'Malley wasn't one to equivocate.

"The money was going into another account. Offshore. Held by Mrs. Edward Kaiser."

"Manstead was putting Edward's money into his wife's offshore account?"

"They were lovers, Ellie."

"Lisa Kaiser and Harvey Manstead?"

"Over ten years. They met when she worked at Riteway. He left his wife because of her, but she married Edward."

"Ouch."

"She kept seeing Harvey on the side. Promised they would run away together if he'd 'fund her venture'." O'Malley shrugged. "He believed her. Especially after she took care of Edward."

"She killed him?"

"Manstead says she used potassium chloride."

"The stuff you throw on your driveway to melt ice?"

He nodded. "It mimics a heart attack if you inject it in the right spot. And it's not hard to liquefy. We found three bags in the garage."

"Inject it? Come on, where's she going to get a syringe? You can't tell me Lew delivered it."

O'Malley bared his teeth, but it wasn't a smile. "One of the treatments for Meniere's Disease is to inject yourself with histamines. We found an entire box of syringes in their bathroom."

My stomach turned over. I went to the sink and emptied my coffee. "Hold on. What about the picture? The photo of the farmhouse?"

"What about it?"

"How did she get that?"

"She must have wangled it from Manstead and sent it to herself."

"And then brought it to me." I put the mug in the dishwasher. "But Manstead does drive a red Lincoln. I checked."

"She made it up, Ellie. No one else saw the car, and he has a solid alibi – he was at a board meeting."

I straightened up. "She didn't want to share the wealth with his kids."

"Looks that way."

"So she killed her husband and set up her lover."

"And left him holding the bag."

"And I helped."

O'Malley didn't answer.

I looked over, grateful for his silence. "What's the next step?"

"The Feds 'll throw the book at Manstead. Fraud. Embezzlement. Whatever else they can hang on him."

"What about Lisa?"

"They'd pick her up if they could find her. After all, she did commit murder."

I thought about it. "She won't leave any tracks. She's obviously been planning this for years."

O'Malley shrugged again. "You never know."

***

Over the next few weeks, jonquils sprouted, and the drip of melting ice off the eaves promised renewal, but my gut was a congealed mass of anger. Susan was contrite, too, and our walks included long spates of silence. Like everyone else,

I'd underestimated Lisa Kaiser. Her stint in corporate PR had served her well. She'd analyzed her audience – me -- and suckered me in with just the right mix of reticence and modesty. All the while pulling slick moves on everyone else.

I was making dinner one night, wondering whether I'd ever learn that sharing space and time with someone doesn't automatically confer trust, when I called up to Rachel. "We're ready, sweetie."

"Be right there." I heard the soft click of keys on the computer. "I just want to finish this message."

"I thought we agreed. No IM before homework."

"This isn't IM. I'm e-mailing Sam."

"Sam Kaiser?"

"Yeah – but his mother doesn't know."

I raced up the stairs and burst into her room. "You're in touch with Sam Kaiser?"

Rachel looked up and nodded. "After they moved, his mother said he couldn't email anyone, but he figured out a way."

"How?"

"He's using his neighbor's computer."

I stared at Rachel. I knew she didn't realize the significance of what she'd just said. E-mails can be traced. Especially by the Feds.

"Pretty slick, huh?" She said.

I smiled as I picked up the phone. "You said it, kiddo."

THE END

THE MURDER OF KATIE BOYLE

My sixth novel, DOUBLEBACK (October 2009), features both Ellie Foreman and Georgia Davis as co-protagonists, and I'm often asked how they originally met. Georgia made an appearance in A PICTURE OF GUILT, and then more substantively in AN IMAGE OF DEATH, but they already had a passing acquaintance. How they met is explained in this story, written and published in 2009, even thought it takes place before AN EYE FOR MURDER (2002). The story was published in a limited numbered edition and can be found on audio at www.sniplits.com.

Katie Boyle had a perfect body, a beautiful face, a terrific sense of humor, and a law degree. So it wasn't surprising that lots of women hated her. Still, when I found her body in the closet of Bodyworks, her exercise studio, on a sunny spring morning, I was stunned. Murders don't happen on the North Shore of Chicago – not often, anyway.

I wouldn't have found her at all if I didn't have the annoying habit of being early. Promptness on the set is non-negotiable in my video production business, and it's spilled over into the rest of my life. When I'm early, as was the case that Monday, I help Katie haul out the weights, bands, and other paraphernalia she uses to torture us.

The studio occupies an area of the village we euphemistically call downtown, but is really not much more than a couple of strip malls on both sides of the street. I parked in the lot, went inside, and climbed the steps to the second floor. I stopped in the hall. The door to the studio was unlocked, but the lights were off. I was mildly surprised. Katie usually arrived well before class, steaming cappuccino in hand.

I flipped on the lights and went into a tiny reception area. I love the smell of coffee even more than the taste, but there was no rich, dark aroma wafting through the air. Instead, I noticed a stuffy smell, as if the studio had been full of people and needed airing out. But there'd been no early class this morning.

Maybe she was in the bathroom. "Katie?" I called out. "It's Ellie."

No answer.

I peeked into the studio. It was a large comfortable room with a thick rug -- one of the only carpeted exercise studios I'd ever seen—and mirrored walls. As I looked around, I caught a glimpse of myself frowning.

"Katie... " I called again. "You there?"

Still no answer.

I ran a hand through my hair. Maybe she went back to her car for a pair of socks or a headband. I checked the clock. Still eight minutes until class. Mondays are usually an interval class combining aerobics and strength training; I should pull out the equipment from the closet. I went over and twisted the door handle. I felt a weight on the other side. I opened it. That's when Katie's body tumbled out, her head bloody and misshapen.

***

Georgia Davis was just sitting down for breakfast with Matt at the village diner when the call came in. Part of her wanted Matt to ignore it. Although they were both on the force, he was a detective; she was patrol. During the day their paths rarely crossed, and if they did, they were careful to keep their relationship quiet. The force had strict fraternization rules. Matt's partner, Dan O'Malley knew – how could he not? But to everyone else, they were just cop-friends, who, like other cops, would rather share a meal with each other than civilians.

She stole a glance at Matt. People should only know what else they shared. He gave her back one of the looks he usually kept private. Her stomach flipped. Physically, they were opposites: his black wiry curls so different from her straight blond hair; his dark eyes so different than her Nordic blues. His softness. Her sharp edges. Different. Still, she couldn't get enough. She ached for his touch, his smile, his attention. It went way beyond sex, even beyond passion. Which was why she hated anything or anyone who stood in her way.

Matt's cell kept chirping. He shrugged regretfully, as if he could read her mind, and picked up. He was quiet. Then, "The one right around the corner? You're shitting me. Okay. I'm there." He disconnected, slid out of the booth, and looked at Georgia. "You're not going to believe this. Apparently, we have a homicide. I'll tell dispatch you're coming with me."

***

Ten minutes later, the morning quiet was shattered by a phalanx of cops, detectives, and technical-looking types in biotech uniforms. I learned later they were all part of a North Shore Task Force that was activated whenever there was a homicide or violent crime. Meanwhile, the dozen or so women who showed up for class were shooed home, but they saw me inside, and I reckoned I'd have a slew of calls on my machine when I got home.

I hunched nervously in a corner. I'd already been questioned by a uniformed cop when two more showed up, a woman in uniform, and a man who wasn't. Although the woman stayed in the background, she watched every move the man made. When he approached me, she took a step forward. I couldn't tell whether she was protecting him or just wanted to eavesdrop.

"Ms. Foreman, I'm Detective Matt Singer. I understand you found the vic – I mean Ms. Boyle."

I nodded.

"I know you've already told Officer Parker what happened. But do you mind telling me again?"

I shook my head. "Are you – do you know how she died?"

His tone was surprisingly gentle. "Officially, we won't know until the autopsy results, but it looks like blunt trauma to her head."

"Someone bashed her head in."

"Something like that." He cleared his throat. "Now, it's your turn."

He prompted me with questions, many of which I'd already answered, but I got the sense he was really listening, so I didn't mind. The other officer who'd questioned me had looked bored.

"Were you a friend of– Ms. Boyle?"

I nodded. "I liked Katie."

"Did she have a lot of friends?"

I bit my lip.

Detective Singer caught it. "What?"

"Katie was – well…" I glanced at the female officer.

Singer looked over his shoulder, as if just now noticing she was there. "Oh, this is Officer Davis. She's with me."

A thin smile flitted across Davis's face. I caught that. He turned back to me. "You were saying…"

"Katie – well, Katie was one of those people you either love or hate."

"How so?"

"She is – was – a beautiful woman. And smart. And fit. She has two great kids. A nice house in Glenview. The whole nine yards." I glanced at Davis. "You know what I mean?"

Davis's face stayed blank. Singer answered for them both. "No. Tell me."

I blew out air, feeling flustered. "It's – well – I feel kind of uncomfortable saying this -- but I could understand some women being jealous."

"Jealous." He repeated.

"You know, the woman who has everything." I looked at Davis again. She gave nothing back.

"Were you jealous?" Singer asked.

I sputtered. "M—me? No. I wasn't. I'm not. Wasn't."

"Because…"

I paused. "Because Katie's life – wasn't as perfect as she let on."

One of his eyebrows arched. "How so?"

I hesitated. Then I sighed. "Katie and her husband were divorcing. It was -- acrimonious."

"Why?"

I paused, longer this time. "She was having an affair. With Paul Munson, one of the instructors here."

***

"I want you to take the lead," Matt said as Georgia headed west to Waukegan Road an hour later. Georgia was driving the cruiser; Matt was riding shotgun.

"But I'm not a detective."

"You will be one day. It's good practice."

She flashed him a smile. Matt always looked out for her.

He pulled out a pocket notepad, put on his glasses, and thumbed through his notes. Georgia liked it when he wore his glasses. They gentled him.

"So, what did you think of Ellie Foreman?" Matt asked.

"In what way?"

"Any observations? Was she a reliable witness? Was she hiding anything?"

Georgia felt her brow furrow. "She's was okay, I guess. One of those North Shore women."

"What does that mean?"

She could tell from his tone he was edgy. She shook her head. "Nothing."

"Sweetheart, you can't keep that chip on your shoulder. Just because you didn't grow up here. I didn't either."

She looked over. "That's not true. Skokie is on the North Shore."

"By a whisker."

"Still, it's a far cry from the West side."

Matt changed the subject. Probably figured it was better than having an argument. "I liked her."

"Who?"

"Foreman," he said. "You can tell she's a video producer. She sees things. Picks up details."

A pang of jealousy stabbed Georgia. She forced it back down. Foreman was no threat. She was only a witness, for Christ's sake. A witness in a homicide.

Still.

She pulled up to a four-story apartment building in Glenview. She and Matt got out of the car, went inside, and pressed the buzzer opposite the name Paul Munson.

There was no response. Georgia rang again. Then a third time. Finally the buzzer sounded back and the door unlocked. They took the stairs to the third floor.

The man who opened the door looked like he'd just woken up. Wearing a gray t-shirt and white shorts, he was young and handsome, and seemed to be in great shape. Thick sandy hair, sculpted arms, and blue eyes that, even sleepy, were checking her out. Georgia could tell he liked what he saw.

"Paul Munson?" She said.

His eyes turned guarded. "Yeah?"

"I'm Officer Davis. This is detective Singer. Do you know Katie Boyle?"

"She's my boss." He didn't appear to be dissembling. He looked confused.

"When was the last time you saw her?"

"Last night..." He stopped suddenly, as if he'd realized he shouldn't be so free with information. His chin jutted out. "Why? What's wrong? "

Georgia took a breath. "I'm sorry to tell you, but Katie Boyle has been the victim of a homicide. She's dead."

Munson's hand flew to his mouth, and he reeled back. He looked sincere to Georgia, although she wasn't experienced enough to tell when someone was acting. Or what they were thinking. No. That wasn't true. She could always tell what was on Matt's mind by the look in his eyes or the set of his mouth. She forced herself back to Munson. His face went ashen, and he clutched the door for support.

"May we ask you a few questions?" Once the words were out of her mouth, she realized it should have been a statement, not a question. He didn't appear to notice. In fact, he opened the door wider. "Of course."

His apartment was what you'd kindly call spare. She and Munson sat on a threadbare brown couch. Matt took the only chair.

When Munson wasn't teaching three classes a week at Bodyworks, he said, he conducted personal training sessions for wealthy North Shore women. Business was good. Everyone wanted to be fit.

"What about your personal life?"

"What about it?"

"You're not married. Are you seeing anyone?"

His answer surprised her. He looked at Georgia, then Matt. "You mean, was I sleeping with Katie?" He slumped. "Katie and I were – well, yes. We were lovers. She was in the process of leaving her husband for me."

"You and she were going to be—together?"

He nodded. Georgia picked up on his pained expression. "We were making plans."

"Who knew about your affair?"

"No one. Well, maybe one or two of the women who come to class."

"Why do you say that?"

"It's hard to keep your hands off someone you love when you work with them every day."

Georgia felt her cheeks get hot. She wondered if Matt's were too. She didn't dare look. "What about her husband? Did he know?"

"Eventually. Katie told him when they separated."

"How did he take it?"

"He was furious. Threatened to take the kids from her. Said he'd make her pay."

"Tell me what you know about him."

"Steve is volatile. He can't keep a job. That's why Katie went to law school. She had to support the family. She was looking for a job when --" He stopped abruptly and swallowed. "That's how we -- the affair -- started. We were having a beer after class one night, and she poured out her heart. I'd always thought she was so together, you know?" Tears welled in his eyes. "She made me feel like I was the only one who could -- patch her up. Put her back together." A tear rolled down his cheek. He was either a terrific actor, or was extremely distraught. "And now, you tell me she's gone? What am I going to do?"

***

Sure enough when I got home, I found at least five messages on my machine. I returned all the calls and commiserated with my fellow exercisers. They might not be close friends, but when you work out with someone every morning for ten years, you get to know them. Then I called Susan Siler, my best friend.

A few minutes later we were hiking around the village, an activity during which we solve the world's problems as well as our own. Katie Boyle's life might have looked perfect, but Susan's really *is*. Her husband Doug is a lovely man, she has cute kids, and she works part time in an art gallery. She's gentle, modest, and creative enough to put Martha Stewart to shame. Her only flaw is that her voice squeaks when she's upset. At the moment, she sounded like a trapped mouse.

"I can't believe it! Who would want to kill her?"

"She was having an affair."

Susan looked down her nose at me. "Really." It wasn't a question.

"With one of the exercise instructors."

We power walked around the corner. "Male?"

My turn to look down my nose at Susan.

"Did her husband know?"

"They separated because of it."

"Bingo."

"I'm not so sure." I was in middle of a contentious divorce myself. That was one of the reasons Katie and I had became friends -- we had a lot in common. My soon to be ex, whom I'd found in bed with his secretary, was making life impossible. Still, I wasn't out to kill him. He was Rachel's father.

"Is there something you're not telling me?"

I sped up. "I am not having an affair. Although sometimes I wish I were. It would make life more fun."

Susan kept pace and peered at me. She never criticizes, but one of her looks says it all.

"Anyway, Steve Boyle has an alibi. Apparently he was bowling the night Katie was killed. Then he went to Hanson's for drinks. Lots of people saw him."

Susan was quiet. Then, "How is Rachel these days?"

"It's rough. Most of the time she sequesters herself in her room and talks on the phone. When we do interact, she's angry. You know how it is." Susan was a child of divorce. That's why I knew she and Doug would stay together forever.

"Maybe she should see someone."

"I don't have a lot of discretionary income these days. And Barry's no help."

Her voice held a cautionary note. "She's your daughter, Ellie."

***

Katie Boyle's husband Steve *looked* volatile, Georgia thought. And Irish. Stocky and squat, he had carroty hair, a bristly mustache, and pale blue eyes locked in a perpetual squint. Georgia and Matt had shown up at the house around dinnertime on Monday, and before they rang the bell, they heard him swearing in a loud voice, presumably at one of his kids. Georgia knew fathers like that – macho men who fell apart when their wives disappeared. She'd had one. She felt for the kids.

"Katie never played well with others," he said once they started questioning him. Georgia fidgeted. Despite her visceral dislike, Boyle's alibi had checked out, and his answers showed no hesitation.

Now Matt asked, "Why do you say that?"

"It was always her way or the highway." He got up and went to the fridge, tripping over a gym shoe as he did. "Christ, Sean." He yelled. "How many times have I told you to leave your goddam shoes at the door?"

Georgia winced. The kid came in and picked up the shoe, a mix of shame and anger in his eyes.

"Sorry champ," Boyle said. "I didn't' mean to yell. It's just the – everything."

The kid looked like he was about to cry. Boyle saw it. "Why don't you go watch whatever you want on TV? Hell, watch all night if you want. You won't be going to school tomorrow anyway."

The kid swallowed and left the room, clutching his gym shoes to his chest.

Boyle grabbed a beer, came back to the table, and stroked his mustache. "Aw, man. I don't know what I'm gonna do." He sat down, silent for a moment, then cleared his throat, as if doing so could make the grief go away. He looked up at them. "You knew, of course, that Katie was about to expand her business."

Georgia sat up. "She was?"

"Yep." He popped the top off the beer. "She was drawing up the contracts. But it wasn't going well."

"What do you mean?"

"Katie wanted to buy out this other woman. But the other woman wanted a partnership." He took a long pull on the beer. "That'd never happen." He snorted. "Not with Katie."

Georgia and Matt exchanged glances.

Thirty minutes later they pulled up in front of a singlewide at what was probably the only trailer park on the North Shore. Even so, neat rows separated each vehicle and there was even a tiny playground in back.

Dana Callaway was petite, dark, and sported a nose ring and several more through her eyebrows. She looked embarrassed when she came to the door, but her demeanor changed to fear when they told her why they were there. "I'm surprised you found me. Not many people know I'm here."

"Katie Boyle's husband told us."

She nodded, as if she wasn't surprised. "I got kicked out of my apartment. Couldn't pay my rent. It was Katie's fault."

"Sorry?"

"She fucked me over."

"How so?"

"She promised me one thing, but when it got down to brass tacks, she screwed me. I had a nice business. Mostly personal training. We were going to merge. I'd teach classes at Bodyworks, Katie would have access to my clients. But when the papers were drawn up, it turned out I wouldn't be much more than her employee. Screw her. And Bodyworks."

Callaway had an alibi – she'd been training a Glencoe woman in her private gym, and the client, although annoyed to be dragged into a murder investigation, confirmed it.

Back at Matt's place, Georgia undressed. "You think Callaway put it out for hire? I see her as the type."

"Maybe." Matt took off his clothes and got into bed. He didn't sound convinced.

"Why not?"

"What was she gonna pay them with? She's got nothing."

"What if she's hiding it? Or spent it on the hit?" Georgia put on one of Matt's t-shirts and slipped in next to him. "She sure wasn't at all sorry to hear Katie was dead."

"Maybe." His expression was solemn.

Georgia picked up on it. "What's wrong?"

"Remember what Paul Munson said? How he and Katie couldn't keep their hands off each other at work?"

Georgia nodded.

"I feel that way sometimes. About you."

She smiled and rolled on top of him. "I do, too. All the time."

***

"So they all get wasted." Rachel giggled. "And the best part is there are no parents."

I couldn't help overhearing her on the phone. She was in her room; I was in the hall, pretending to iron. To be honest, I was eavesdropping. She's only twelve.

"Somebody's older brother or sister gets the booze. You know, like raspberry flavored vodka. Everyone likes it." Silence. "I guess. A lot of guys are dealing now." My pulse started to race. She was talking about weed. "Why not? No one'll find out." Another silence. "Ooohhhkaaaay." She stretched the word into three syllables. "Catch you later."

I tried to put the ironing board away quietly, but the metal legs squeaked as the folded up. Rachel flung open her door. "You're spying on me!"

"I am not."

"Yes, you were." Her eyes narrowed into slits of fury. "What did you hear?

"Enough to keep you grounded for the next three years."

"I hate you!" She screamed. "You're invading my privacy. I want to move in with Dad."

***

When NORTAF gets involved in a crime, its bureaucracy comes with it. For Georgia that was good news. It meant they hadn't released the crime scene. Despite the fact she wasn't a detective and officially had no business there, the next morning she drove over to Bodyworks and borrowed a key from the shopkeeper next door.

She carefully inspected the studio. It was carpeted, which meant there weren't any shoe or footprints. No prints on the mirrors, either. She supposed there might be some partials on the weights and bands, but they wouldn't necessarily be those of Katie's killer. She sighed and leaned against a wall. *Tell me, Katie. Who killed you? And why?*

She pondered it, then went into one of four stalls in the bathroom. When she finished, the toiled wouldn't flush.

Just my luck, she thought. *Four stalls and I get the one that's broken.* She turned around and jiggled the handle on the tank. Nothing. She exited the stall and looked around for a plunger. There was none. She let out an exasperated breath, went back into the stall, and lifted the top off the tank. She felt her eyes widen. Something was in there, blocking the proper operation of the toilet.

She gingerly dipped her hands into the tank and pulled it out. It was an empty plastic quart bottle. A red label was affixed on the other side. She turned it over. Raspberry flavored vodka. She frowned. What the hell was that doing here? This was an exercise studio, where people presumably came to improve their health, not swill down booze.

She examined the bottle. Was Katie Boyle a closet drinker? It might explain a few things. Then again, it might not. Boyle might not have been hiding empty bottles of booze in the john. But if Boyle wasn't, who was?

***

I was making dinner Tuesday evening -- well, assembling it is a better word since I don't often inflict my cooking on Rachel-- when the police cruiser stopped at the curb. I always have a frisson of panic when I see a cop; I'm convinced I've done something illegal that I don't remember. Thirty years ago I probably did, but I've been a model of lawfulness since. When Georgia Davis slid out of the car, I relaxed.

She looked over the house before coming to the door. *Smallest house on the block*, I imagined her thinking. *She's barely hanging on.*

I opened the door before she had a chance to knock. "Hi."

"Sorry to disturb you, but I had a few questions." I'd expected a chilly attitude. I wasn't disappointed.

"Come on in. Want some coffee?"

"No thanks."

I led her into the kitchen. We sat at my small butcher-block table. I could tell she was gathering her thoughts, trying to figure out how to start.

I tried to make her feel at ease. "I have pop, if you prefer. Diet coke?"

She didn't reply, just stared at me.

Great.

Then, "Did Katie Boyle have a drinking problem?"

I cocked my head. "Katie? Are you kidding? She was the picture of health."

"People hide it. Cover it up."

"Not Katie. She could put it away a few beers, but she only drank once in a while. Why?"

She shook her head.

I waited.

"So," Davis went on. "She only drank beer? No liquor?"

"Not that I know of."

"No vodka?"

"No vodka." I was beginning to be irritated. "Why?"

She hesitated, as if she knew she wasn't supposed to be telling me anything important but didn't know how to get around it. "I found an empty bottle of vodka in a toilet at Bodyworks."

"You're kidding."

"The crime scene techs must have missed it. They probably didn't think to check the women's john." She shrugged. "Got any ideas who might have stashed it?"

I shook my head.

"The other instructors? Clients?"

I mentally ran through the list. Besides Paul, there were only three others, and none of them had a drinking problem, as far as I knew. And I couldn't see any women coming to class to hide booze in the toilet. "That's weird. Vodka, you say?"

"Raspberry flavored." She crossed her arms. "So you can't shed any light on the matter?"

As I shook my head, Rachel bounced into the kitchen, headed to the fridge, and grabbed a can of diet Coke. "Rachel," I said. "Meet Officer Davis."

Rachel, who was in one of her surly moods, hardly looked at Davis. "Hi." She popped the top off the can and disappeared out.

"I apologize," I said. "The Martians landed a while back and stole her brain."

Davis didn't laugh.

"They promised to return it when she's twenty-one."

Still no reaction.

I stood, went to the counter, and picked up the knife I'd been using to chop vegetables. "So, anyway, I'm sorry I didn't --" Suddenly I froze, the knife in mid-air. Rachel's phone conversation. Raspberry flavored vodka. No parents. "Oh shit."

Davis stood up. "What?"

I spun around. "I think I know what's going on."

***

"How did you crack it?" Matt asked Georgia when they were finally back at Matt's that night. She rolled over, sat up, and pulled the sheet around her. She debated how to tell him. She settled for the truth. "It wasn't me. It was Ellie Foreman."

Matt propped his head on his elbow. "The woman we questioned? The video producer?"

She nodded. "She has a teenage daughter. Rachel."

"So?"

"So, it turns out that flavored vodka is all the rage with high school girls these days. They drink it like water. Along with smoking weed, swallowing pills, and whatever else they can get their hands on."

"Was her kid involved?"

"No. But she knew who was."

Matt rolled onto his back and laced his hands behind his head. "And?"

"Remember the woman in Winnetka whose house was trashed by a bunch of high school kids a few months ago? Well, apparently, it's become a game. Kids break into places that aren't occupied to party. Pharm parties they call them. They usually trash the place pretty good before they leave."

"And they broke into Bodyworks?"

Georgia nodded. "No one is there at night. Or Sundays. So some of the kids decided to break in and started partying. The problem was that Boyle showed up. We don't know why. Maybe she forgot something. Maybe she just wanted a place to be alone. Anyway, the kids were there, and they were high." She shrugged. "One of them whacked her with a baseball bat. The other shoved her hard. She fell and cracked her head on a heavy weight. They didn't mean to --"

"Why did they have a bat?"

"One of the guys was on the baseball team, and he'd come to the party from practice."

"And the weight?"

"They pulled some out of the closet to play with."

"Go on."

"When they realized she was dead, they panicked. Dragged her into the closet. Tried to clean up and clear out. That's when someone tossed the vodka into the toilet."

"Jesus." Matt looked thoughtful. Then he sat up and reached for her. "Good work."

She shrugged. "O'Malley did the questioning."

"Yeah, but you did the leg work." He started to run his fingers through her hair.

Georgia smiled. "Stop that."

He cupped her cheeks with his hands. "Never." He kissed her. She let out a little sigh.

After a minute, he asked. "How'd you find out which kids were involved?"

Without missing a beat, Georgia answered. "I questioned Foreman's daughter and got some names. Made a few calls. It was pretty fast. They fell like a row of dominos."

Matt nodded.

"The kids are already lawyered up but one of them spilled everything. We got it on tape."

Matt worked his hands down her shoulders. "You're amazing, you know that?"

"I know." Her voice was husky.

"Still, you owe her."

"Who?"

"Foreman. She did you a *mitzvah*."

She frowned.

"What's the matter? You don't like her?"

"I have this feeling we're not done. Foreman and me."

"I don't know." She shrugged. "It's weird."

Matt smiled and kissed her again. Georgia concentrated on the feel of his lips and forgot about Ellie Foreman.

THE END

PART TWO:
CHICAGO THEN AND NOW:
OTHER PLACES, OTHER TIMES

FOREWORD, PART TWO
By J.A. KONRATH

To read Libby Fischer Hellmann is to love Libby Fischer Hellmann. Her writing is tight, fast, and highly entertaining. When I first read her Ellie Foreman mysteries, I set her as the standard that series fiction should aspire to.

But I had no idea Libby was so versatile. My first inkling of this came a few years ago, when I asked her to contribute a story to an anthology I was editing. Frankly, I didn't think she'd make the cut. While Libby doesn't shy away from being tough in her writing, her Ellie books were not what I'd call hardboiled, and my anthology was a collection of hit man stories. I figured I'd give her a token invitation just to be polite, and I'd never have to reject her because she'd never submit anything.

Boy, was I wrong. Her story, DETOUR, was pure, adrenalin-fueled noir, and wound up being one of the best of the book. Perhaps that was a catalyst, because soon after DETOUR Libby began writing some seriously diverse and seriously good yarns in various genres and sub-genres. She also edited the acclaimed hardboiled anthology, CHICAGO BLUES. She's still great at the light-hearted suspense she's known for, but the stories here -- all previously published -- offer a wide variety of styles, tones, and topics. Funny. Dark. Poignant. Exciting. Surprising. And yes, even hardboiled.

You'll laugh. You'll cry. You'll have a terrific time with this fabulous collection. And you can thank me for it, because I'm the one who gave her that first push. Come to think of it, maybe she should be paying me royalties...

JA Konrath is the author of over a dozen thriller novels. You can find him at www.jakonrath.com.

YOUR SWEET MAN

My contribution to CHICAGO BLUES (Bleak House, 2007) was way out of my comfort zone, but that's what I love about writing short stories. They allow me to stretch and experiment with different characters, plots, eras, and settings. This story is about a Blues bass player whose ability to love and forgive is tested by events beyond his control. There's also a historical element: the story takes place both in the 1980's and the 1950's. It turned out to be one of the sweetest stories I've ever written.

"Who's Gonna Be Your Sweet Man When I'm gone?
Who you gonna have to love you?"
…Muddy Waters

1982: Chicago

Calvin waited for the man who'd been convicted of killing his mother. Outside Joliet prison the July heat seared his spirit, leaving it as bare and desiccated as a sun-bleached bone. Sweat ringed his armpits, grit coated the back of his neck. Almost noon, no shadows on anything.

He extracted a Lucky from the crumpled pack on the dash and leaned forward to light it. The '74 Chevy Caprice never failed to start up. As long as he kept enough fluid in the radiator, the engine ate up the highway without complaint. Even the lighter worked.

He took a nervous drag. He hadn't seen his father in fifteen years. His granny had made him come when he graduated high school to show him that Calvin had amounted to something, after all. Calvin remembered clutching his diploma in the visitors' room, sliding it out of the manila envelope, edging nervously up to the glass window that separated them. He held it up against the glass, hating the sour smell of the place, the chipped paint on the walls, the fact that he had to be there at all. He remembered how his father nodded. No smile. No "atta boy – you done good." Just a lukewarm nod. Calvin imagined a yawning hole opening up on the floor, right then and there; a hole he could sink into and disappear.

Now, the black metal gates swung open, and a withered man emerged. Calvin was still wiping sweat off his face, but his father was wearing a long sleeved shirt and beige canvas pants. Even from a distance, his father looked smaller than he remembered. Frailer. The cancer that was consuming him, that had triggered his early release, was working its way through his body. He walked slowly, stooped over. His skin, a few shades lighter than the rich chocolate it once was, looked paper-thin, and he blinked like he hadn't seen sunlight in years. Maybe he hadn't. His father looked around, spotted Calvin in the Caprice. He nodded, took his time coming over.

Calvin slid out of the car, tossed his cigarette on the dirt, ground it out with his foot.

"Hello, Calvin..."

Calvin returned his greeting with a nod of his own. Cautious. Polite.

"Appreciate you coming to get me, son."

A muscle in Calvin's gut twitched. He couldn't remember the last time someone had called him "son." "Son" was a word that belonged in the movies or TV, not in real life. Calvin gestured to the gym bag his father was carrying. "Let me take that."

His father held it out. Calvin threw it in the back seat. His father stood at the passenger door but made no effort to open it. Calvin frowned, then realized his father was waiting for permission. Twenty-five years in prison did that to a man. "Just open the door and get in."

His father shot him a look, half-embarrassed, half-grateful, and slid into the car. Calvin waited until his father was settled, then started the engine. As they pulled away from Joliet, he said, "Thought we'd go back to my place."

"You still in Englewood?"

"Hyde Park now. Got ourselves a house near 47th and Cottage Grove."

His father's eyebrows arched. "Well, that's mighty fine."

"Jeanine fixed it up nice. Even got a little garden out back. She's a *good* girl."

His father didn't seem to notice. He should have. It was Jeanine who shamed Calvin into coming in the first place.

"He's dying, Calvin" she'd said. "And he's paid his dues. Twenty-five years of 'em."

Now his father turned to him. "How's that job coming?"

"What job?" Calvin made his way back to the highway.

"The one you was talking about when you come to see me. Janitorial supplies."

"I opened my own company six years ago. I got five people working for me now."

"Well that's mighty fine, son. Mighty fine."

But it didn't feel fine. It felt false. Calvin imagined that black hole opening up even wider. That was why he never wrote or visited his father, except for the Christmas card Jeanine made him sign every year. Any time he thought about him, even a stray fragment, the night his mother was murdered flooded back into his mind. He couldn't help it. Better not to think about it at all, his granny would say. "Just go on and live your own life."

But Granny was dead, and the people at Joliet called *him* when they found the cancer. Calvin stole a glance at his father. He was quiet. Just staring out at the road, a dreamy look on his face. Calvin remembered that look. His father's body might be in the front seat, but his mind was miles away. Calvin knew he was thinking about his mother.

He tightened his grip on the wheel. How dare he? "So... You feelin' okay?"

His father pulled his gaze in and looked at Calvin. "For the days I got left, I'm doing jes' fine."

Calvin turned onto the interstate. "You sure? Jeanine talked to our doctor. He can see you tomorrow if you want."

His father gave him a sad little smile. "Appreciate it son, but don't go to no trouble." His father went back to looking out the window. Calvin turned on the radio. The all news station was blaring out something about Israeli troops in Lebanon. His father didn't react, just kept gazing out. He seemed somehow smaller, less distinct than he'd been just ten minutes ago. Like his shadow was slowly fading from black to gray. At this rate he might disappear altogether.

Calvin snapped off the radio. For a while the whine of the air conditioning was the only sound in the car. Lulled by the air blowing through the vents and the rhythm of his wheels on the highway, Calvin was startled by the abruptness of his father's voice.

"You start making the arrangements?"

Calvin cleared his throat just loud enough. "Not yet." He wasn't sure what to expect. Would his father lay into him? Cuss him out?

But all his father did was to wave a weak hand. "I guess I got to do it myself."

"Why don't we talk about it later?"

His father's shoulders sagged and he closed his eyes. "I ain't got many laters, son."

***

1950's: Chicago

The hot breath of the blues kissed Jimmy Jay Rollins when he was little, leaving him hungering for more. His mama -- he never knew his daddy – took him to church in the morning and the blues joints at night. By the time he was seven, he was playing guitar licks with whoever his "uncle" of the moment happened to be, and by the time he left school at 16, he knew he wanted to play bass guitar.

The bass wasn't as flashy as the electric slide guitar of Little Ed or Muddy Waters, but it was the glue that held everything together. No one could play a 12-bar chorus without him; no one could start a lick or riff. The bass was there through every number, from beginning to end, setting the pace. Steady. Unrelenting. The lead guitar, saxophone, even the drummer could take a break; not so the bass. Willie Dixon became Jimmy Jay's personal hero.

By day, Jimmy Jay worked in a steel factory near Lake Calumet, but at night, he bounced around playing gigs on the South side. You could smell stale cigarette smoke and yesterday's beer in the air, spot a few guns and knives if you looked real close. But none of that mattered when the music started. The Blues flowed through his veins, transporting him to a place where he could let go, soar above the world, tethered only by an electric guitar, wailing horn, or harmonica.

He was jamming at the open mike set in the Macomba Lounge one hot summer night, a thick cloud of smoke, perfume, and sweat choking the air, when a wisp of a girl – she couldn't have been more than 18 -- came up to the stage. She was wearing a red dress that skimmed her body just right. A curtain of black hair shimmered down to her waist, and her skin looked pale blue in the light. She tentatively took the mike and asked them to play in G, then launched into a bluesy version of "Mean to Me," an old Billie Holiday song.

By the middle of the second verse, people set their glasses down, stubbed out their cigarettes, and a hush fell over the room. Her voice was raw and unpolished but full of surprises. At first a sultry alto, she could hit the high notes in a silver soprano, then dip two octaves down to belt out the Blues like a tenor. At first he thought it was a fluke – no one had that range and depth. He tested her, moving up the scale, changing the groove, even throwing her a sudden key change. She took it all with a serene smile, bobbing her head, eyes closed, adjusting perfectly. Her voice never wavered.

After a few numbers, the band took a break, and Jimmy Jay bought her a whiskey. As he passed her the drink, he noticed the contrast between her face, soft and round, and her eyes, dark and penetrating. Her name was Inez Youngblood, she said, and she'd just moved here from Tennessee. She was part Cherokee, once upon a time, but mostly mountain white.

"A hillbilly?" Jimmy Jay joked.

She threw him a dazzling smile that made his insides melt. "A hillbilly who sings the Blues."

"Why Chicago?"

"I listen to the radio. Chicago Blues is happy Blues. You got Muddy Waters. Etta James. Chess Records. Everybody's here. Sweeping you up with their music. There just ain't no other place to sing." Those dark eyes bored into him. "And I got to sing."

By their third drink, he began to imagine the curves underneath that red dress, and what she looked like without it. She had to know what he was thinking, because she smiled and started to finger a gold cross around her neck. Still, she didn't seem put off. More like she was teasing him.

Another set and half a reefer later, a fight broke out in the back of the bar. Inez, who was singing "Wang, Dang, Doodle" took it in stride, even when knives glinted and someone pulled out a piece. She just pointed to the fighters, asked the bartender to shine a spot in their direction, and leveled them with a hard look. The brawl moved into the alley. Jimmy Jay was impressed.

It was almost dawn when they quit playing. Someone bought a last round of drinks, and Jimmy Jay was just thinking about packing up when Inez came over.

"You're pretty damn good, Jimmy Jay."

He grinned. "Thanks, Hillbilly. You got a set of pipes yourself."

She laughed. "We oughta do this again."

Jimmy Jay suppressed his elation. "I could probably get us a couple of gigs."

She nodded. "I'd like that."

He nodded, just looking at her, not quite believing his good fortune.

She offered him a slow sensual smile. "Meanwhile, I got a favor to ask you, baby."

Jimmy Jay cleared his throat. "Yeah?" His voice cracked anyway.

She turned around, and lifted her hair off the back of her neck. "Help me take off my cross."

She ended up in his bed that night. And the next. And the night after that. She might only have been 18, but she was all heat and fire. All he had to do was touch her and she shivered with pleasure. When he ran his fingers slowly up her leg, starting at that perfectly shaped ankle, past her knee, stopping at the soft, pliant skin of her thigh, she would moan and grab him and pull him into her. Sliding underneath, rocking him hard, like she couldn't get enough.

"You are my sweet man," she would whisper when they stopped, exhausted and sweaty. "My sweet, sweet man."

***

They were a team for almost ten years. Inez, the hillbilly, soaring like an angel in one number, moaning like a whore in another; and Jimmy Jay, steadfast and sturdy, setting the beat, making her look good. Inez drove herself hard, and her talent grew. Her timing was impeccable. She rolled with the band, but could carry the show. If someone missed a chord, she covered them, and if they messed up their solo, she'd make light of it by singing scat, humming a chorus, or talking to the crowd.

Before long they were headlining at places like the Macomba before it burned down, South Side Johnny's, and Queenie's. Their only disagreement was over Chess Records and the two white owners who wanted to sign them. Jimmy

Jay was all for it -- not only did his idol Willie Dixon work for Chess, but a record contract was something he'd dreamed of all his life. Inez kept saying they should hold out for a better deal. So far they had.

Even Calvin's arrival didn't slow them down. Calvin was a good baby who turned into a good boy. The same face and nappy hair as his Daddy; the high cheekbones and coffee-with-cream skin of his Mama. Inez seemed thrilled. She cooed and sang to him all day, but if Jimmy Jay figured she might retire, he figured wrong. Calvin came with them to the clubs on the South and West side, even to Peoria and East St. Louis. They'd bring blankets and put him to sleep in the back room on a ratty sofa, sometimes the floor. When he was older, Jimmy Jay or Inez would drop him off at school before they went to bed themselves. Jimmy Jay didn't mind. His own mama had brought him to all the Blues joints.

Inez started calling them both her sweet men. Jimmy Jay would grin. They were happy. Real happy. Until the gig at Theresa's.

***

It was late autumn, and a chilly rain had been falling for two days, flooding the viaducts and lots of basements. Jimmy Jay and Inez were headlining at Theresa's Lounge on South Indiana. The place wasn't as upscale or as large as Macomba's, and the regulars, mostly people from the neighborhood, treated the place like home, dancing and talking with the players during the set. Tonight the smell of wet wool mixed with the smoke and booze and sweat.

A promoter from Capitol Records was in town and supposedly coming down that night. Inez was excited -- Capitol was huge, much bigger than Chess. Jimmy Jay was glad he'd talked a new lead guitar into playing the gig with them. Buddy Guy had just come up from Baton Rouge, and everyone was saying he was gonna change the face of the Blues.

It was a knockout performance. No one missed a chord and the solos kicked. There were no amp or mike problems. Jimmy Jay and the drummer locked into a tight groove, and Buddy Guy's guitar was by turns brash, angry, and soulful. Inez's voice was as rich and mellow as thick honey. Even with the lousy weather, the place was packed, everyone swaying, dancing, bobbing their heads. It was like great sex, Jimmy Jay thought. Hot, sticky sex that trembled and throbbed and built, and ended in a long, fiery climax.

During the break, a white guy came up to the stage. He'd been at one of the back tables, smoking cigarettes. With his baby face and eager expression, he couldn't have been much older than Jimmy Jay. But his tailored suit and hair, slicked back with Bryl Crème, said he was trying to look well off. He bought the band a round of drinks and nodded to Jimmy Jay. Then he turned to Inez and started talking quietly but earnestly. She looked from him to Jimmy Jay, then back at him. When she nodded, he took her hand and covered it with thick fingers. She didn't pull away. After the next set, Jimmy Jay caught them talking behind his back. By the last set, Inez was favoring him with the same smile she'd shot Jimmy Jay the first night at Macomba's ten years ago.

By the time Inez left town with him a week later, the rain had changed to snow. Jimmy Jay went to fetch Calvin at school. When he got back, she was gone. At first he thought she was at the store, picking up something for dinner, but when she didn't come home by six, an uneasy feeling swept over him. He checked the closet and drawers. Most of her things were gone. Except her gold cross.

Word got around that she'd run away with Billy Sykes. He hadn't worked for Capitol, it turned out. He did work in the record business, but dropped out of sight after he shorted some men who'd been financing a label with mob money. He reappeared a year later as a promoter. No one could say who his clients were.

That winter Jimmy Jay sat for hours on the bed, running Inez's gold cross and chain through his fingers. His mother moved in to look after Calvin who, at nine, was just old enough to realize his world had shattered. Word filtered back -- someone had seen her in Peoria, someone else heard she was in Iowa. Jimmy Jay tried to play, but he sounded tired and flat. Inez was inextricably bound up in his music and his life; with her gone, it felt like part of his body – worse, his soul -- had shriveled up and fallen off.

One day Calvin came in and saw him on the bed, fingering the cross with tears in his eyes.

"Don't be sad, Daddy." He came over and gave Jimmy Jay a hug. "I know what to do."

Jimmy Jay gazed at his son.

"Mama just got lost. She don't know how to get home. All we got to do is find her."

Jimmy Jay smiled sadly. "I don't think she wants to come home, boy."

"Granny says every mama wants to come home. All we needs do is find her.   Once she sees us, it'll be just fine. I know it. "

Jimmy Jay tried to discourage him, but Calvin clung to his idea like a leech to a man's skin. He talked so much about finding his lost mama that after a while, his intensity infected Jimmy Jay. Could it really be that simple? Maybe Calvin was right. Sure Inez wanted to be a star, but she had a family. If they went after her, maybe she *would* realize what she'd given up and come home.

The following spring Billy Sykes brought Inez back to Chicago for a show on the West side – no one on the South side would book her. She was singing with some musicians from St. Louis, Jimmy Jay learned. They were staying at the Lincoln hotel, a small shabby place near the club.

Jimmy Jay waited until Calvin was home from school and had his supper. Then they both dressed in their Sunday best and took the bus to the hotel. Jimmy Jay slipped an old man at the desk a fiver and asked which room Inez Rollins was in. The man pointed up the steps. Jimmy Jay and Calvin climbed to the third floor and knocked on #315.

A tired female voice replied, "Yes?"

"It's me, Inez. And Calvin."

The door opened and suddenly Inez was there, her body framed in the light.

"Mama!" Calvin ran into her arms.

Her face lit, and she clasped Calvin so tight the boy could hardly suck in a breath. When she finally released him, she turned to Jimmy Jay.

"Hello, Jimmy Jay."

She looked washed-out, Jimmy Jay thought, although it gave him no pleasure to see it. Gaunt and nervous, too. Her eyes were rimmed in red, and her black mane of hair wasn't glossy. He thought he saw a bruise on her cheek, but she kept finger-combing her hair over the spot.

"Hello, Inez." He looked around. "Where's Sykes?"

"He's at the club. Getting ready for tonight."

Jimmy Jay nodded. He got right to the point. "We want you to come home. We are a family. Calvin needs you. So do I."

At least she had the decency to look ashamed. Her eyes filled. She gazed at Jimmy Jay, then Calvin. Then she shook her head.

"Why not?"

"Remember what I told you the first time we met?"

"You told me a lot of things."

"I need to sing, Jimmy Jay. And Billy's gonna make me a star."

Jimmy Jay saw the determination on her face, as raw as the first time he'd met her. His heart cracked, but he struggled to conceal his grief. *He* might have lost her, but Calvin didn't have to. "Take the boy. He needs his mama. I'll – I'll pay you for him, 'ifin you want."

"I'll think about it." Inez looked down at Calvin, trailed her fingers through his hair, and smiled. Calvin snuggled closer. "I'll talk to Billy when he gets back."

Jimmy Jay nodded. "I'll leave the boy with you. I'll pick him up at the club when you start your gig. We can talk more."

Inez looked sad but grateful. Calvin looked thrilled.

***

Two hours later, the band had finished setting up but there was no sign of Inez. Or Billy Sykes. Or Calvin. Jimmy Jay saw the uneasiness on the musicians' faces, heard one of them say, "Where are those damn fools?"

He retraced his steps to the Lincoln Hotel.

No one was behind the desk when Jimmy Jay got there. He went up the stairs and down the hall. Music blared out from Inez's room. The radio. Benny Goodman's orchestra, he thought. He was about to knock on the door when he saw something move at the other end of the hall. Something small. He wheeled around and squinted.

"Calvin? Is that you?"

The figure trotted toward him. Calvin, looking small and lonely.

"What you doin' out here, son? Where's your mama?"

Calvin didn't say anything, just shrugged.

"Is she inside?" Jimmy Jay pointed to the door.

Calvin nodded.

"Is Sykes back?"

Calvin nodded again.

Jimmy Jay turned back to the door, leaned his ear against it. The music was loud. He knocked. No one answered. Probably couldn't hear him above the music. He knocked again, and when no one responded, started to push against the door.

"Inez, Sykes…. Open up!"

Nothing. Except the music.

Jimmy Jay looked both ways down the hall, then threw his weight against the door. It almost gave. He backed up, turned sideways, and rammed himself against it again. This time the door gave, and Jimmy Jay burst into the room.

***

He was still holding the gun when the police arrived. Inez's body was at the foot of the bed, but Sykes' was half way to the door. A pool of blood was congealing under each of them.

1982: Chicago

Three weeks later, Jimmy Jay no longer had the strength to get out of bed. Calvin was putting in twelve-hour days. He knew it was an excuse for not dealing with his father, but he couldn't bear to come home to a place where death hovered in the air.

One night, though, was different. As he trudged inside, Calvin heard music from upstairs. And laughter. When he climbed the steps, he saw that Jeanine had moved their stereo into Jimmy Jay's room. An old album revolved on the turntable. His father was in bed, eyes closed, snapping his fingers. Jeanine was sitting in the chair smiling too, her head bobbing to the music. Calvin peered at the album cover. Chess Records. Muddy Waters.

His father opened his eyes. "Hey, Calvin." His face was wreathed in smiles. "There ain't nothing like Muddy for an old soul. With Willie Dixon and Howlin' Wolf on back up. Lord, it makes me see the gates of heaven."

"Don't talk that way, Dad."

Jimmy Jay dismissed him with a wave of his hand. When the song came to an end, Calvin lifted the needle and turned off the stereo. Jeanine went downstairs, claiming dishes that needed to be washed.

"Calvin," his father said, "We can't put it off no more. It's time to talk about the arrangements."

Calvin stiffened. He dug in his pocket for his Luckys, pulled one out and lit it. He sat in the chair. "I don't know why you want to be buried there."

His father eyed him. "She was my wife, Calvin. And your mama."

"She was white trash!" Calvin exhaled a cloud of white smoke. "White trailer trash."

"Don't you ever talk that way 'bout your mama!" His father's voice was unexpectedly strong. "And she was from the mountains of Tennessee, boy," his father added. "The Smoky Mountains."

But Calvin wasn't mollified. "She ran out on us. You and me. She left us. And for what?"

His father just looked at him. Then he turned his head toward the window. "She was my woman," he said quietly, his burst of energy now dissipated. "And I was her sweet man."

Calvin felt his stomach pitch. The black hole was opening up again, and all he wanted to do was jump in and let it consume him. He stubbed out his cigarette, letting the window fan clear the smoke. Jeanine ran it all the time, even though it didn't do much cooling. Beads of sweat popped out on his forehead .

"I still miss her, son."

Calvin swallowed. "Pop, don't."

"I ain't got no regrets." His father said. "At now, in a little while, if the good Lord is willin', I'll see her again."

Calvin's throat got hot. He felt tears gather at the back of his eyes. He tried to blink them away hoping his father wouldn't notice. But he did.

"Why you crying, Calvin? You're a good son. And Jeanine is a good woman. She been taking good care of me."

"It's not that." The words spilled out.

His father cocked his head. The slight movement seemed to require more energy than he could muster.

"I – I got to tell you something."

110

His father's body might be wasted, but his soul seemed to expand. His eyes grew huge, taking over his entire face. "What's that, son?"

The black hole widened. Calvin had to take the plunge. "That – that night..." Calvin's words were heavy and sluggish, as if the hole was already sucking him down. "The night mama died ...." Calvin whispered. "It was my fault. I killed Mama."

An odd look registered on Jimmy Jay's face.

"After you left ..." Calvin's voice was flat and hard."... Mama sang to me. And hugged me. It felt – so good... So right."

"Your mama had the voice of an angel."

Calvin held his hand up to stop him. "Then Billy Sykes come back. He was pissed when he saw me. 'What's that kid doing here?' He yelled. He and Mama -- well, she told him she wanted to take me with them. Sykes wouldn't have none of it. 'Are you crazy?' He said. 'It's bad enough that you're a hillbilly. And part Injun. I ain't taking your nigger kid, too. Get rid of him.'

"Mama begged him. 'He won't be no trouble,' she kept saying and looked at me. "Will you, sweet man?"

"But Sykes kept saying no. 'I put too much of my money in you to throw it away. What are people gonna think when they see you with a nigger kid?'

"Mama and me were on the bed. She was hugging me real tight. 'I want my son,' she said.

"'He'll be in the way,' Sykes said. "You want to be a star? You got to make a choice. Me or the kid.'"

Jimmy Jay didn't say anything.

Calvin shuddered. "Mama said, 'Don't make me do that. I'm his Mama!'"

"'Then I'll make the choice for you.' Sykes says. And he pulls out a gun and aims it at my head.'" Calvin looked at the floor.

"What happened then, son?" Jimmy Jay asked, his voice almost as flat as Calvin's.

Calvin covered his eyes with his hand. "Mama got up from the bed. She looked scared. 'All right. All right. Put that gun away, Billy. I'll send Calvin back to his Daddy. Just put the gun away. Before someone gets hurt.' Then she looked from me to Sykes. She didn't say nothing more."

Calvin pressed his lips together. He couldn't look at his father, but he knew his father was staring at him.

"Sykes started to put the gun away, but then -- I don't know, Pop -- something came over me. I jumped up and tackled Sykes. Right there in the room." He hesitated. "The gun went off. And Mama dropped off the end of the bed. Just dropped dead right in front of me."

His father whispered. "And then?"

"Sykes was like a crazy man. It was like he couldn't believe what happened. He started screaming, first at mama. Kept telling her to get up and stop foolin' around. But she didn't, Pop. She never got up." Calvin's voice cracked. "Then he dropped the gun and started for the door. He was gonna take off! Just leave her there." Calvin paused again. "I just couldn't let that happen. I couldn't. When he was half way to the door, I picked up the gun and shot him in the back."

Calvin felt tears streaming down his face.

Jimmy Jay, his eyes veiled, let out a quiet breath. Calvin heard the hum of traffic through the window above the fan.

After a long time, Calvin said haltingly, "I guess it's time to go to the police."

"You won't do nothing of the kind, son." His father raised himself on one elbow. "I already done the time. For both of us. And..." His features softened. "...I figured out what happened a long time ago."

"You knew?" Calvin's stomach turned over. "How?"

"There was no way your mama could do anything to hurt you. Or you her. I knew it had to be an accident. At least with her. And Sykes... well..." Jimmy Jay shrugged as if it didn't matter.

"You knew? All these years?" Calvin felt his features contort with anguish. "I killed them, and you took the rap for me?"

Jimmy Jay nodded. "And I'd do it all over again."

Calvin searched his father's face for an explanation. The silence pressed in.

"You were just a boy," Jimmy Jay finally said, gazing at him with an expression of infinite sadness, compassion, and love. "I done the time for you both...so you would grow up and turn into her sweet man. Now..." He paused. "We got to get back to that plannin.' The Lord 'll be givin' Inez back her other sweet man, and I needs to be ready. We still got a lot of music to make together."

THE END

Libby Fischer Hellmann

THE JADE ELEPHANT

The Jade Elephant was first published in the EXPLETIVE DELETED anthology (Bleak House, 2008) edited by Jen Jordan. I loved researching the seamier, sleazier parts of Chinatown where menus are stained, kitsch is king, and even walking down the street after dark is risky. Add in two older criminals seeking redemption, and the result was irresistible. At least to me.

Gus stared at the jade elephant in the window of the pawnshop, wondering if it could be his salvation. A soft translucent green, about ten inches tall, its trunk curled up in the air as if it was trumpeting the joy of existence. Charlieman, his fence, said that meant good luck. Charlieman was Chinese.

Gus folded his newspaper under his arm. There wasn't much to distinguish this from any other pawnshop in Chinatown. Tucked away in a building with an illegal gambling operation upstairs, it was a grim and dingy place. Faded yellow Chinese characters -- who knew what they said? – covered the window. A shabby dragon sat above the door spitting imaginary fire.

He trudged down chalky cement blocks uninterrupted by shrubbery and pushed through the door of the restaurant. One of the few that hadn't fled to the suburbs, it was a dimly lit place. That wasn't all bad -- at least you couldn't see the stained yellowed napkins or the scratches on the tables.

Pete was in the second booth, slurping his soup. The only other customers were three Asian men at a back table. Chinatown's Chamber of Commerce would have you believe the place was bustling with commerce, but much of that commerce was conducted by dubious "businessmen" in alleys or street corners or greasy Chinese spoons like this. Rumor was the mayor had finally slated Chinatown for urban renewal. Sure. Gus snorted.

Pete stopped slurping and looked up. "What kept you?"

"Traffic." Gus slid into the seat across, wondering why they still came here at all. Habit, he figured. Inertia.

His partner grunted and went back to his soup.

"How is it?"

"Like always."

A waiter came over and offered Gus a laminated plastic menu whose edges curled away from the page. Gus waved it away. "The usual, Chen."

"You want egg roll or soup?" he asked, rolling his "r's" so they sounded like "l's."

Gus pulled his coat more tightly around him. The December cold had seeped into his bones. "Soup."

Chen nodded and disappeared through a swinging door that squeaked when it flapped.

Pete looked over. "So?"

Gus leaned his elbows on the table. "It was benign."

Pete cracked a smile. "Attaboy!"

"I was lucky."

"It's all that clean living." Pete laughed. "What'd the doc say?"

Chen came out from the kitchen, carrying a steaming bowl of soup. He set it down in front of Gus. "That it happens when you get old."

"We're not old." Pete sounded defiant.

"You're pushing sixty, and so am I," Gus said. "He said I could get another in a couple of years. With the stress and all."

"Stress causes tumors?"

Gus nodded. "Said I should take better care of myself. Build up my immune system."

"Eat your vegetables," Pete laughed.

"That's what he said."

Pete took a bite of his egg roll and chewed slowly. "But hey. You dodged the Big C. Time to celebrate!" He twisted around. "Hey, Chen. You got any champagne in that lousy kitchen of yours?"

Chen's face scrunched into a frown. "Sorry. No champagne. Next door. I go?"

"Naw. Don't bother," Gus called out. He looked over at Pete. "It's not worth it."

"You sure?" Pete looked like he wanted to argue, but then thought better of it. "Well, at least have some Dim Sum."

"I don't –"

"Chen. Bring the man one of your fucking Dim Sum, okay?"

Chen disappeared into the kitchen.

"So you ready to get back to work?" Pete asked.

"Why? You got something?"

"I got lots of somethings." Pete grinned. "I was waiting to hear about you. There's this sweet job out in Barrington, for openers."

Chen brought the Dim Sum on a plate. Gus studied the puffy white thing, not sure how to eat it, then palmed the whole thing and took a bite. It was surprisingly good.

"There's this trader. Mostly retired now, see. Lives in a mansion, but they're gone most of the year. You know, snowbirds in winter, Michigan in summer, Europe in between. The place is empty. We get Billy to disconnect the alarm, and take our time --"

"Not Billy. Christ. He's a maniac on wheels. Remember the last time? He nearly got us picked up."

"I know." Pete made a brushing aside gesture. "But he's good with electronics. The best." When Gus didn't answer, Pete said, "Okay. Lemme think about it." He hesitated. "Hey. There's something else we need to talk about."

"What's that?"

"I think we got a problem with Charlieman."

Gus shot him a look. "What kind of problem?"

"Well, you probably didn't notice, what with being preoccupied with your—your situation. But I got a feeling something's – well, he's just not himself. I think he's in

117

trouble. I'm thinking he made a deal with the devil. Maybe even surveillance. So, I found this other guy, but he's not in Chinatown, see? And I —"

"No." Gus shoved his bowl of soup away.

"What do you mean, 'no'?"

"Charlieman would have warned us. We've been working with him a long time."

"I don't know, Gus. He's different."

Chen came with their food: chicken chow mein for Gus, sweet and sour pork for Pete. Gus sprinkled crunchy noodles from a wax paper bag on top. For a few minutes, the only sound was the clink of forks on plates. They never used chopsticks.

After a while, Pete blurted out, "Hey, man, what's the matter?"

"Nothing."

"Don't try to con a con. I know you twenty years."

Gus stopped eating. "You're right." He laid his fork across his plate. "When I was sitting in the doc's waiting room, there were all these patients there. Most of them were really sick, you know? You could – I could tell from their faces."

Pete nodded.

"The doctor was over an hour late. I don't know why the assholes can't get their act together, know what I mean?"

Pete giggled nervously. "If we were that late, our asses would be warming the benches at Cook County."

Gus nodded. "I'm antsy, you know? I hate hospitals. So I decide to take a walk down the hall. So there I am walking, and there's this pay phone at the other end. I walk past it and I see this woman on the phone."

Pete speared a chunk of pineapple.

"She was in a hospital gown, and she was crying."

"Fuck. I hate to see a woman cry."

"Me, too. So I turn around and go back the other way, but as I did, I sneak a look at her." Gus paused. "There was something familiar about her. I don't know. Something about her face. Her voice, too. I'd heard it before."

"Yeah?" Pete shook out a cigarette from the pack he kept in his shirt pocket.

"I walk away real slow, but I can still hear her, you know? Turns out she's talking to her insurance company. Asking them to pay for a new kidney. But they don't want to. She's begging them, Pete. Says she don't got nothing left. She's got to get some help, or she'll die."

Pete struck a match and lit the cigarette. "That's tough."

"She looked bad, too. Scrawny. Pale. All bent over." He sighed irritably. "I mean, the woman's looks like she's about to keel over any minute, and no one lifts a finger to help."

"Maybe her – what d'ye call it – maybe she reached her limit."

"I dunno. Well, I'm just turning around on my way back to the doctor's office, when it dawns on me how I know her."

"How?"

Gus licked his lips. "We, pal. She was one of our marks."

"What?"

"You remember the job we did in the high rise downtown? About six months ago?"

An uneasy look came over Pete. "The one where the woman was in her bedroom and we had to --"

"Yeah. The one where we scored the jade elephant."

"No, man. You gotta be wrong. What are the odds --"

"I'm telling you it was her. I was the one..." He paused. "...who took care of her, remember?"

"I remember." Pete frowned. "Hey, do you think that was how --?"

"I don't think anything. Except that she's gonna die because she can't pay for a goddamn kidney transplant."

"Shit. That's Twilight Zone stuff, you know?" Pete shook his head. "But we didn't make her kidney dry up. All we did was rip her off."

"You think?" Gus went quiet.

"Hey." Pete went on. "This ever happen to you before?"

"No."

"Me neither, but Pauly... remember Pauly?"

"We worked a couple jobs with him, right?"

"Yeah. So he's doing a job out on the North Shore. Something looks real familiar. He can't place it. Then all of a sudden, he realizes he ripped off the place five years earlier. The same place. But this time, he trips a silent alarm and some guy comes after him with a shotgun. He got five to ten."

Gus kept his mouth shut.

"Hey, don't get all squirrelly on me. Nothing about how God put her in your path. It's just the way it goes. Her luck ran out. Yours didn't." Pete wiped a napkin across his mouth. "By the way, my new fence, Mike, says he could get us ten grand or more for that elephant."

"That much?" Gus asked.

"That's what he said." Pete nodded.

***

They did the job in Barrington the following week, and another in Winnetka after that. Gus insisted they use Charlieman to fence the goods, but Pete wasn't happy about it. He wouldn't even go into the pawnshop. Gus had to handle the negotiations. While he was there, Gus scoped out the place, looking for tiny cameras, bugs, or recorders, but he didn't see a thing. The place looked like it always did: shabby and crowded with junk. He did ask Charlieman how much he wanted for the jade elephant, but Charlieman said it wasn't for sale.

The next few weeks flew by. The city glittered with lights, music, and tinsel. Even the shop windows in Chinatown were decked out, and if you walked down Cermak, you could hear a tinny rendition of "Silent Night" from somewhere. Pete convinced Gus to have lunch at a new restaurant in the Loop, but the waitresses were too young for the attitude they copped, and the food was too rich.

After lunch Gus bought himself a new coat and gloves at Field's and started walking. He noticed the squealing kids and their parents in front of the department store windows. The Salvation Army volunteers shaking their bells. People gliding around the skating rink, sappy smiles on their faces. Why was everyone so damn cheerful? Come January, all the unkempt promises that littered the streets like garbage would come back. Now, though, the promise of hope and deliverance floated through the air. Gus fastened the buttons on his new coat.

He hadn't planned it – or maybe he did – but just before dusk he found himself in front of a condo off Michigan Avenue. It was prime property, the middle of the Gold Coast. That's why they'd cased it in the first place. They'd hit more than one place in the building, and truth was, it had been a good day. In addition to the jade elephant, they'd scored some jewelry and a roll of bills some idiot had stored in his freezer.

"Got us some cold cash," Pete laughed afterwards.

"Everyone's a comedian," Gus replied.

Now, he peered up at a series of porches that jutted out from the building like horizontal monoliths. She lived on the eighth floor, he remembered. He counted out eight slabs. Light seeped around the edges of the window shades. What was she doing? He was surprised to realize he hoped she wasn't alone. That someone was looking in on her. He wondered how she got the jade elephant in the first place. Did she travel to some exotic spot to buy it? Was it a gift? He lingered on the sidewalk, half-expecting to see some sign she had found a way to pay for her kidney. But all he saw were flat granite facings, slabs of porch, and light seeping around the window shades.

He took the subway and then the bus to his apartment on the West side. He turned on the tube to some tearjerker about a lost baby and a frantic mother. Ten to one there'd be a "Christmas miracle" where they found the little bugger. A few minutes later, he snapped it off and pulled out a bottle half-filled with bourbon.

An hour later, the bottle was empty. He dug out a Christmas card he'd bought at Field's, signed it, and licked the envelope closed.

***

The next night Pete told Gus he couldn't meet him for dinner. Just as well, Gus thought. He wolfed down a sandwich and a brew at his neighborhood bar. Then he went home, and dressed in dark clothes, gloves, and a stocking cap. He filled his pockets with a knife, picklock, and flashlight. Opening a drawer, he lifted out his 38 Special. He raised it to eye-level and sighted. He'd cleaned and oiled it for the Barrington job, but they hadn't needed it. He lowered the gun, feeling its heft against his palm, and slid it into his holster. He belted the holster around his waist. Then he slipped the greeting card into his pocket.

It was after midnight when he got off the Red Line at Chinatown. The Hawk was hurling blasts of arctic air that sliced through him like a blade. Halfway to the pawnshop, he heard footsteps behind him. He moved into the shadows. Three Asian goons swaggered down the block like they owned it. They probably did, thanks to an uneasy alliance with the Russians. The street was full of Boris's and Wan Chu's these days; Tony and Vito had been relegated to benchwarmers.

Gus waited until they were gone, then snuck into the alley behind the pawnshop. A lamppost spilled weak light on Charlieman's back door. The smell of garbage was strong. He pulled out his picks and was about to start working the lock when he noticed the door was slightly ajar. Curious. Charlieman never forgot to lock up. Gus put his ear against the door. He heard a faint rustling. Mice? Then he heard a couple of steps. Not mice.

Gus stuffed his picks back in his pocket. If Charlieman was working late, his lights would have been on.

So it wasn't Charlieman. Maybe it was one of the Asians? Charlieman had been talking about getting a silent alarm, but Gus figured he was too cheap to spring for it. Still, he crept out of the alley and went around to the front. Shit. The jade elephant which usually sat in Charlieman's window was gone!

Suddenly the overhead lights snapped on, and a harsh fluorescent glare poured over everything. In the stark illumination, Gus saw Charlieman at the back of the store, aiming a gun at someone. Gus squinted and craned his neck. The gun was pointed at Pete, who was standing near the back door, a bulky bag over his shoulder. In his free hand he held the Jade Elephant.

Gus froze, unsure what to do. He thought banging on the window and yelling, "Hey, Charlieman, don't shoot." He thought about pulling out his 38, but he knew he couldn't get to it in time. How could he shoot his fence anyway? Maybe he could buy Pete some time. Make a disturbance. Take Charlieman's attention off his friend. He started toward the front door, shouting, "Stop. Both of you."

Pete looked his way, surprised. So did Charlieman. Gus jiggled the doorknob. "Listen, this is all a misunderstanding. We can work it out."

Charlieman's gun hand waved dangerously from side to side, and wild Chinese exclamations spewed out of his mouth. But Pete took the hint. He feinted left, then broke right and lunged. He even managed to throw open the back door. Charlieman whirled around and pulled the trigger. The flash of blue made Gus blink. Pete dropped the bag and bent over so far his face nearly touched the floor. Then he lurched through the open door.

Gus ran back into the alley. Pete had collapsed on the ground. He was still clutching the jade elephant. Gus crouched next to his friend.

"What were you thinking, pal?" he said softly. "Why now?"

The only thing that came out of Pete's mouth was a gurgle.

Sirens whined in the distance. Gus looked up. Charlieman was at the back door yelling hysterically in Chinese and making big swooping gestures. But Gus was so far back in the shadows he was sure Charlieman didn't recognize him.

The phone rang inside the shop. Charlieman backed up to answer it. Pete lay curled up on his side. If it weren't for the dark pool of liquid underneath, he might have been asleep. Gus gazed at the jade elephant. By some miracle, the thing wasn't broken, but Gus could see streaks of red marring its green surface. Merry Christmas.

The sirens grew louder. The flashing lights were only a block away. Gus tried to ease the elephant out of his partner's hands, but Pete's grip was too tight. Gus had to pry back one finger at a time before he it came loose. Clutching it to his chest, he scrambled up and hurried away from the shop.

***

The next morning, Gus wrapped the elephant in newspaper, stuffed it in a shopping bag, and headed downtown. The streets were full of beggars. Everyone had their hand out this time of year. He tried to steer around an old woman hunkered down on the pavement. She had a black kettle in front of her and a hand-lettered sign that said "Need money for food."

When the doorman made him cool his heels in the lobby, Gus grew uneasy. He shouldn't be here. This was crazy. He was just about to leave when the doorman got off the intercom and pointed him to the elevator. The numbers on the car's panel blinked as he flew up, but the door was slow to open. When Gus finally stepped off, the woman was waiting for him in the hall. She looked every bit as pitiful she did at the hospital.

He handed her the shopping bag. "This belongs to you. Merry Christmas."

She peeked into the bag then set it on the floor. "I'll be damned. I didn't think it would end like this."

"What do you mean?"

"I remember you. And your partner."

Gus swallowed. "He's dead."

"Too bad." She said it almost cheerfully. Then a steely look came into her eyes. "I remember what you did to me. The rope. The gag. And the rest of it. You almost killed me, you know."

"That's why I'm here. I'm – well -- I hope this helps." He looked down.

Silence pulsed between them. "I saw you at the hospital," she said. "While I was on the phone."

Gus looked up, surprised. "You did?"

"Afterwards I went to the nurse to get your name. I even got your address when the nurse wasn't looking. I was going to call the cops, turn you in."

Gus fingered the button on his coat. "But you didn't."

"No."

"Why not?"

"I had a better idea." She cocked her head. "Why did you come here?"

"I told you. I wanted to give this back to you. It's worth a lot of money."

She eyed him curiously. "You trying to turn over a new leaf?"

He shrugged. "Maybe."

"Aren't we all." She laughed, but it was a hollow sound, and something about it pricked the hair on his neck.

"So are we square?" He asked.

She didn't say anything for a moment. Then, "We will be."

It was Gus's turn to cock his head.

"I've been thinking about this for a long time."

"About the jade elephant?"

"No." She slipped her hand in her pocket and pulled out a 22. "Did you know we have the same blood type?"

Gus frowned. "Huh?"

She laughed. "I'll say one thing. You saved me a trip to your place." She aimed at his head, so as not to damage his kidneys.

THE END

DUMBER THAN DIRT

This story was first published in 2000 in Blue Murder Magazine, which has since disappeared. It was reprinted in Twilight Tales' BLOOD AND DOUGHNUTS, and most recently in the ONCE UPON A CRIME ANTHOLOGY edited by Gary Bush. An "only in Chicago" story, it's goofy and noir at the same time.

Derek's father used to call him dumber than dirt. His mother said he wasn't the sharpest knife in the dishwasher. Both of them said he had more luck than brains. Like the time he accidentally shoved the gearshift in reverse and backed his father's '78 Dodge Challenger into a wall. No one got hurt, but eight-year-old Derek felt his sore bottom for days. He felt something else, too. He'd only gripped the wheel for a few seconds, but the thrust of the engine was so powerful, his sense of control so profound, that Derek immediately got hooked on cars.

As he grew up, his passion deepened. He didn't care much about the engineering or the technology. But the cold sleek lines of a classic design, the supple leather of a bucket seat, the hum of a perfectly tuned engine triggered an urgent need in him -- a need that could only be met by flooring it every chance he got. He spent his high-school years happily scouting, admiring, and borrowing the objects of his desire, sometimes without the owner's permission. But Derek never thought too much about the consequences of his actions, and when his friends went off to college, Derek went off to East Moline for two to five. He swore afterwards he'd never be seduced by a V-8's siren song again.

The summer he got out, he found a job at Lindsey's, a pub on Chicago's north side. Lindsey's sported lots of polished oak, soft lights, and a dartboard in back. They served tiny steaks with blue cheese on top, and the place was always crowded. Chuck Lindsey was a Sixties liberal who thought everyone deserved a second chance. He hired Derek to wash dishes and sweep floors. Derek found a room a few blocks away and walked to work. In Lakeview, most folks did, and the dearth of cars helped Derek avoid temptation. He cheerfully joined the throngs of pedestrians hoofing it down the street, another skinny young man with long hair and a slightly sleepy expression.

He was on the early shift one morning, rinsing out pots, when he heard a knock at the door. He walked out to the front and squinted through the window. It was Brady, a regular who sat with Lindsey almost every night, sharing jokes and stories and drinks. The bus boys said Brady threw money around like water. Once in a while Brady's wife, a hot blond number, came in too. Today, though, Brady wasn't smiling. As Derek opened the door, he felt waves of tension eddying out from Brady.

"Lindsey in back?" *No "hello, how are you, pal."* Brady never looked at you when he spoke, as if people were annoying things you swatted away like flies.

"He's not here."

"He must be." Brady sounded irritated, as if it was Derek's fault, and brushed past him. Derek started sweeping. Last night, he was loading the dishwasher when he heard loud voices coming from Lindsey's cramped office next to the kitchen. Then there'd been silence. A few minutes later Derek saw Brady slink down the hall, his face half-hidden by a baseball cap pulled low across his forehead.

Now Brady pushed past him again. "You hear from him this morning?"

Derek shrugged. "Nope."

Brady opened the door. "When he comes in, have him call me." Not a request. An order.

"Sure thing, Mr. Brady." The door slammed.

A few minutes later, Derek caught a gleam of silver wedged between a barstool and the foot rail. Thinking it was a gum wrapper, he leaned over to pick it up. It was a set of car keys. A small tag asked the finder to return them to Ian Brady at a post office number. Derek turned them over in his hand. One key was silver, but the other was that new kind of key that wasn't a key at all, just a finger of black plastic. Mercedes made them. Derek laid the keys on the bar. Brady would be charging back in as soon as he realized he'd dropped them.

He finished sweeping the floor. Then he unloaded the dishwasher. Half an hour passed. Brady hadn't come back. Derek started to itch all over. He stayed in the kitchen and tried not to think about the keys. Twenty minutes later the itch was still there, and his face felt hot. He checked the clock. Lindsey would be in any minute, along with the lunchtime crew.

He walked back to the bar. The keys glinted in a shaft of sunlight. He ran his thumb and forefinger around his jaw-line, stroking an imaginary beard, a habit he'd picked up that made him feel smart. He stared at the keys. Then he scooped them up and let himself out the door.

The Benz couldn't be too far away. Derek walked up one block and down another. No car. Puzzled, he doubled back through the alley behind the restaurant. There it was, parked in the spot Lindsey usually kept vacant for suppliers. A navy blue coupe that looked like it just came off the showroom floor. Cream interior. Deep pile carpeting. Fat seventeen inch tires. It had to be over five hundred horsepower. That thing would fly.

He skulked in the narrow shadow from an overhanging eave, his eyes scanning the buildings across the alley. This was the hottest summer since the year all those people died, and today was already a scorcher. Everyone must be holed up next to their air conditioners with the blinds down. Derek sauntered up to the car and pressed the dot of raised plastic on the key. The locks snapped up. He swung himself into the car. The leather seat yielded to the contours of his back, as though it was custom tailored for him. He gripped the wheel and turned over the engine. It caught right away. He nudged the car out of the alley.

He headed east to the Drive, handling the Benz as gently as one of Lindsey's crystal glasses, the ones he saved for special occasions. The slightest touch of his hand prompted an eager response, as if the car was just waiting for his next command. The ride was well balanced and stable, and it cornered on a matchstick. He cruised down the Drive, getting the feel of the car, then turned south on Fifty-Five.

The road opened up a few miles later, and Derek floored it. The car hesitated for a fraction of a second, then lunged forward. Derek hunched forward and let the car eat up the highway. There was always a moment when he could tell whether a set of wheels was worth it or whether it had some defect, some flaw that made it a clunker. But this baby was perfect. Derek blew out his breath. It felt like he hadn't really breathed in years. His fingers drifted over the walnut-trimmed instrument panel, the velvety smoothness of the seats. He wasn't sure where the car ended and his flesh began.

***

When Derek smelled it, he thought it might be fertilizer from a nearby field until he spotted the warehouses flanking the highway. Then he popped open the glove compartment, thinking Brady left a burger or hot dog inside. He found lipstick, tissues, and a garage door opener, but no food.

The odor grew more rancid, and he opened the windows. That helped for a while, but when he closed them to crank up the A/C, it came back. An uneasy feeling twisted his stomach. He veered off the highway at the next exit and stopped. The smell was strongest near the trunk. He got out and opened it up.

He jumped back as if he'd singed his fingers, then took a tentative step forward. The body of a man was curled up inside. There were brown stains all over his khaki pants and polo shirt. On his feet were black Converses, the kind Lindsey wore. The hair on the back of Derek's neck rose. It *was* Lindsey.

The sudden roar of a passing car reminded Derek the trunk was wide open. He pushed it down. His pulse raced. This had to be a bad dream. If he opened the trunk again, it would be empty. He did. It wasn't.

Then he glimpsed a patch of red plastic peeking out from under Lindsey's body. He pulled it out. It was a shopping bag from one of those fancy Lakeview stores. Inside was a crumpled white shirt with the same brown stains, and a large butcher's knife, it too stained with blood. Derek froze. The knife was from the restaurant's kitchen.

He stiffened. He had a big problem, and grand theft auto was just the beginning. A minute passed. He walked up to the passenger side and pulled the tissues out of the glove compartment. He edged around to the back and slid the knife out of the bag, using the tissues to keep his prints off. Clutching the knife, he jogged to a wooded area set back from the road, found a patch of dead leaves and twigs, and buried the knife underneath.

Seconds later, he was back behind the wheel heading south on Fifty-Five. Calmer now, he turned on the radio and twisted the dial to a country station. Tim McGraw was singing *I Like It, I Love It*. Derek thumped the wheel to the beat. Then he noticed the cell phone built into Brady's car. His hand flew to his chin and stroked it for a moment. He punched in a number.

"Louie? It's Derek." Louie was from East Moline. They'd worked in the laundry together, listening to country all day long. It was Louie who told him McGraw was married to Faith Hill.

"Derek, my man. Still keeping your ass clean?" Louie guffawed. He knew Derek was a dishwasher.

"Louie, I got a problem."

"Hold on, lemme get to another phone."

Derek heard a shrill voice in the background. "You already had one lousy break today. This better not take long."

"Don't mess with me, woman," Louie's voice snapped. Then he was back. "What's happening, man?"

Derek told him. There was a long silence.

"Where are you now?"

"In the car."

"Man, are you crazy? You calling me from some dude's car? What's the matter with you? Get to a pay phone and call me back." There was a click and the line went dead.

Derek drove to the nearest gas station, but a few people were filling up their tanks, and he couldn't risk someone getting a whiff of Lindsey. He sailed past it then redialed Louie's number.   "You at a pay phone?

"Er, yeah, Louie."

"It don't sound like it."

Derek took a breath. "Louie, I don't know what to do."

"Only one thing to do. Get your ass out of that car. Fast. Dump it."

"Can you help me?"

"No way, man. Ditching cars is one thing. Dead bodies is somethin' altogether different. Screw it man. You shouldna' called me."

"Louie, don't hang up. Please."

More silence.

"Louie?"

"Yeah?"

"Where do I dump it?"

"Anywhere man. Just do it." Louie sounded impatient. "Shit. You got no clue, do you?"

Derek shook his head, not realizing Louie couldn't see him.

"All right. Listen to me good now, Derek. You remember that movie we saw in the joint?"

"What movie?" Derek loved movies. When he could follow the plot.

"Think. The one about Bernie. You remember?"

Derek thought hard, his lips pursed together with the effort. It was something about two guys trying to figure out what to do with a dead body. *Weekend At Bernie's.* "Yeah." He was proud of himself. "I remember."

"Well, where's the one place we thought they shoulda' ditched him, but they didn't?"

Derek thought he recalled some of the guys acting like they knew all about dumping stiffs, but he couldn't remember what they said. "I - I dunno."

"Man, do I have to spell it out for you?"

Derek hung his head.

"Listen. I'm not gonna say it straight out -- you never know who's listening. But you get yerself out to the airport, you hear?"

The muscles on his face relaxed. "I got it. Thanks, Louie."

"And we never talked, you got it?"

"Sure."

"Derek?"

"Yeah, Louie?"

"Long term parking."

"Right."

Derek cut northeast towards O'Hare. He might catch on slow, but he knew what to do now. He'd ditch the Mercedes then race into the airport like he was boarding a plane. Then he'd make a one-eighty and take the subway home. His problems would be over. He turned up the radio and whistled along with Garth Brooks.

But when he got to long term parking, he realized they'd just finished renovating the lots. There was now a booth next to the automatic gate, and inside sat a black man, or a Double-A , as Louie called them. Derek pulled up and waited for his ticket.

The man stared at Derek with narrowed eyes, and Derek felt a jolt of recognition. The guy was an ex-con. Louie said you could always tell. There was something in the eyes, something that marked you as a former inmate, and it never went away, no matter how long you'd been out. Derek realized he should have waited until dark. The booth might have been empty, or even if someone *was* there, they'd probably be jammin' to the music from their headphones, taking no notice of a guy in a Benz. He circled the lot and pretended to change his mind. As he looped back to the highway, he felt the guy staring after him.

Derek cruised through neighborhoods where the same house reproduced itself in different hues of paint. After an hour or so he came to an industrial area dotted with warehouses and factories. He sat up straighter. The road dead-ended just ahead. Beyond it was a field, waist high with prairie grass. Nothing else. He stopped and got out of the car. There was no traffic. Or people. He was about to toss the keys into the field and run like hell when he heard a voice behind him.

"Nice wheels, man."

Derek whipped around. A kid on a bike. The kid braked to a stop.

"A Cl600 with a V-12 engine, right?"

Derek didn't know what model it was, but he dipped his head anyway.

"I know a guy has one of those new CLK350s, but your baby is wicked sweet."

Derek grunted. The kid went on about independent suspension, torque, and power transmissions, clearly trying to impress Derek with his knowledge. But Derek didn't want to shoot the breeze. He had to split before the kid smelled Lindsey.

"What are you doing around here, anyway?" The kid wrinkled his nose.

Derek's stomach flipped. He shrugged, struggling to act nonchalant. What should he say? Luckily, the kid gave him an out.

"You work around here?"

"Yeah," Derek said, almost grateful. "Yeah. I do."

"Oh. You must have just started, right? 'Cause I never seen your car before."

Derek nodded. Then a thought came to him. "You know what time it is?"

The kid shook his head.

"I gotta go. They dock you an hour's pay if you take too long on break."

He got back in the car and tried not to lay down any rubber as he pulled away.

By late afternoon, the stench from the trunk was turning his skin clammy. Blasting the A/C didn't help, and the hot angry air whipping through the window scalded his arm. He sped up Ninety-Four to Milwaukee, then backtracked south. He'd missed his shift; he hoped Lindsey wouldn't fire him. Then he giggled. Lindsey wouldn't be firing anyone anymore. By nightfall, though, he was drained. He was a prisoner in the Benz, just as surely as he'd been in the joint. He was hungry and tired, and he didn't know what to do.

It wasn't until three in the morning, occasional headlights winking past him on the Skyway, that he had an epiphany. This wasn't his problem. It was Brady's. Brady killed Lindsey. He, Derek, was guilty of only one thing: taking the car for a joy ride. If he could somehow undo that, he'd be in the clear. He played with the idea, turning it over in his mind, like a new car you want to baby until you know its limits.

The sun was just streaking the sky with pink when Derek drove east on Fullerton in Lincoln Park. He found Brady's home easily – his address was in the glove compartment. It was a neat brick townhouse, surrounded by a wrought iron fence in front and a small garage on the side. A discreet sign mounted on the gate asked visitors to announce themselves. He parked the car, got out, and left the keys in the ignition. He pressed the buzzer and then sprinted to the corner where he crouched behind a shuttered newsstand and peeked out.

Brady's door opened; Brady and his wife emerged. Brady's wife was in a bathrobe, her blond hair in tangles, but

Brady was wearing the same clothes he'd worn yesterday. Both of them looked shocked to see the Benz. His wife waved her arms in the air, then pointed a finger at Brady. Brady's arms flew up as if he thought she might hit him. He gestured to the house and hurried inside.

His wife waited until the front door closed. Then she strolled up to the driver's side, looked in both directions, and took the keys out of the ignition. Back at the trunk, she inserted the key and raised the hood. Ten seconds passed. Then Derek heard her scream, loud enough to carry a full block away. She slammed down the trunk and ran up the driveway, clutching her stomach with her hands. Derek thought she was going to throw up. He waited until he heard the sirens approaching before he left. He thought he might have forgotten something, but he didn't know what it was.

***

Derek couldn't decide whether to show up for work. If he didn't, someone would wonder where he was, but if he did, they'd ask where he'd been yesterday. He decided to go in and say he'd been sick. He needed the money.

The sign said Lindsey's was closed, but the place was crawling with cops. A couple of uniforms shielded the door. When he told them his name, they said to duck under the yellow tape stretched across the front. A man in a fancy suit and silk tie stood at the bar, talking into a cell phone. His skin was the shade of cocoa, his nappy black hair grizzled at the sides. His eyes were fearless.

"I know, but it's the closest thing we got to a crime scene." His eyes locked on Derek trying to slip through the door. "This is the last place anyone saw him alive." The man pointed to a table. Derek sat down. A guy taking pictures was just finishing up, while another guy started to smear black powder all over everything. "Call me back when you have something." The man who'd been talking snapped the phone closed and dumped it in his jacket pocket.

"Luke Woolston. Area Three Detectives." The man nodded to Derek. "Who are you?"

Derek stammered. "D-Derek Schindler."

"They told me you missed work yesterday."

"Yeah." Derek refused to meet the detective's eyes.

Woolston took a swivel stick off the bar, stuck it in his mouth. "How come?"

Derek gazed past the detective. The guy with the briefcase was dusting the top of the bar with white powder. "I got no A/C. I couldn't breathe."

Woolston twirled the swivel stick in his mouth. "You go to the ER? See a doctor?"

Derek shook his head.

"But you made a miraculous recovery." The detective curled his lip.

"I took lots of showers."

Woolston sat down across from Derek. "When was your last shift?"

"Yesterday morning."

"Where did you go afterwards?"

"Home."

The detective's cell phone rang. Woolston pulled it out of his pocket. "Good. Keep on it." He laid the phone on the table, his eyes never leaving Derek's face. "We've got a problem."

Derek looked at the cell phone.

"Yesterday we got a report of a stolen Mercedes. Brand new car. Then, less than twenty-four hours later, the car shows up. With Mr. Lindsey in the trunk." He took the swivel stick out of his mouth and pointed to the phone. "Now I hear you did two to five for stealing cars."

Derek blinked.

"You see the problem?" Woolston twirled the swizzle stick. "Let me try out a theory on you, son." He stood up, walked around to Derek, laid a hand on the back of Derek's chair. Derek had to twist around to see him. "I'm prepared to believe that whoever killed Lindsey didn't intend to kill him. I

137

think the offender --" Woolston took his time with each syllable-- "was just out for a joy ride. And you know, I can understand that."

Derek cocked his head.

"I was into cars myself," Woolston smiled. "I was runnin' a 327 in a 'Fifty-Four Bel Air. Nothing like the feel of a Hurst shift in your hands, you know? 'Course that was a while back."

Derek felt his lips curve up in a smile.

"So," Woolston went on, "Lindsey might have seen this person in the act of -- shall we say--liberating-- Brady's car. And the person panicked. He knew he'd be sent back inside. So he did the only thing he could think of. He stabbed Lindsey with a knife." Woolston wandered back to his own chair. His eyes gave away nothing. "What do you think of that theory, Derek?"

Derek's foot started tapping the floor under the table. He tried to stop; he knew it didn't look good. He couldn't.

"You come down to station with me, son. You can tell me all about it."

"Brady and Lindsey had a fight," Derek blurted out.

Woolston raised an eyebrow.

"Two nights ago. I was loading the dishwasher. Lindsey's office is right next to the kitchen. I see Brady comin' out of the office. All sneaky like. Then, when I'm on the early shift yesterday morning, he shows up looking for Lindsey."

Woolston sat down and nodded, as if he'd heard it all before. "What about the car, Derek? You take it for a ride?"

Derek shrugged.

The detective's cell phone rang again. He listened, disconnected, then inclined his head toward Derek. "You sure there's nothing else you want to tell me?"

Derek shook his head. His foot was still tapping.

"Like how did your prints end up on the steering wheel and the trunk of the Mercedes?"

Derek flinched. That's what he'd forgotten to do at Brady's house. It was all over.

Woolston ignored him. "Where's the knife, son?"

"I didn't kill him."

"Did you have help?"

"I didn't do it. I was set up."

"It's your word against Brady's." He dropped his chin, but kept his eyes on Derek.

"I found the keys in the bar."

"So you *did* steal the car?"

Derek said nothing. It was quiet except for his shoe tapping.

"Son, if you confess, it'll go easier on you. I'll tell the States Attorney you cooperated."

"I didn't kill anyone. You can't prove it."

Woolston stood up. "You may be right. But I can put you away for theft of a motor vehicle. And with a dead body in the trunk, I can also charge you with concealing a homicide. That's a Class Three felony. With your priors, son, you're looking at some serious time."

***

The ceiling of the cell was dimpled with tiny white pebbles that seemed to be glued onto the tiles. Derek tried counting them as he lay on his bunk but then gave up. Some of them were so tiny he wasn't sure whether they were part of the design or just mistakes. They'd transferred him downtown after the arraignment and assigned a public defender, but his lawyer, a woman who looked too young to know what she was doing, wanted him to cop a plea. She told him it was only a matter of time until they charged him with homicide. The only reason they hadn't was the absence of a weapon. When he told her he didn't do Lindsey, she shook her head and said it didn't much matter.

He wondered whether to tell her about the knife. It wouldn't have his prints on it, but the fact that he knew where it was might work against him. He should try to be smart about this. But he wasn't feeling very smart. Or hopeful. He should never have taken the job at Lindsey's. He'd always wanted to be a lifeguard. He should have tried for that. His parents were right. He was stupid.

He was still lying on his bed thinking how you couldn't tell day from night inside when they came to get him. Woolston was waiting for him in the interview room.

"We're letting you go," the detective said wearily.

Derek whipped his head up. "Did Brady confess?"

"No."

"Someone else did it?"

Woolston shook his head.

Derek was confused. "What happened, then?"

Woolston stared at Derek, then shrugged his shoulders. "I shouldn't be telling you this—but Brady's wife found a bloody shirt of Brady's stuffed in a bag in his closet."

Derek's chin jutted forward. "A bloody shirt?"

"Yeah. It seems that Brady and Lindsey were lovers. The wife's known about it for a while. When Lindsey showed up dead, she claims she wrestled with her conscience, hoping they could put their marriage back on track. You know, forget about the past. But when she found the shirt, she realized she couldn't."

Derek thought about it for a minute. "What does Brady say?"

"He admits that he and Lindsey were lovers. And that they had a fight the other night. But he says they made up a few minutes later. In Lindsey's office." Woolston cleared his throat.

So, that was the silence Derek heard the night he saw Brady coming out of Lindsey's office. Embarrassed, he made circles on the floor with his foot.

"Of course, Brady denies killing Lindsey, but we've got this shirt..." Woolston's voice trailed off. "And now his wife doesn't want to press charges about the car." Derek got the feeling Woolston didn't believe a thing he'd just said but didn't care enough to go on with the case. "So we're letting you go. You got lucky."

Derek smiled.

"Do me a favor, though. Get out of Chicago. It's not your kind of town."

***

Derek took Woolston's advice and packed his things. He'd catch a bus south. Or west. But he had one thing to do before he left. He wanted to thank Mrs. Brady for not pressing charges. Apologize for the trouble he'd caused. Tell her he hoped there were no hard feelings.

She answered the door in a halter-top and skimpy shorts. Her blond hair was swept up on top of her head.

"I've been wondering when you'd show up."

She stood close enough that he could smell her perfume. Then she turned to a small table and picked up an envelope. "I'll bet you're interested in this." She smiled mysteriously and dangled it in front of him.

"What's that?"

"You know."

"No, ma'am, I don't." He was bewildered

"Don't play dumb with me. Where is it?"

"Where's what, ma'am?" He'd been hoping to impress her with his good manners, but she didn't seem to be noticing.

"Look Derek, or whatever your name is, you almost screwed this up for me. Big time. But I managed to make it work anyway."

He shifted his feet.

"Why do you think I dropped the theft charges?"

At last, she was saying something he understood. He replied eagerly. "That's why I'm here, Mrs. Brady. I wanted to-
-"

She cut him off. "You're damn right that's why you're here." Derek felt like he was in one of those movies where he couldn't follow the plot. "I did you a favor. Now it's your turn. Where's the knife?"

The knife?" Derek involuntarily took a step backwards. How could she know about the missing knife? Unless -- he concentrated hard -- unless she knew who put it there. Which would mean she knew who killed Lindsey. Or maybe-- He met her eyes and saw the answer to his question. "You killed Lindsey."

"A real genius aren't you?" She sneered, checking her nails as if she'd just had a manicure.

"Why?"

"You think I'm just gonna sit by while my husband makes a fool of me? With another man?"

Derek thought fast now. "The keys. Brady didn't lose them. You planted them. To frame him."

She flashed him a cold smile. "After he went to sleep the other night, I took the car to the restaurant and killed Lindsey."

Derek frowned.

"Oh, I had some help." She twisted around. Derek could just make out the shape of a shirtless man sprawled on a couch in the living room. "Then we planted the keys, sopped up the shirt with Lindsey's blood and threw it in the bag with the knife. I knew Brady'd be back at Lindsey's the next morning. He was so crazy about that man he called him first thing every morning. God forbid Lindsey wasn't there, he'd run over like a damn puppy dog to find him."

"But then--"

"But then you stole the car. You really had me going for a while." She tossed her head. "I had to improvise."

Derek stuck his hands in his pockets.

"Thank God it all turned out. Now there's only one loose end left."

She opened the envelope and peeled off a few bills. "Consider this a down payment." She handed them to Derek. "You bring back the knife, the rest of it is yours, too."

He took the cash. Ten grand. And ten more later. He held the bills in the palm of his hand. She waited, an expectant smile on her face, while he thought it through. He stared at the floor, tiled in black and white. Then he lifted his eyes. She folded her arms across her chest. "Well?"

He chose his words with care. "You know something, Mrs. Brady? I'm right sorry, but the truth is, I just don't remember where it is. It could be anywhere." He smiled innocently.

Her smile faded.

"And if anything happens to me, the police might find a note telling them where the knife is and who used it... " His voice trailed off. He flipped up his hands.

She eyed him with suspicion, her hands on her hips. Derek bit his tongue. Finally, she sighed and handed over the rest of the cash. "You leave me no choice."

Derek slid the bills into his pocket.

"How do I know you'll be back?" she asked uncertainly.

"Oh, I wouldn't worry about that, ma'am," he said slyly. "I reckon you'll be seeing a lot more of me from now on."

She slammed the door in his face, but Derek didn't mind. He whistled as he skipped down the street. He patted the twenty grand in his pocket. So what if he was dumber than dirt? Who cared if he wasn't the sharpest knife in the dishwasher? His parents were right. He had more luck than brains.

THE END

THE WHOLE WORLD IS WATCHING

This story was written and published in the SISTERS ON THE CASE anthology edited by Sara Paretsky (Signet, 2007). I originally wrote this as an exercise in preparation for a thriller that takes place – in part -- during the 1960's . I hope that, like a delicious hors d'oeuvre, it whets readers' appetites by capturing the passion, the hope, and the fury of that era.

"'The whole world is watching.'" Bernie Pollak snorted as he slammed his locker door. "You wanna know what they're watching? They're watching these long-hair commie pinkos tear our country apart. That's what they're watching!"

Officer Kevin Dougherty strapped on his gun belt, grabbed his hat, and followed his partner into the squad room. Bernie was a former Marine who'd seen action in Korea. When he moved to Beverly, he bought a flagpole for his front lawn and raised Old Glory every morning.

Captain Greer stood behind the lectern, scanning the front page of the Chicago Daily News. Tall, with a fringe of gray hair around his head, Greer was usually a man of few words and fewer expressions. He reminded Kevin of his late father, who'd been a cop too. Now, though, Greer made a show of folding the paper and looked up. "Okay, men. You all know what happened last night, right?"

A few of the twenty-odd officers shook their heads. It was Monday, August 26, 1968.

"Where you been? On Mars? Well, about five thousand of them -- agitators -- showed up in Lincoln Park yesterday afternoon. Festival of Life, they called it." Kevin noted the slight curl of Greer's lip. "When we wouldn't allow 'em to bring in a flatbed truck, it got ugly. By curfew, half of 'em were still in the park, so we moved in again. They swarmed into Old Town. We went after them and arrested a bunch. But there were injuries all around. Civilians too."

"Who was arrested?" an officer asked.

Greer frowned. "Don't know 'em all. But another wing of 'em was trying to surround us down at headquarters. We cut them off and headed them back up to Grant Park. We got -- what's his name – Hayden."

"Tom Hayden?" Kevin said.

Greer gazed at Kevin. "That's him."

"He's the leader of SDS," Kevin whispered to Bernie.

"Let's get one thing straight," Greer's eyes locked on Kevin, as if he'd heard his telltale whisper. "No matter what they call themselves -- Students for a Democratic Society, Yippies, MOBE -- they are the enemy. They want to paralyze our city. Hizzoner made it clear that isn't going to happen."

Kevin kept his mouth shut.

"All days off and furloughs have been suspended," Greer went on. "You'll be working overtime, too. Maybe a double shift." He picked up a sheet of paper. "I'm gonna read your assignments. Some of you will be deployed to Grant Park, some to Lincoln Park. And some of you to the Amphitheater and the convention."

Bernie and Kevin pulled the evening shift at the Amphitheater, and were shown their gas masks, helmets, riot sticks, and tear gas canisters. Kevin hadn't done riot control since the Academy, but Bernie had worked the riots after Martin Luther King's death.

"I'm gonna get some shut-eye," Bernie said, shuffling out of the room after inspecting his gear. "I have a feeling this is gonna be a long night."

"Mom wanted to talk to me. I guess I'll head home."

Bernie harrumphed. "Just remember, kid, there's more to life than the Sears catalogue."

Kevin smiled weakly. Bernie'd been saying that for years, and Kevin still didn't know what it meant. But Bernie was the patrolman who broke in the rookies, and the rumor was he'd make sergeant soon. No need to tick him off.

"Kev..." Bernie laid a hand on his shoulder. "You're still a young kid, and I know you got – what -- mixed feelings about this thing. But these, these *agitators* – they're all liars. Wilkerson was there last night." He yanked a thumb toward another officer. "He says they got this fake blood, you know? They holler over loudspeakers, rile up the crowd, then pour the stuff all over themselves and tell everyone they were hit on the head. Now they're threatening to pour LSD into the water supply." He faced Kevin straight on. "They're bad news, Kev."

Kevin hoisted his gear over his shoulder. "I thought they were here just to demonstrate against the war."

"These people want to destroy what we have. What do you think all that flag burning is about?" Bernie shook his head. "Our boys are over there saving a country, and all these brats do is whine and complain and get high. They don't know what war is. Not like us."

***

Kevin drove down to Thirty-first and Halstead, part of a lace-curtain Irish neighborhood with a tavern on one corner and a church on the other. When he was little, Kevin thought the church's bell-tower was a castle, and he fought imaginary battles on the sidewalk in front with his friends. One day the priest came out and explained how it was God's tower and should never be confused with a place of war. Kevin still felt a twinge when he passed by.

His parents' home, a two-story frame house with a covered porch, was showing its age. He opened the door. Inside the air was heavy with a mouth-watering aroma.

"That you, sweetheart?" A woman's voice called.

"Is that pot roast?"

"It's not ready yet." He went down the hall, wondering if his mother would ever get rid of the faded wallpaper with little blue flowers. He walked into the kitchen. Between the sultry air outside and the heat from the oven, he felt like he was entering the mouth of hell. "It's frigging hot in here."

"The A/C's on." She turned from the stove and pointed to a window unit that was coughing and straining and failing to cool. Kevin loosened his collar. His mother was tall, almost six feet. Her thick auburn hair, still long and free of gray, was swept back into a pony tail. Her eyes, as blue as an Irish summer sky, his father used to say in one of his rare good moods, looked him over. "Are you all right?"

"Great." He gave her a kiss. "Why wouldn't I be?"

"I've been listening to the radio. It's crazy what's happening downtown."

"Don't you worry, Ma." He flashed her a cheerful smile. "We got it under control."

Her face was grave. "I love you, son, but don't try to con me. I was a cop's wife." She waved him into a chair. "I'm worried about Maggie," she said softly.

Kevin straddled the chair backwards. "What's going on?"

"She hasn't come out of her room for three days. Just keeps listening to all that whiney music. And the smell – haven't you noticed that heavy sweet scent seeping under her door?"

Kevin shook his head.

His mother exhaled noisily. "I think she's using marijuana."

Kevin nodded. "Okay. Don't worry, Ma. I'll talk to her."

***

As he climbed the stairs, strains of *Surrealistic Pillow* by the Airplane drifted into the hall. He knocked on his sister's door, which was firmly shut.

"It's me, Mags. Kev."

"Hey. Come on in."

He opened the door. The window air conditioner rumbled, providing a noisy underbeat to the music, but it was still August hot inside the room. Kevin wiped a hand across his brow. Her shades were drawn, and the only light streamed out from a tiny desk lamp. Long shadows played across posters taped on the wall: the Beatles in Sgt. Pepper uniforms, Jim Morrison and the Doors, and a yellow and black sunflower with "War is Not Healthy for Children and Other Living Things."

Maggie sprawled on her bed reading the *Chicago Seed*. What was she doing with that underground garbage, Kevin thought? The dicks read it down at the station. Said they got good intelligence from it. But his sister? He wanted to snatch it away from her.

"What's happening?"

Maggie looked up. She had the same blue eyes and features as her mother, but her hair was brown, not auburn, and it reached half way down her back. Today it was held back by a red paisley bandana. She was wearing jeans and a puffy white peasant blouse. She held up the newspaper. "You want to know, read this."

She slid off her bed and struck a match over a skinny black stick on the windowsill. A wisp of smoke twirled up from the stick. Within a few seconds, a sickly sweet odor floated through the air.

The music ended. The arm of the record player clicked, swung back, and a new LP dropped on the turntable. As Maggie flounced back on the bed, another smell, more potent than the incense, swam towards him. Kevin covered his nose. "What is that awful smell?"

"Patchouli oil."

"Pa—who oil?"

"Pa-chu-lee. It's a Hindu thing. Supposed to balance the emotions and calm you when you're upset."

Kevin took the opening. "Mom's worried about you."

"She ought to be worried. The country is falling apart."

Bernie had said the same thing, he recalled. But for different reasons. "How do you mean?"

"Idiots are running things. And anytime someone makes sense, they get assassinated."

"Does that mean you should just stay in your room and listen to music?"

"You'd rather see me in the streets?"

"Is that where you want to be?"

"Maybe." Then, "You remember my friend Jimmy?"

"The guy you were dating..."

She nodded. "He was going to work for Bobby."

"Who?"

"Bobby Kennedy. They asked him to be the youth coordinator for Bobby's campaign. He was going to drop out of college for a semester. I was, too. It would have been amazing. But now..." She shrugged.

"Hey..." Kevin tried to think of a way to reach her. "Don't give up. What would Dad say?"

"He'd understand. He might have been a cop, but he hated what was happening. Especially to Michael."

Kevin winced. Two years ago their older brother Michael had been drafted. 25th Infantry. Third Brigade. Pleiku. A year ago they got word he was MIA. Their father died three months after that, ostensibly from a stroke. His mother still wasn't the same.

"Dad would have told you that Michael died doing his job," he said slowly.

"Launching an unprovoked, unlawful invasion into a quiet little country was Michael's job?"

"That sounds like something you read in that – in that." Kevin pointed a finger at the *Seed*.

Maggie's face lit with anger. "Kevin, what rock have you been hiding under? First Martin Luther King, then Bobby. And we're trying to annihilate an entire culture because of some outdated concept of geopolitical power. This country is screwed up!"

Kevin felt himself get hot. "Damn it, Mags. It's not that complicated. We're over there trying to save the country, not destroy it. It's only these – these agitators who are trying to convince you it's wrong."

"These 'agitators' as you call them are the sanest people around."

"Throwing rocks, nominating pigs for president?"

"That's just to get attention. It got yours." Maggie glared. "Did you know Father Connor came out against the war?"

Kevin was taken aback.

She nodded. "He said it's become the single greatest threat to our country. And that any American who acquiesces to it, actively or passively, ought to be ashamed before God."

Kevin ran his tongue around his lips. "He's just a priest," he said finally.

She spread her hands. "Maybe you should have gone into the army instead of the police. What good is a deferment if you don't understand why you got it?"

"I'm the oldest son. The primary support of the family."

"Well then, start supporting us."

He stared at his sister. "Dad would be ashamed of you, Maggie."

"How do you know? Mother came out against the war."

"What are you talking about?"

"You should have seen her talking to Father Connor after church last week. Why don't you ask her how she feels?"

"I don't need to. I already know."

Maggie shook her head. "You're wrong. It's different now, Kevin. You're gonna have to choose."

He averted his eyes and gazed at an old photo on the window sill. Of himself, Mike, and Maggie. He remembered when it was taken. He and Mike were eleven and twelve,

Maggie seven. Mike had been wearing mismatched argyle socks. He was scared his father would notice, and he begged Kevin not to tell. Kevin never did. It was their secret forever.

***

Monday night Mayor Daley formally opened the 1968 Democratic National Convention. Marchers set up a picket line near the Amphitheater, and thirty demonstrators were arrested. But there was no violence, and it was a relatively quiet shift. Kevin didn't need his riot gear.

It was a different story at Lincoln Park, he learned the next morning, as he and Bernie huddled with other cops in the precinct's parking lot.

"They beat the crap out of us," Wilkerson said. "See this?" He pointed to a shiner around his left eye. "But don't worry." He nodded at the sympathetic noises from the men. "I gave it back." He went on to describe how hundreds of protestors had barricaded themselves inside the Park after the eleven o'clock curfew. Patrol cars were pelted by rocks. Demonstrators tried to set cars on fire. When that didn't work, they lobbed baseballs embedded with nails. The police moved in with tear gas, the crowd spilled into Old Town, and there were hundreds of injuries and arrests. Wilkerson said the Mayor was calling in the Guard.

"What did I tell you?" Bernie punched Kevin's shoulder. "No respect. For anything." When Kevin didn't answer, Bernie spat on the asphalt. "Well, I'm ready for some breakfast."

They drove to a place in the Loop that served breakfast all day and headed to an empty booth, still wearing their uniforms. Two men at a nearby table traded glances. Kevin slouched in his seat.

One of the men cleared his throat. "Look...." He folded the newspaper and showed it to his companion. Even from a distance, Kevin could see photos of police bashing in heads. "Listen to this," the man recited in a voice loud enough to carry over to them. "'The savage beatings of protestors were unprecedented. And widespread. Police attacked without reason, even targeting reporters and photographers. For example, one reporter saw a young man shouting at a policeman, 'Hey, I work for the Associated Press.' The police officer responded, 'Is that right, creep?' and proceeded to crack the reporter's skull with his nightstick.'"

Bernie drummed his fingers on the table and pretended not to hear. When their food came, Kevin pushed his eggs around the plate. "My parish priest came out against the war," he said.

Bernie chewed his bacon. "I'm sure the Father is a sincere man. But has he ever seen any action?"

"Not In 'Nam."

"What about Lincoln Park... has he ever dealt with these – these *demonstrators*?" Bernie lowered his voice when he spoke it, as if the word was profane.

Kevin shrugged.

"Well, then." Bernie dipped his head, as if he'd made a significant point.

I'll call your shiner and raise you an MIA? How could you compare Vietnam to Lincoln Park? "Maybe they have a point," Kevin said wearily.

"What point comes out of violence?"

"Couldn't they say the same about us?"

"We're soldiers, son," Bernie scowled. "We have a job to do. You can bet if I was on the front line..." He threw a glance at the two men at the next table, then looked back at Kevin. "Hey, are you sure you're up for this?"

"What do you mean?"

"You seem, well, I dunno." He gazed at him. "I got this feeling."

Kevin tightened his lips. "I'm fine, Bernie. Really."

***

The cemetery hugged the rear of the parish church. It was a small place, with only one or two mausoleums. Unlike the Dougherty's, most Bridgeport dignitaries chose Rosehill, the huge cemetery on the North side, as their final resting place. Kevin avoided going inside the church; he didn't want to run into Father Connor.

Despite the blanket of heat, birds twittered, and a slight breeze stirred an elm that somehow escaped Dutch Elm disease. He strolled among the headstones until he reached the third row, second from left. The epitaph read: "Here lies a good man, father, and guardian of the law."

Life with Owen Dougherty hadn't been easy. He was strict, and he rarely smiled, especially after he gave up drinking. But he'd been a fair man. Kevin remembered when he and his buddy Frank smashed their neighbor's window with a fly ball. Frank got a beating from his father, but Kevin didn't. His father forked over the money for the window, then made Kevin deliver groceries for six months to pay him back.

He sat beside his father's grave, clasped his hands together, and bowed his head. "What would you do, Dad?" Kevin asked. "This war may be wrong. It took Michael. But I'm a cop. I have a job to do. What should I do?"

The birds seemed to stop chirping. Even the traffic along Archer Avenue grew muted as Kevin waited for an answer.

***

Tuesday night Kevin and Bernie were assigned to the Amphitheater again. The convention site was quiet, but the rest of the city wasn't. On Wednesday morning Kevin heard how a group of clergymen showed up at Lincoln Park to pray with the protestors. Despite that, there was violence and tear gas and club-swinging, and police cleared the park twice. Afterwards, the demonstrators headed south to the Loop and Grant Park. At 3 AM the National Guard came in to relieve the police.

Greer transferred Bernie and Kevin to Michigan Avenue for the noon to midnight. Tension had been mounting since the Democrats defeated their own peace plank. When the protestors in Grant Park heard the news, the American flag near the band shell was lowered to half-mast, which triggered a push by police. When someone raised a red shirt on the flagpole, the police moved in again. A group of youth marshals lined up to try and hold back the two sides, but the police broke through, attacking with clubs, Mace, and tear gas.

As darkness fell, demonstration leaders put out an order to gather at the downtown Hilton. Protestors poured out of Grant Park onto Lake Shore Drive, trying to cross one of the bridges back to Michigan. The Balbo and Congress bridges were sealed off by guardsmen with machine guns and grenades, but the Jackson Street bridge was passable. The crowd surged across.

The heat had lost its edge, and it was a beautiful summer night, the kind of night that begged for a ride in a convertible. When they were teenagers, Kevin's brother had yearned for their neighbor's yellow T-Bird. He'd made Kevin walk past their neighbor's driveway ten times a day with him to ogle it. He never recovered when it was sold to someone from Wisconsin.

"Hey, Dougherty. Look alive!" Kevin jerked his head up. Bernie's scowl was so fierce his bushy eyebrows had merged into a straight line. About thirty cops, including Kevin and Bernie, were forming a barricade. Behind the police line were guardsman with bayonets on their rifles. A wave of kids broke toward them. When the kids reached the cops, they kept pushing. The cops pushed back. Kevin heard pops as canisters of tear gas were released. The kids covered their noses and mouths.

"Don't let them through!" Bernie yelled. Kevin could barely hear him above the din. He twisted around. Bernie's riot stick was poised high above his head. He watched as Bernie swung, heard the *thwack* as it connected with a solid mass. A young boy in front of them dropped. Bernie raised his club again. Another *thwack*. The boy fell over sideways, shielding his head with his arms.

The police line wobbled and broke into knots of cops and kids, each side trying to advance. Kevin caught a whiff of cordite. Had some guardsman fired a rifle? The peppery smell of tear gas thickened the air. His throat was parched, and he could barely catch his breath. He threw on his gas mask, but it felt like a brick. He tore it off and let it dangle by the strap around his neck. Around him were screams, grunts, curses. An ambulance wailed as it raced down Congress. Its flashing lights punctuated the dark with theatrical, strobe-like bursts.

Somehow Kevin and Bernie became separated, and a young girl suddenly appeared in front of Kevin. She was wearing a white fluffy blouse and jeans, and her hair was tied back with a bandana. She looked like Maggie. Young people streamed past, but she lingered as if she had all the time in the world. She stared at him, challenging him with her eyes. Then she slowly held up two fingers in a V-sign.

Kevin swallowed. A copper he didn't know jabbed her with his club. "You! Get back! Go back home to your parents!"

She stumbled forward and lost her balance. Kevin caught her and helped her up. She wiped her hands on her jeans, her eyes darting from the other cop to Kevin. She didn't seem to be hurt. She disappeared back into the crowd. Kevin was relieved.

A few yards away a group of cops and kids were shoving and shouting at each other. Rocks flew through the air.

"Traitors!" An angry voice that sounded like Bernie's rose above the melee. His outburst was followed by more pops. As the tear gas canisters burst, a chorus of screams rose. The protestors tried to scatter, but they were surrounded by cops and guardsmen, and there was nowhere to go. The cops closed in and began making arrests.

Coughing from the gas, Kevin moved in. He was only a few feet away when the girl with the long hair and peasant blouse appeared again. This time she was accompanied by a slender boy with glasses. He was wearing a black t-shirt and jeans. The girl's bandana was wet and was tied around her nose and mouth. She was carrying a poster of a yellow sunflower with the words "War is Not Healthy for Children and Other Living Things."

The boy looked Kevin over. He and the girl exchanged nods. "What are you doing, copper man?" His eyes looked glassy.

Kevin kept his mouth shut.

"You don't want this blood on your hands. She told me how you helped her up. Come with us. You can, you know." The boy held out his hand as if he expected Kevin to take it.

Wisps of tear gas hovered over the sidewalk. Kevin tightened his grip on his club. He stared at the kids. The girl looked more and more like Maggie.

Suddenly, Bernie's voice came at them from behind. "Kevin. No! Don't even look at 'em!"

Kevin looked away.

"Don't listen to him, man!" The boy's voice rose above Bernie's. "You're not one of the pigs. You don't agree with this war, I can tell. Come with us."

"Get back, you little creep!" Bernie moved to Kevin's side and hoisted his club.

The boy stood his ground. "You know you don't belong with..." He waved a hand. "... him."

A commander in a white shirt at the edge of the barricade yelled through a megaphone. "Clear the streets. Do you hear me, men? Clear the streets. Now!"

Someone else shouted, "All right. Grab your gear. Let's go!"

A line of police pressed forward, but the boy and girl remained where they were. Everything fell away except the sound of the boy's voice. In an odd way it felt as silent as the cemetery behind the church.

"Time's running out, man," the boy said, his hand half covering his mouth. "How can you defend the law when you know it's wrong?"

Bernie's voice slammed into them like a hard fist. "Kev, don't let him talk to you like that."

Kevin spun around. Bernie's face was purple with rage. Brandishing his riot stick, he swung it down on at the boy's head. The boy jumped, but the club dealt a glancing blow to his temple. The boy collapsed.

"Bernie, no!" Kevin seized Bernie's arm.

Bernie snatched his arm away. "Do your job, Dougherty." He pointed to the kids with his club. "They are the enemy!"

The girl turned to Kevin with a desperate cry. "Make him stop!"

Kevin strained to see her face in the semi-dark. "Go. Now. Get lost!"

"No! Help me get him up!" She knelt beside the boy.

"What are you waiting for, Dougherty?" Bernie's voice shot out, raw and brutal. He clubbed the boy again. The boy lay curled on his side on the ground, moaning. Blood gushed from his head. His glasses were smashed.

"Do something!" The girl screamed at Kevin. "Please!"

Her anguish seemed to throw Bernie into a frenzy. His eyes were slits of fury. He raised his stick over his head.

Kevin froze. Everything slowed down. Images of Maggie floated through his mind. She could be in the crowd. Maybe Father Connor. Even his mother. He thought about Mike. And his father. What Bernie was doing. What *his* duty was. His duty was to serve and protect.

The moment of clarity came so sharply it hurt. His chest tightened, and his hands clenched into fists. For the first time – maybe in his entire twenty-three years -- he knew what that duty meant.

"Dougherty," Bernie kept at him, his voice raspy. "Either you do it, or I will!"

Kevin stared at his partner. Then he dropped his club and threw himself over the girl. She groaned as his weight had knocked the wind out of her. Her body folded up beneath him, but it didn't matter: she was safe. Kevin twisted around and caught a glimpse of Bernie. His riot stick was still raised high above his head.

Kevin wondered what his partner would do now. He hoped the whole world was watching.

THE END

HOUSE RULES

This darkly humorous Keystone cops-like story was written for the MURDER IN VEGAS anthology (Forge, 2006) edited by Michael Connelly. It was subsequently nominated for both the Agatha and Anthony Awards for Best Short Story. You can also find it on audio at www.sniplits.com.

If Marge Farley had known what was in store during her vacation to Las Vegas, she might have gone to the Wisconsin Dells instead. At the very least, she might not have taken the side trip into the desert. But she'd been craving something new and different, which was why they'd come to Vegas in the first place. And she'd surprised her husband Larry with a trip to Red Rock Canyon to cheer him up.

But Larry ignored the petrified sand dunes, the waterfalls cascading into the canyons, and the red-tailed hawks soaring high above the Mojave. Polishing off both bottles of water, he stomped back to the car. "This isn't fun. It's too hot. And dusty. Let's go back." He swiped beads of sweat off his forehead. Wet bands ringed the back of his shirt.

Marge tried to focus on the craggy rock formations in the distance. The desk clerk at the hotel concierge said this was the place to visit. And Dr. Phil said there were times you had to decide what was important in a relationship. Lord knows, she was trying. But Larry'd had what you might call a setback last night. A fifteen thousand dollar setback.

"It's not fair." He moaned when they'd stumbled out of the casino. "Why couldn't we have Benny Morrison's luck?"

She'd heard the story a thousand times. How their friend Benny took his wife to Vegas and won fifty grand at the tables before they even unpacked. How he flew up to their room, grabbed their bags, and told Frances they were going home – that very minute -- to build a swimming pool in their back yard. Larry still did a slow burn every time the Morrison's invited them over.

But Larry had never had much luck. Marge pulled the visor of her cap down and contemplated a pink cactus flower not far away. So they'd skip the next vacation. Postpone the bathroom remodeling. Life wasn't about money, anyway. It was a spiritual journey. Like they said on "Oxygen." In fact, hadn't some woman said something about mantras last week? How they made for peace and tranquility? She should share that with Larry. As she tried to remember exactly what the woman had said, something near the flowers glinted in the sun and broke her concentration. "Look at that!"

Larry grudgingly turned around. "What is it now?"

Marge took off her sunglasses. "Something's over t here. By the flowers. It's glittering."

"It's probably a frigging gum wrapper."

She headed over. "Then we should definitely pick it up. How could someone even think of littering in a place like this?"

"Marge…" Larry followed her over, bumping into her when she came to a sudden stop. "What the --?"

"Look!" Marge pointed. Behind the flowers a piece of metal was sticking out of the sand.

"Lemme see." Larry squinted and crept closer. "Looks like some kind of box." He peered at it, then felt around it with his shoe. They heard a metallic thump. Larry's eyebrows shot up. He bent over the box.

"Wait!" Marge cut in. "Don't touch it." She hugged her arms and looked around. "You have no idea what's in there."

Larry looked up. "For Christ's sake, Marge, it's just a box." He squatted down beside it.

"Hold on. Stop. Isn't—isn't this where they dump all the radiation stuff?"

"Huh?"

"You know, spent fuel rods, the waste from reactors? Like they talk about on TV? They transport it into the desert and dump it in places where nobody lives."

"Marge, that's in Wyoming. And you're talking about huge containers. The size of railroad cars. Not little boxes."

"Still..." She pleaded. "You never know."

Larry shot her one of his looks, the kind where the lower part of his jaw pulsed, the way it did when he disagreed with her.

An uneasy feeling fluttered her stomach. "You were right, Larry. This isn't fun. Let's go back to the car. We'll get a nice, cold drink at the hotel."

Instead, he knelt down and started scooping up chunks of dry, hard-packed sand.

"Honey, didn't you hear what I said?"

But he kept scrabbling through the sand. Then he stopped digging and sat back on his haunches. Jiggling it to pry it loose, he lifted up a gray tackle box about a foot square and five inches deep. Its surface, at least the part not covered with sand, was dingy and battered.

Marge was just about ready to go back to the hotel without him. Let *him* get poisoned by some weird biological toxin. "Larry, you just leave that thing right there."

His response was to shake the box from side to side. A swishing noise could be heard.

"Larry." Marge started to feel anxious. "It doesn't belong to you."

He looked around, a strange light in his eyes. The sun was casting long shadows across the desert, suffusing everything with a rosy, warm light. No one else was in sight. "It does now." Cradling the box under his arm, he started back toward the car. "Let's go. And for the love of God, don't say a word to anyone."

Marge pursed her lips. She knew better than to argue. She'd spent her whole life following the rules. School rules. Secretary rules. Wife in the suburb rules. She pasted

"Hints from Heloise" into a scrapbook. She knew ten ways to get out stains, how to keep potatoes from budding, how to keep her husband happy. And anything she didn't know, she learned on Oprah. Rules were there for a reason. You play by the rules, you find what you're looking for. So what if she'd been a little restless recently? That didn't mean she was looking for trouble. She stole a worried look at her husband. She never understood rebels.

As they hurried back to the parking lot, a man in a car at the edge of the lot flicked a half-smoked cigarette out his window. He seemed to be watching them, Marge thought. She shook her head. She must be imagining things.

***

Mirrored bronze panels reflected a series of chandeliers that drenched the hotel lobby in a giddy display of light. The casino was off to one side. Larry gave it a wide berth and headed for the elevators, but Marge peeked in as she passed.

A room as big as a football field, the perimeter was rimmed with slot machines for the little old ladies and pigeons. Circular pits for poker, roulette, and blackjack took up the center, with rectangular crap tables around them. It was barely six o'clock, but coins were already clinking, cards were being dealt, roulette wheels clacked. Loud electronic music made it impossible to think. But then, that was the point, wasn't it? Hundreds of greedy souls flocked to the place every night, each thinking they were the exception to the rule. They would beat the house. Larry had been one of them, Marge thought.

As she crossed to the elevator, she wondered how long it would before someone noticed the bald, pudgy man with a dingy box under his arm. He did look suspicious. She slipped in front to shield him. She knew this wasn't a good idea.

"But I had it when I checked in." A brassy redhead in tiger-striped pants complained loudly at the front desk.

"Ma'am, I'm doing everything I can." The desk clerk's tuxedo was wrinkled, and stringy hair grazed his shoulders. He fingered one of several earrings in his ear. Marge wasn't partial to men with earrings, but she knew she was supposed to be tolerant.

"I talked to housekeeping," he was saying. "Put up a notice in the employee lounge. I even put a reward out for the bracelet."

"Sure you did." The woman glared. "You got some nerve, you know? Our money's not good enough for you. You gotta steal everything that's not nailed down."

The desk clerk broke eye contact with the woman and – impolitely, Marge thought – looked around. His eyes swept past them but then came back and focused, Marge realized with a start, on Larry and his package. She stepped closer to her husband, but it was too late. The lady in tiger pants was still carping, but the desk clerk couldn't take his eyes off Larry. As the elevator doors opened and they stepped inside, he picked up the phone.

***

Back in their room, Larry took the box into the bathroom. He wiped it down with a damp towel, then felt around the seam.

Marge stood at the door. "Please, Larry. It's not too late. Don't open it. What if it's anthrax?"

"Marge." He growled. "If you aren't gonna help, at least get out of the way."

Her mouth tightened. Then, "At least let me try to find you some gloves."

"Huh?"

"Rubber gloves. I saw a drugstore around the corner off the Strip."

Larry shook his head. He didn't care about germs. Something was inside that box. It was a sign. And it couldn't have come at a better time. What with the lousy economy, he hadn't made his quota last quarter. Then there was last night. He needed a break. And God was finally sending him one.

"At least, let me wipe it with a little bottle of bleach." Marge persisted. "It's destroys viruses."

He caught his wife's reflection in the mirror. She'd always been a little loony, but lately it had become big time. Quoting all those bimbos on TV. Yakking away about the environment. Refusing to let him eat fries or Capn' Crunch. Too many carcinogens. He didn't know what she wanted any more. It wasn't like he hadn't been trying. He'd agreed to come here, even though he liked the Dells just fine. But Marge wanted something new. Exotic. Well, he scowled, she sure got that in spades. He picked up the box and looked underneath.

"At least let me put some alcohol on it." Marge pulled out a bottle of alcohol from her travel kit. Saturating a cotton ball, she dabbed it on the box. A sharp, antiseptic smell filled the room.

"For cryin' out loud, Marge."

He snatched the box out of her hands. She was acting like Donna Reed on steroids. He wanted to pry open the box, but the lock seemed to be warped, bent at an odd angle. Even with the right tools, it would be tough to open. But he didn't even have a screwdriver. He wondered if he should call a repairman. An "engineer," they probably called them here. A fancy place like this probably had a slew of them, all expecting to pocket a huge tip just for changing a frigging light bulb.

He grabbed the faucet and splashed cold water on his face. In the mirror he saw Marge paw through her bag again. Frigging thing was big enough to hold an entire drug store. She pulled out a small, chunky red plastic object. With a white cross on it.

A Swiss Army knife! He spun around. How the --

She smiled as if she was reading his mind. "I was reading this survey of female travel writers – you know, in *New*

Woman magazine? It said if you don't have a travel alarm or a Swiss Army Knife, you're not properly packed." She handed it over. "Most women like the scissors and the small blade, but I kind of like the bottle opener."

Larry swallowed his astonishment – every once in a while, his wife still amazed him. Snapping it open, he started levering the blade in and out of the box.

"One woman actually fixed the engine of her rental car with it," Marge went on. "Another fixed her hair dryer. Of course, you have to check it in your luggage nowadays. But it's worth it."

Larry ignored her. Jimmying the blade, and then the screwdriver, he slowly widened the space between the lid and the base. Finally, a sharp upward tug of the screwdriver sprang the lock, and the box flew open. Larry took a breath, said a prayer, and looked in.

"My god!"

"What is it?" Marge crowded in behind him.

He lifted out a large plastic bag. Inside were at least a dozen smaller baggies, all filled with a white, powdery substance. He gingerly opened one of the bags, stuck in his pinkie, and brought it to his tongue. It tasted bitter and tingly. Maybe a slight numbing sensation.

He gazed up at the ceiling and smiled.

***

The knock on the door made Marge jump. She and Larry exchanged looks.

"I'll take care of it." Larry started toward the door, closing her in the bathroom. "You stay in here. And keep the door shut."

"But what if—"

"Just do what I say."

Marge obediently sat on the toilet. Shivering, she draped a towel over her shoulders. They always kept these rooms too cold. Through the door she heard muffled voices. Larry's and someone else. A woman's.

"No thank you," he was saying. But the heavily- accented voice – Spanish, Marge thought -- drifted closer.

"I turn down beds. And put towels in bathroom." Marge pictured a Hispanic woman with dark hair and a gold cross at her neck.

"No!" Larry yelped like a wounded dog. "I'm sorry," he added. "I mean – my – my wife's in there. She's not feeling well."

"I give towels. She feel better."

Something jingled as she swished across the carpet. Keys. Maids carried those big silver rings, didn't they? The jingling was followed by a smacking sound. Marge knew that sound. Whenever Larry was upset, he slapped the palms of his hands against his thighs.

Larry's hands smacked back and forth. The jingling edged closer.

Marge's heart thumped. If she didn't do something, the maid would burst through the door. Jumping up from the toilet, she locked the bathroom door and slid open the door to the shower. She carefully stowed the box in the bathtub as far away from the shower head as she could, then turned on the water. As a cold spray gushed down, she slid the door shut and plopped back on the toilet.

The jingling stopped.

"See, I told you," Larry said weakly. "She's not feeling well."

Silence. Then, "Ees okay. I help."

Good Lord, Marge thought. The woman wouldn't give up. She quickly grabbed the towel and bunched it in front of her face, hoping her voice would sound like she was inside the shower stall. "Just leave them outside."

"You sure, meesus? I get medicine."

She was about to issue a sharp retort when it occurred to her the woman was just doing her job. Following the rules. Marge was annoyed with herself-- she should be more tolerant.

"Thank you. I'll manage. Just leave the towels on the floor."

Eventually, the jingling retreated, and the door to their room slammed. Marge waited a full minute before coming out of the bathroom. Larry was looking through the peephole, still slapping his thighs. The scent of cheap perfume hung in the air.

"That was close." He whispered.

"Is she gone?"

He nodded and headed back toward the bathroom. Marge grabbed his arm. "Larry, we can't do this. It's wrong. We've got to hand it over to the police."

"Are you crazy?"

"It's not worth it. If we get caught..."

His nervous laugh cut her off. "It's a little late to worry about that."

"It's never too late to do the right thing. We all do things we wish we hadn't."

"But this isn't one of them. Anyway, what cop in his right mind 'll believe we found this in the desert?"

"But we did."

"Sure. And while you're at it, don't forget to tell 'em it was your Swiss Army knife that got it open."

"What's that supposed to mean?"

"It means you're in this up to your neck, too. You're an accomplice, Marge."

Marge stiffened. All she'd done was pack her toiletry bag according to *New Woman's* rules: a little detergent, cotton balls, and, of course, the knife. How could that make her a co-conspirator? Larry had to be wrong. Maybe this was some kind of test. Of their values. Their relationship. She lifted her chin.

"I'm going to the police."

His eyes narrowed. "You can't."

"We have to follow the rules." She started for the door, but Larry caught her by the arm.

"Marge, don't. Please. The box -- it's a sign. I know it."

"A sign?" She searched his face hopefully. Hadn't she just been thinking the same thing?

"We can make a killing if we're careful. Do you know how much that stash is worth?"

Her spirits sank. "I don't care."

" It could be worth millions!"

Money. She looked away. They weren't even on the same planet. Dr Phil said there was a point you had to rescue a relationship or it died. They'd discussed it at her women's workshop: Marge, a newly pronounced lesbian, and two others so bitter over their divorces they couldn't possibly launch, much less, rescue a relationship.

"Our luck is about to change. All we have to do is find someone to sell it to."

"But that would make us..." She whispered hoarsely. "...dealers."

"N...no. Not really," he said. "It wasn't ours to begin with."

"Exactly. That's why we can't do this, Larry. We've got to play by the rules."

Before he could stop her, she wriggled out of his grasp and bolted through the door.

***

Marge crossed the lobby, aware that the desk clerk with the stringy hair was watching her. She picked up her pace.

Outside darkness was falling, but it was a false, noisy darkness. Gaudy neon displays sputtered. Fountains gurgled. Horns blared. Electronic dings spilled out from the casinos. As she pushed through the dense crowds on the Strip, she grew uneasy. She didn't like this city where night was day and darkness was light. An air of abandon, a go-for-broke chaos, permeated everything, all of it sizzling in the oppressive desert heat. Marge fanned herself with the flaps of her sweater.

Finally, she caught sight of a black and white cruiser on the next block. Two cops lounged against its side. She was hurrying to flag them down when she felt a presence beside her. She quickened her pace, but the figure loomed closer. When she tried to break into a run, he clamped a hand on her arm. She started to scream, but her attacker grabbed her around the waist and buried his mouth on hers in a hard kiss. With the other hand, he jabbed something hard and cold in her side. She knew without seeing that it was a gun.

**

Alone in the room, Larry paced and slapped his thighs. The stash would more than make up for his losses. All he had to do was unload it. But he was a salesman from the Midwest. Where could he find a drug dealer in Las Vegas?

He pulled out the shirt Marge bought him before they came. You can't wear a golf shirt and chinos in Vegas, she'd said. Even if everyone else does. He slipped it over his head and checked himself in the mirror. Some slinky yellow material. He looked like a frigging Italian.

Italian. Everyone knew the casinos were fronts for the Mafia. The Mafia ran drugs. If he went down to the casino, maybe he could find someone -- a card dealer maybe -- who knew somebody. But what would he say? "Hey, you want to score – it's upstairs in my room?"

He pulled on the new pair of pants that matched the shirt. A tan weave. At least they weren't white. Damn. He sounded like Marge with all her frigging rules. He opened the box, took out one of the baggies, and stuffed it into his pocket. She hadn't always been this way. She'd been quite a number when he spotted her in the secretarial pool twenty-five years ago. When had she changed? The kids were living their own lives. You'd think she would have loosened up.

He closed the box and looked for a place to stash it. The safe? No. That would be the first place someone would look. Under the bed? No. That was for amateurs. He looked around, his gaze settling on the mini bar. Twisting the key, he opened the tiny refrigerator, took out the nuts, candy, sodas, and tiny bottles of booze, and slid the box in. It fit perfectly. He threw the food into a laundry bag and shoved it under the bed.

A moment later, he opened the door to the room. He half-expected to see the maid standing there, her arms full of towels, but the hall was empty. He rode the elevator down and crossed the lobby, nodding to the desk clerk as he passed. His luck was about to change. He knew it.

***

The moment she was accosted Marge wondered why she ever thought a trip to Vegas would be fun. She should have gone to the Dells. Larry and she could have stopped at the water park, like they always did, then shopped for cheese. They might even have taken a boat ride.

Now the man growled in her ear. "You've got something that belongs to me."

Funny how your mind works, she thought. Here she was on the Vegas Strip, a gun poking her ribs, and she was thinking about the Dells.

The man jabbed the gun in her side. "You hear me?"

"The box?"

"I want it back." His voice was raspy, as if he'd smoked too many cigarettes.

"You can have it."

He positioned himself behind her so she couldn't see his face, but she thought the pressure on her ribs might have eased. "Smart move, lady. So where do I find it?"

"In our room."

"Good." The raspy voice croaked in her ear. "You just keep nice and quiet, see, and no one 'll get hurt."

As he hustled her down the strip, the greasy smell of fries and burgers from a fast food joint made her stomach grumble. She realized she hadn't eaten since lunch.

"And tell your husband to stop takin' things that don't belong to him."

She nodded, swallowing her hunger. Maybe this could still work out. If she could somehow flag down the policemen at the cruiser, she'd say the box belonged to this goon. Which, according to him, it did. So let him take the rap. She and Larry would be in the clear. Then they could start over. Together. She nodded again, to herself. Dr. Phil would approve.

***

Larry tried to look nonchalant as he strolled down the strip, but his armpits were damp and sticky, and sweat crawled on his neck. He checked out each passer-by, but most of their faces said they had more important things to do than notice a man in a yellow shirt.

He bought a beer at a dimly-lit place off the strip. Two customers were hunched over the bar: a black man with a "they do it better in Vegas" T-shirt and a woman with frizzy gray hair. Larry considered approaching the guy and tried to remember some rap. Home guys? Homies? He changed his mind when the man glared at him in the mirror.

Back on the strip, the crowd was thick and boisterous. Larry elbowed his way into a resort with cobblestone streets and quaint cafes. Supposed to be a mock up of Paris, he remembered. Wandering past a "French" bakery whose warm scented bread set his mouth watering, he spotted a scruffy-looking man on a bench. The guy's knee jerked up and down, but he wasn't making eye contact with anyone. He shook out a cigarette from a crumpled pack. Touching a match to it, he sucked down a drag. Took his time waving out the match.

Larry walked over. The man threw him a surly glance and scuttled farther down the bench. His movement waved the scent of Patchouli oil through the air. Larry remembered Patchouli oil. A three-day fling in college with a hippie who never said much more than "far out" and "dig it." She'd had a perpetual buzz, and she reeked of the stuff.

He took a swig of his beer. Maybe this guy was the one. Then again, if he was wrong, it could all go south. He remembered how much he'd lost at the casino. He thought about the box and how much it was worth. He wiped a hand across his mouth and sat.

"I have some stuff I need to move." He muttered. "Think you could help?"

The guy didn't move. Or even look over. Larry wondered whether he'd made a mistake. Two cops were leaning against their cruiser half a block away. Too close for comfort. He resisted the urge to slap his thighs. He stole a look at the guy. No response. Rows of slats pressed against his shoulder blades. He was about to bolt, melt into the crowd, when the guy gave him a tiny, almost imperceptible nod.

Larry's pulse started to race. It was working! "You – you want in?"

"What's the deal?" The man said.

Larry threw his arm over the back of the bench. The guy's lips were pencil thin, and his upper lip didn't move when he spoke. In fact, Larry wasn't sure he'd spoken at all until he repeated himself.

"What's the deal?"

Larry told him.

"Where is it?"

"In my hotel room."

"Hotel? What the hell is it doing in a —"

Larry cut him off, surprised at how brazen he felt. "It's a long story. And I don't have all day. Yes or no?"

Silence. Both of them stared at a trash can, one of those fancy, shiny ones that reflected lights from the hotel marquee. The man on the bench ran a hand over his head. Twice.

"You're on."

***

174

The elevator doors opened, and Marge and her assailant made their way down the hall, the barrel of the gun still prodding her in the ribs. As they skirted a housekeeping cart outside her door, Marge remembered the maid with the towels. Was she in the room now? If she was, maybe there was some signal Marge could send her, something that would tell the woman to get help. Thinking furiously, Marge swiped her card key and pushed through the door.

To her surprise, the lights in the room were on, and a reedy voice called out from the bathroom. "So, what are you waiting for? Check the cabinets."

Seconds later, the maid stomped out of the bathroom. When she caught sight of the man with the gun, she threw her hands in the air.

"*Santa Madre de Dios*!"

A noise came from the bathroom. "Estella…what the --"

Fear knifed through Marge. "Who else is in there?" She shouted anxiously. "Get out of my bathroom!"

Silence.

Marge glanced at her attacker, seeing him for the first time. He had thick dark hair, matted and bushy, jeans, denim shirt, and skin so bad it made bubble wrap look smooth. She wished he'd do something to help. But he just stood there, confusion stamped on his face. She'd have to save herself. But how? She frowned and arched her back, hoping to slip through his hold, but his grip was too strong. Then the bathroom door slowly opened, and the desk clerk with stringy hair and too many earrings emerged.

"You?" Marge planted her hands on her hips, her fear turning to anger. "Why are you here? Where is my husband?"

The maid unleashed a stream of rapid-fire Spanish, followed by a flood of tears.

The concierge fingered an earring, not at all perturbed. "The guest in the room below complained of a leak in their bathroom ceiling," he said over the maid's wails. "We were just checking it out." Flashing a look at the man with the gun, he added, "See? Nothing to worry about. So now, if you'll –"

The man with the gun suddenly seemed to snap out a trance and pointed the gun at the desk clerk. "Stay where you are." He barked. "Not another step. "

The desk clerk shot him a strange look. Almost as if they knew each other, Marge thought. She crossed her arms. "Where's my husband?"

"No one was here when we came in."

Marge fixed him with an icy stare. He looked defiant, but he could be telling the truth. At least about Larry. But then, where was her husband? And where was the box?

Her assailant waved the gun at the maid. "Stop bawling, woman. And get out of here." He turned to the desk clerk. "You too. And you ain't seen nothing. Or no one. If you know what's good for you. Got it?"

"Wait!" Marge yelled. "You can't do –"

Her attacker waved the gun at her. "You… up against the wall."

"But what about --"

"Shut up." He turned back to the desk clerk. "You got a problem with your hearing?"

"No."

Marge saw the look they exchanged. "Do you know each other?"

The two men didn't answer. She frowned. The sobbing maid was her last hope. She turned to her, trying to telegraph an SOS, but the desk clerk grabbed the maid's arm and shoved her out into the hall. As the door slammed, Marge heard him ream her out in Spanish.

"You got exactly thirty seconds to find that box." Her assailant snarled.

Marge sagged against the wall. She knew it was a waste of time. The box wasn't here. But she searched anyway, sliding open the shower stall, the closet door, drawers.

Nothing.

Until she found the bag of snack food under the bed. Who did Larry think he was fooling? Still, maybe it would all work out. She hauled out the bag from under the bed and stood up.

"Try the mini bar."

"Open it." The man pointed to the cabinet.

"I don't have the key."

The man shot her a look and kicked the cabinet. It flew open, revealing the box.

Marge opened the refrigerator and pulled it out.

The man grabbed it from her and slid it under his arm. Then he cocked the gun. "Tough break. Now I have to shoot you. You know too much."

Marge blew out a breath. He was right. It was over. She resigned herself to her fate and squeezed her eyes shut, waiting for the bullet to end her life. Still, she couldn't help thinking how humiliating it was to die in Las Vegas. And how none of this would have happened if Larry had played by the rules.

***

They both heard the click of the key card. Her attacker shoved her into the bathroom with the box. Jabbing the gun into her ribs – it almost felt familiar by now -- he raised a finger to his lips.

Marge pasted her ear against the wall. Larry was talking. To a man. Drawers slid open and closed. The closet door slammed.

"I can't believe this. It's gone." Larry's voice took on a high-pitched, nasal whine.

"What do you mean, it's gone?" The man's voice was deep. And angry.

"I- I was only out of here for a few minutes." Larry stammered.

Then, "OK, Pal. Game's over. Get your hands in the air."

"What – what are you talking about?"

"I'm Officer Dale Gordon, Las Vegas police. And you're under arrest. You have the right to remain silent…"

"A cop!" Larry yelped. "You're an undercover cop!"

"That's right, pal. And you're in serious trouble."

Marge gasped. A police officer. It was a sign. She lunged for the door. As she did, she elbowed her attacker by accident, and something metal dropped into the toilet. The gun. She must have knocked it out of his hand. Out of the corner of her eye, she saw the thug trying to retrieve it from the bowl. He was cursing under his breath.

Banging her fists on the door, she yelled. "Help! Help me please!"

Footsteps raced over. The door was flung open. A scruffy-looking man who didn't look much like a policeman to Marge crouched in a shooter's stance, his gun pointed straight at her.

Her hands shot up in the air. "Don't shoot!" She heard the click of his gun.

"Who the hell are you?"

***

Marge was about to tell him when she heard a rattle out in the hall. The door opened, revealing the maid with a gun in her hands. She seemed to size up the situation right away and pointed her gun at the undercover cop. "Drop the gun. Now." Her English was perfectly unaccented.

The cop complied.

The maid pointed at Marge with her head. "Get me the box."

Marge scurried into the bathroom, picked it up, and handed it over.

The maid nodded and folded it under one arm. "Nobody moves for the count of ten."

She let the door close with a thud.

There was an instant of shocked silence, and then pandemonium broke loose. Everyone shouted at once. The cop whipped out a cell phone. So did Marge's attacker. Larry accused everyone of ripping him off. The chaos stopped only when they heard more shouts in the hall. The undercover cop ran to the door and flung it open. The two uniformed cops

Marge had seen lounging against the cruiser stormed into the room.

"Took you long enough!" The undercover cop snarled. "Did you see her?"

The back-up cops exchanged a look. "Who?"

"The maid, dammit! She took it! Not even a minute ago!"

One of the cops gasped. "The door to the stairwell! It was just closing!" He bolted down the hall to the exit. The other cop followed.

***

They caught her before she hit the ground floor, but she didn't have the box with her, and she refused to say where it was. In fact, she clammed up and didn't say a word in English or Spanish. After listening to Marge's story – several times – the cops searched the room, then took everyone into custody, including the desk clerk. Everyone except Marge.

They'd been trying to crack this narcotics ring for months, they said. They knew the drops were made at Red Rock Canyon late at night. They'd even busted one of the mules, but the other suspects got away. Apparently, they'd buried the stash under the sand, figuring they'd come back for it when they could. The cops assured everyone they'd turn the hotel upside down to find the box. But even if they didn't have the evidence right now, they had enough to make everyone's life unpleasant, thanks to Marge.

She promised the cops she'd call if she found the stash and told Larry she'd get bail money wired tomorrow. She watched them shuffle down the hall, all of them in cuffs. She was about to close the door when she noticed the maid's housekeeping cart wasn't there any more. But it had been -- when she and her attacker had come back to the room. For a fancy hotel, they sure didn't keep track of their equipment very well. Shaking her head, she closed the door.

A moment later, she opened it again. Scanning the hallway, she noticed that the door to the hotel room door closest to the stairwell was seeping light around its edges. Marge crept toward it. The door was unlatched. She pushed it open. There was the cart, draped in skirting, probably to hide all the cleaning supplies. Marge bent over, raised the skirt, and smiled.

She picked up the box. A grimy smell clung to it. No matter. She had a bottle of *Jean Nate* in her bag. *New Woman* said it was just the thing after a day in the hot sun. She looked both ways and stole back to her room.

She was in the bathroom dousing the box with perfume, the TV chattering from the other room, when an author started to talk about her book, "Your North Star: Claiming The Life You Were Meant To Live." Marge straightened up. A few hours ago, she wasn't sure she'd have a life to reclaim. Was this a sign?

Slowly she examined herself in the mirror. Then she turned sideways. Fluffed up her hair. When you really got down to it, there wasn't anything that a beauty shop, new clothes, and a few aerobics classes couldn't fix.

Her gaze returned to the box. Maybe she'd pay a visit to the maid tomorrow. Make her a small proposition. After all, the woman had almost out-smarted them all. Marge was sure she'd know what to do.

She nodded to herself in the mirror. Yes, that was a good plan. She'd go see the maid. Maybe even bail her out of jail. Then she'd buy that book, read it from cover to cover, and start to reclaim her life. After all, she always played by the rules.

THE END

DETOUR

This story was written for my friend Joe Konrath's anthology, THESE GUNS FOR HIRE (Bleak House, 2007). As he said in the introduction, this was one of my first attempts at hard boiled, and I found it liberating. In fact, it pushed me in an altogether new direction. You can also find it on audio at www.Sniplits.com.

I wasn't expecting a hit that hot August morning. I was barreling east on a stretch of Ninety-four between Indiana and Michigan that just begs you to floor it. Newly paved, two wide lanes, it's practically uninhabited at six in the morning. Compared to Ninety-six, or even Sixty-nine, you feel like you're about to take off, like the frigging crows on the power lines at the side of the road. At least the ones that haven't been dropped by West Nile.

I'd headed out from the Michigan shores before dawn. I hadn't slept much -- Christ -- I hadn't even changed my clothes. I was still trying to figure out what the old lady was up to. I hadn't seen her – or the place -- in ten years. Why did she invite me back? I'd been living in the Motor City, trying to keep a low profile, when all of a sudden the phone rings, and there she is with that high-class way of talking. You know, the kind that reminds you of your fourth grade teacher. Asking could I please do her the honor of visiting?

The honor?

It'd been too long, she said, with just a trace of regret. We needed to catch up. I could stay overnight. She'd put me up in the guest cottage, she said, and we could bond. What was I, Elmer's Glue?

So I met her yesterday afternoon for tea. Tea, for Christ's sake. So bitter that even with sugar and cream it sucks out the insides of your cheeks. She had those stupid little sandwiches and biscuits. Scones, she called them -- all arranged on a silver tray you only see at weddings. She also had this thick white stuff in a bowl. Clotted cream, she smiled. "You'll like it. It's sweet."

As she poured, she made small talk. How was I, Teresa dear? What was I doing? Such a shame about my father. Hey -- no one calls me Teresa. It's Terry. Tare, sometimes, or TJ. But never Teresa. Who did she think she was, the Queen of England?

Afterwards I meant to grab a burger and a couple of boiler-makers in town to rinse the taste of the tea out of my mouth, but I took a walk along the lake instead. The old lady's place went on forever now. Much farther than it used to. She'd bought up even more of her neighbors' land. I couldn't understand why. She didn't have any kids. What was she gonna do with it when she croaked? What is it they say, the rich get richer, and we get screwed?

It was after midnight when I got back to my room. I lay down on the bed, and the next thing I knew some bird was chirping outside the window, and it was four in the frigging morning. I took a quick shower and left. I wasn't looking forward to the drive home.

Once I was on Ninety-four, I pulled into a truck stop for breakfast. Not only was I wiped, but I was starving. That's probably where he picked me up. I was wolfing down three eggs over easy with toast and bacon. A bunch of farmers in plaid shirts, jeans, scuffed boots were there. Plus one creep in a yellow slicker, even though the sun was blistering hot. There was a map of the state on the wall with one of those "you are here" pins stuck to it. Christ. I knew where I was. And where I was going. But I didn't think it meant trouble.

Thirty minutes later I was back on I-94, the oldies station blasting. My head was bobbing to Del Shannon's "Runaway" like one of those sappy little dogs you see in the back of cars when I caught him. At first I thought it was just some jerk riding my tail. A kid coming down from a wild night. Or a trucker in a car instead of eighteen-wheeler. I switched lanes and slowed down, thinking the asshole would blow by me. But he didn't. He switched lanes, too, and slowed down.

He was in a blue Buick. Who drives a Buick any more? I was in a gray Camry I'd ripped off last week. Had to be nearly six years old, but it still drove like a champ. I checked the rear view mirror. A man. Older, from what I could tell. Maybe fifty. Shades covering his eyes. Looked like he was wearing a sports coat. I frowned. It was close to ninety degrees already.

I floored it. The Camry hesitated for a second, like the transmission was about to go AWOL. But then it gathered itself together and surged ahead. The lane dividers flashed past so fast the stripes ran together into one straight line. Kind of like the blades on a prop plane. Speaking of flying, I realized I was clocking almost a hundred. I checked the rear view. The creep was still on my ass.

I gripped the wheel. Who knew I was here? I thought about the last job I'd pulled. It'd been riskier than usual. I'd taken all the normal precautions. Stole some plates. Wore a disguise. Made sure to use a throw down. But I didn't figure the mark would have his kid with him. I don't do kids. I had to wait until he dropped the kid off. Which meant tailing him all afternoon. First to some fancy toy store in the mall whose name I couldn't even pronounce. Then to a bookstore. And then the Dairy Queen.

Too much time is a danger in my line of work. Things change. People take notice. Someone could have picked me up. He did have two bodyguards, but for all I knew, there could have been another-- a guy who was supposed to watch the watchers.

I slowed and checked the rear view again. Still there. I fished out my cell phone and punched in a number. "Hey."

"Hey, babe. What's happening?" His voice was as smooth and mellow as always.

"You get the package for the last job?"

"Just came today. And very sweet it is. You do fine work."

"Yeah, well, you hear about anything strange going down?"

"What do you mean?" A trace of caution crept into his voice.

"Some guy's riding my ass." I explained what was going on.

"There's nothing on the street. In fact, I got another job for you. It's all lined up. You know, the jerk's probably just a redneck having some grins. You see that a lot in the country."

"I don't think so, Johnny."

There was a beat of silence. "Well, if makes you feel better, why don't you take the long way home?" That was code to hole up for a few days. "I'll be waiting for you whenever you show up. We need to spend time together."

I smiled as I disconnected. Johnny D was my boss. And my man. It didn't matter he was twenty years older than me. Or that he'd been one of Pop's buddies. His partner, as a matter of fact. Johnny D taught me a lot about my job. And after Pop died, he taught me other things. A shiver of pleasure ran up my spine.

I took another look in the rear view. The Buick was still there, but it was holding steady fifty yards back. Maybe Johnny D was right. Maybe this was just some joker getting his rocks off by scaring me. Like I said, I didn't get much sleep last night. I could be a little paranoid. I decided to hang tight for a few more minutes.

I thought back to my visit with the old lady. There was a lot of history between us. Pop used to do jobs for her. When he wasn't using a gun he was using a hammer, and for a long time he was the caretaker at her place. A huge estate overlooking Lake Michigan, it was in the kind of neighborhood no one pays much attention to. Mostly because the rich families who live there make sure of it. Private roads. Private beaches. Private clubs. There's a shitload of Detroit money up there, Pop used to say. And the old lady's place is sitting pretty, right in the middle of it.

Once I asked my father how he met her. He said he knew her husband first, and had promised Grayson – what kind of a name is Grayson? -- that he'd look after the old lady if anything happened. And, wouldn't you know it, Grayson up and died one night. Helped along by the 38 slug that blew his brains over the desk and against the wall. But that was a long time ago, when I was still a little girl. After that we started to visit the old lady a couple of weeks in the summer. To make sure she was okay, Pop said.

At first my mother came too, and we stayed in the guest cottage. My mom, my dad, and me. Mom tried to pretend I was one of *those* girls. She even bought me this fancy white dress with lace all over it. Except I got a big fat blueberry stain on the front the first time I wore it. I never put it on again.

I always wondered if that's why she took off. It was only a few days later. Pop and I had been fixing a pipe in the old lady's kitchen, and we went back to clean up for supper. Mom wasn't there, but there was a note on the table. Pop read the note, then crumpled up the paper and pitched it into the trash. He didn't read it to me, and I was too scared to ask. I thought she left because the stain wouldn't come out of the dress. When I was older, though, I figured she just couldn't hack it. Pop once told me she liked living on the old lady's estate. Said it made her feel respectable. But I guess when you can't have what you want all the time, you want it even more. And when there's no chance in hell of getting it, you just give up.

Which is why I try not to want anything.

I checked the rear view again. The asshole was still there, but now he was closing. Christ. I didn't think a Buick had that much in it. Who was this creep? Who sent him? Johnny D said everything was quiet back in Detroit. Unless one of the mark's bodyguards had one of those bugs you stick to a car to track someone. I'd been thinking of getting something like that myself. Make my job a whole lot easier. Damn. I should have looked under the Camry at the truck stop.

But what if it wasn't the guy or his men? The only other person besides Johnny D who knew where I'd been was the old lady.

Think, Tare. What happened yesterday?

After the preliminaries, she started to talk about my father. She had this strange way of describing his work, using plain words but weird inflections, kind of like a drama queen, to get her point across. Either she didn't want to admit what he did, or she wasn't sure if I knew. Which made me realize she didn't know what I did, either. Then again, how could she? I hadn't seen her since I was fifteen, well before I started following in Pop's footsteps.

I decided two could play her game, and when she asked what I was up to, I kept it vague. "A little of this, a little of that," I said, shrugging my shoulders.

"Do you have any thoughts of going back to school, Teresa dear?"

"It's a little late for that."

"You're only thirty. It's never too late for an education," she smiled.

I shrugged again. "I never was much good in school."

"I see." She stirred her tea with this tiny little spoon, then set it down on her saucer.

We were circling each other like two wary cats. I guess she realized it too, because, all of a sudden, she came out with it. Did I know the kind of work Pop did?

"I think so." I answered cagily. "He worked for you."

She pressed her lips together. Did I ever hear from my mother?

"Nope." I shook my head.

Now, I looked in the rear view mirror. The tail was only thirty yards back. Much too close. I hunched my shoulders and squinted through the windshield. I was cruising over eighty, and there weren't any other cars on the road. No rest stops, either. But Pop taught me not to panic. "All you need is a plan, TJ. You got a plan, nine times out of ten, you can get out of a tight spot."

I tried to focus. Trees and billboards zipped by. A green sign said I was forty miles from Kalamazoo. It could have been forty million for all the good it'd do me. But then, on the side of the road, an orange sign flashed. Detour Ahead. A smaller sign underneath said that Route 131 was closed for repairs.

I was still in the left lane; I twisted around. Nothing on either side except the Buick. The detour was only half a mile ahead. I kept my foot on the gas. Pop used to say never advertise your plans. I tightened my seat belt. A quarter mile. I sucked in a breath. A few hundred yards. I veered sharply to the right and tore up the exit ramp. I threw myself off balance, but I managed to hold onto the Camry. I glanced at the speedometer. I was clocking in at 82.

As I charged up to the stop sign, I heard the screech of brakes. He'd overshot the exit! The plan had worked – I'd bought myself some time. I looked both ways down the road. On the left was a gas station and quick mart, then the entrance back to Ninety-Four. On the right, nothing but farmland.

I turned right and nudged the Camry up to sixty. I sped by fields of chest-high corn that alternated with hayfields that had rolls of the stuff curled up like pinwheels. A farmhouse with a barn on the side. In between the fields were woods with lots of trees. Ahead of me on the left was a farmer riding a tractor. He stared at me as I passed. For him, it was just another day with nothing but work to do.

I opened the glove compartment and slid out my Sig. The nine has always been my favorite. Hardly any recoil. I slammed in the clip, then set the gun on the passenger seat.

I felt him before I saw him. A chill on the back of my neck. When I looked in the rear view, I tensed. He was only a speck in the distance, but he'd be closing fast. I passed a few dirt paths that bisected the road on the edge of the fields. They probably led back to homes or barns or storage sheds. Plenty of cover back there. Getting to it was the problem. Everything was out in the open. Too risky.

I kept driving. The Buick was gaining. My hands grew slick with sweat. Ahead of me were more woods. They ended at the side of a cornfield, but continued around the back. At the far edge of the field was a dirt road. As I got closer, I could see it led back into the woods.

I slowed and swerved onto the dirt path. Trails of dust blew up behind me. Damn! I might as well send up smoke signals. But I had no choice. I kept going. The path was studded with rocks, and the Camry lurched unevenly. I heard a squeal from the chassis. I couldn't think about it now. The woods were just ahead. A few more seconds. I let myself glance back at the road. The Buick was making the turn.

When I pulled into the woods, the Camry was swallowed up by trees and underbrush. No way was I going any farther. I braked and switched off the ignition. I opened the car door, grabbed the Sig, and launched myself into the brush. I thrashed through bushes, ignoring the branches and brambles that scratched my skin. The thicket was so dense I couldn't see much in any direction. I squatted on the ground and pointed the Sig back toward the road.

A minute later the Buick drove up. I heard the engine idling. I pulled back the slide on the Sig. He knew I was hiding. He wouldn't get out of the car without reason. Still, the longer he waited, the edgier he'd get. Another lesson from Pop. Be patient and let him come to me.

I was ready. It was silent. Even the bees stopped buzzing. My calves started to cramp. All that crap about women crouching in the fields to give birth and then getting up to work was bullshit. No way could you stay in this position for long. I swatted away the gnats and tried to work out why the old lady sent him. I thought back to her questions. She'd been fishing -- she wanted to know how much I knew.

What she didn't know is that I was fishing too. See, when Pop died last year, he left me a letter. Written in a scrawl with all those spelling mistakes, it said he wanted to clear the record. Seems as if after her husband died, one of her neighbors put some heat on her to sell her land. She asked my father for help, and two month later, the neighbor dropped dead of a heart attack. Instead of the neighbor buying her out, she was the one who bought. A few years after that, when the neighbor on the other side tried the same thing, he died in a car accident. The old lady ended up with a compound that stretched over a mile of lakefront property.

But I knew all that before I went to see her. In fact, that's why I went. Pop's death had been real sudden. One night he was fine, and the next morning, he keeled over. The doctors said it was a heart attack. He *was* almost seventy, he liked booze and cigars, and he ate all the wrong things. But there are chemicals that can simulate heart attacks, and any professional knows how to use them. So when Pop said he had visited the old lady before he died, well, let's just say coincidence isn't a word in my vocabulary.

But now I realized she must have figured out I knew. Don't know how. I thought I'd been careful not to spill anything. Unless Pop told her I knew before he died. Which meant the guy following me was hers. She had the connections -- hell, Pop probably gave 'em to her. "Use him for back-up," I could hear him saying, "if I'm not around to help you out."

A car door squeaked. I tore myself back to the present. With one hand I grasped the end of a branch and carefully pulled it back. I caught a glimpse of the Buick. The driver's door was open, but there was no sign of the goon. I kept perfectly still. Just one opening. That's all I needed.

Suddenly he stepped in front of the car door, his gun drawn. He started toward the bushes. Christ. Had he spotted me? My heart went ballistic, and it was tough to breathe. Then he stopped, uncertain, maybe, which way to go. It was only a brief moment, but it was enough. I raised the Sig, aimed, and squeezed the trigger.

I waited until I knew he wasn't going anywhere, then scrambled to my feet. I rolled him and found a few hundred in his billfold. I stuffed them in my jeans. I didn't expect to find any ID, and I didn't. The road looked deserted, but I dragged his body back into the woods. When I got back to Camry, I stripped the plates and wiped all the surfaces. Then, just for the hell of it, I checked under the car. No bug. I got all my stuff out of the back then inched the car as far into the brush as I could. With luck they wouldn't find it for a few weeks. Hell, maybe the whole season.

The door to the Buick was still open, and the keys were in ignition. I slid into the front with the Sig beside me. I backed out onto the road, running through the checklist Pop taught me. Everything was accounted for. Even the farmer I passed on the way had left.

***

It wasn't hard to take care of the old lady. She was still in her bathrobe, her clothes laid out on the bed. She didn't scream or struggle when I broke in -- it was almost like she was expecting me. I didn't say anything, and I was quiet when I used the pillow. I didn't want one of the maids barging in. I wore gloves, and made sure there were no marks. With luck they'd think she had a heart attack. But even if they didn't, the only thing the cops would have was a description of a blue Buick, not a Camry. Afterwards, I slipped out the door and for second time that day, headed back to Ninety-four. I ditched the Buick just outside Detroit and hitched the rest of the way.

I lay low for a few days in case there was any heat. I didn't even call Johnny D. I saw something in the paper about the old lady's death -- they said it was a heart attack -- but there was nothing about a Camry or a body in the woods near a cornfield. After four days I was running out of clothes and money, so I decided to go home. I staked out the place until two in morning before I went in. Nothing suspicious.

I didn't check my messages till the next morning. There were three: two from Johnny D and the third a thin nasally voice I didn't recognize. Said he was Kenneth McCarthy, the old lady's lawyer. I grabbed some clothes, stuffed them in a gym bag, then pried up the floorboard next to the bathroom. I threw my entire stash into the bag, grabbed the keys to my Honda, and bolted.

It took an hour of driving around to realize I probably panicked for nothing. If someone out there had made me, the call would have been from the cops, not a lawyer. And theirs would have been in person. This had to be something else. I drove to a diner for some food. Behind the register were these crummy little paperweights with tiny dogs and cats and butterflies suspended inside a glass ball. The butterfly had some silver stuff on its wings, and it sparkled in the light. I could hardly take my eyes off it.

After I ate, I called the man from a pay phone.

"Teresa Nichols?" The nasally voice asked after I'd waited about a year on hold.

"You got her."

"Yes, well.." McCarthy cleared his throat but when he spoke again, his voice was still nasally. Almost whiny. "It seems as if you've been named the sole beneficiary of my client's will."

"What?"

"My client has left everything to you. The estate. The bank accounts. The investments. Even her jewelry. Over ten million dollars in assets."

"Are you fuck – I mean are you out of your mind?"

He cleared his throat again. "There's a letter for you from her. It's marked confidential. If you'd like to come down to our offices, I can give it to you personally."

Yeah, right. I wasn't born yesterday. "Why don't you read it to me?"

"As I said, it's marked confidential."

"You got my permission."

"You won't mind putting that in writing?"

"What the – sure – whatever."

"In that case, well...." I heard the rip of an envelope, the crackle of paper. His tone was so emotionless he could have been reading a grocery list.

"Dearest Teresa,
After Grayson died, your father was my
confidante and closest friend. But you were
the most precious thing in his life. He always
wanted to give you a better life, and he never
stopped trying. He talked about you so much I
felt like I knew you. And though I wasn't your
birth mother, I loved you, too. Now that I'm
gone, I'm in a position to help your father
express his love for you. Just consider it my
way of repaying all the favors."

The lawyer was quiet. I stared out at the street but to this day, I don't remember what I saw.

"Miss Nichols, are you there?"

"Yeah." I grunted after a pause.

He started spewing details about what I was supposed to do and when, but I wasn't paying attention. He said he'd send me a registered letter and checked my address. I hung up the phone and started to walk back to the car. My head was spinning. The old lady didn't order the hit. I took out the wrong target. And now I was rich. I massaged my temples.

But if she didn't do it, who did? I stopped. There was only one other person who knew where I was going. Johnny D. Pop's partner. He knew everything about my father,. He'd been there when Pop died. He was the only man I trusted. We'd even had our wills done together. He'd promised Pop, he said. It was the best way to protect me from the occupational hazards of our jobs.

I walked around some more, then headed back to the car. I had one more job to do. It would probably be my last. But I'd do it, and I'd do it well. Pop would have wanted me to. The old lady, too. But first maybe I'd go back to that diner and buy the frigging butterfly.

THE END

THE RAINFOREST MESSIAH

This was originally published in the WORLD WIDE WRITERS Magazine, (UK, November, 2000). It was republished in the webzine, Mysterical-E, in January 2001, and was voted one of the best five stories of that year. It was one of the first stories I wrote that wasn't set in Chicago.

Tumbleweeds skitter across the desert at random, like dust motes caught in a shaft of light. Zack swallows as he drives, but the air is so dry his tongue is coated with dust. The huge Texas sky hangs down on all sides of him like the flaps of a tent. When he was little, he felt tucked up and secure in tents, but this one is too vast, too relentless. His eyes hurt when he looks up.

He bears down on the gas. The Pontiac shudders, then shoots forward. Past uneven fence posts linked by barbed wire. Past an abandoned oil derrick rising out of the brush. He tries to shake it off, this unease, but it has already penetrated, like water seeping through a leaky roof.

A distant ribbon of grey detaches itself from the horizon. A few minutes later, it puckers into geometric shapes. He has reached the outskirts of Laredo. He cruises south past a cluster of ramshackle buildings. *Colonias,* they call them, inhabited by Mexicans who cross the border to work at menial jobs for less than minimum wage. Third-world shantytowns are more like it. He slows and parks next to a cantina. A chalk-board with several letters missing announces cold beer inside. As he opens the door, a gust of cool air slaps him. He tries not to think of the old westerns where the bad guy swings through the saloon doors. A radio blares out a tune by the Judds. On one side is the bar, a slab of splintered wood which will pierce his skin if he isn't careful. Folding chairs and card tables sit on an uneven floor. Except for a Budweiser sign, a dusty mirror, and a Texas map with Webb County outlined in black, the walls are bare.

He glances at his reflection. With his Nikes, Dockers, and Polo shirt, he has Yankee written all over him. He lifts his sunglasses and scans the place without seeming to, the way he's been trained. A stocky Mexican woman lounges behind the bar with a bored expression. The only other customer sits at one of the tables, a long-necked Bud in front of him.

Zack studies him. A beard covers his face, making it hard to take in his features. He wears a buckskin jacket and camouflage pants, and his long hair is tied back with a leather headband. The man is a cross between Davy Crockett and one of the weirdoes Dennis Hopper always plays.

Zack steps up to the bar. "I'll have a beer."

The woman fishes a longneck Corona out of a cooler and holds up five fingers. Zack digs out a five. He knows he's being ripped off. She stuffs the bill inside her shirt. He tips his head back for a long swig, hoping to rinse the grit from his throat and glances at the man. The man stubs out a cigarette. Zack takes that as a sign of greeting and nods.

"Long ride?" The man asks.

"Long enough." Zack walks over and pulls out a rickety chair. "Why here?" He waves the Corona in the air.

"It is what it is."

Zack sits down. It doesn't really matter where the meet is. Or the cross-over. He'll be well out of it by then.

The man thumps a pack of Camels on the table. "So I put out feelers and one name comes back to me. Just one. Zack Mueller. Special Agent, FBI."

Zack shifts in his chair. The man has a flat Midwestern accent, but he affects a twang, as if he wants Zack to think he's a Bubba.

The man slips a fresh Camel between his lips. "How does an upstanding federal law enforcement agent turn into a gun runner?"

"Hard work and initiative."

The man's eyes narrow. "How do I know you're not fixin' to set me up?"

Zack shrugs. It has taken time and effort to get this far. But he is prepared. He keeps his mouth shut. The man, perhaps sensing a stalemate, lights his cigarette.

A flash of light strobes Zack's peripheral vision. Someone has opened the door to the cantina. A young Hispanic woman, dressed in cargo shorts, a white shirt rolled up to her elbows, and desert boots. The man with Zack nods to her. She closes the door. In the dim light the girl's skin is the color of burnished copper. Her dark eyes glow like polished obsidian.

"You made good time," the man calls out.

She calls to the woman behind the bar. "*Mamacita*," she says. "*Como te a ido?*"

The woman smiles, revealing a mouth with several teeth missing. She turns down the radio. "*Estoy bien a veces. Un poco causada pero.*" I'm okay. A little tired.

"*Trabajas demaciado.*" You are working too hard.

"*No tengo otra alternativa.*" I have no choice.

The girl nods sympathetically. "*Una Pepsi.*"

The woman opens a cold Pepsi. The girl throws a dollar bill on the bar, hikes the bottle to her mouth, then joins the men at the table.

"You know her?" The man jerks his head in the woman's direction.

"No," the girl says. "Yes." She eyes Zack. "I'm Dora. Dora Anuncion."

"Zack Mueller."

They both look at the man. His turn. "I'm what you might call -- an agent too," he laughs. "For some Indians in the Maya Rain Forest. They have endowed me with the – uh -- authority to buy them a shitload of guns."

"What do we call you?" Zack asks.

"You can call me Elvis."

"Elvis?"

"The Indians think I'm their king—no, their fucking messiah. You know. Gonna save them." A half-smile plays on his face. Zack wonders if he's pasted it on for effect.

"You know the Rainforest?" Elvis asks. Zack knows it's in southeastern Mexico, Belize, part of Guatemala. "A lot of in-di-ge-nous," Elvis draws out each syllable, "Indians down there. You know the type. Running around naked. Never saw a white man 'till twenty years ago." Elvis shifts in his seat. "But now it seems progress has come."

"How's that?" Zack asks.

"An American oil company thinks there's a gold mine under the forest. They're fixin' to come in and drill. At the invitation of the Mexican government." Elvis glances at the girl.

Dora clears her throat. "The government wants to jumpstart the economy of the region, create jobs."

"But the Indians don't want it," Zack finishes for her.

"Right. The drilling will destroy their homes, their sacred ground. Not to mention what it will do to the habitat."

"I met Dora in the jungle." Elvis takes over again, Zack notices. He doesn't like to relinquish control for long. "She's on our side. Now the Indians, see, they started out saying they were gonna commit mass suicide if the oil company comes in. But we changed their minds." He chuckles again.

"You're encouraging armed insurrection."

Elvis points a finger at Zack. "Your words."

Zack rolls his beer on the table. "How'd you get to me?"

Elvis glances at Dora. She takes a breath. "I'm an environmental anthropologist. Before the Maya Forest I was in Colombia."

Zack nods. He remembers Colombia. The Indians there kept blowing up the pipeline to keep the multinationals out. When that didn't work they escalated to kidnapping, then to Russian arms. He was in the middle of it.

"But that's jack-- Zack -- compared to what we want to do." Elvis smiles at his little joke. "Can you help us?"

Zack scratches his cheek, pretending to think. "Depends on what you want."

"Don't they got AK47s, stun grenades, rocket launchers, explosives down in Colombia?"

"They placed an order."

Elvis fingers his beard. "One from Column A, one from Column B." His smile fades. "Who the hell are you, man?"

Zack drains the last of his beer. "I've been with the Bureau twenty-five years. Retiring next year." He is ready. He feels it. The fatigue of too many years at the same job. "My daughter has cerebral palsy," he lies. "She needs care. Insurance won't cover it. So I started moonlighting."

Elvis tilts his head as if he can somehow divine the truth of Zack's words. "What's your connection?"

Zack smiles. "I can't tell you that." Mentally he flashes back to Petrovsky, the Russian general who didn't speak a word of English. Always in uniform, as if it proved he was once an important man. Petrovsky, accompanied by Sergei, his younger partner, who did speak English. And wore those cheap, shiny Euro knock-off suits.

They'd negotiated a small deal, the three of them. It went down without a hitch. Afterwards Zack lured Petrovsky to Atlantic City with promises of wine, women, and more business. The Bureau nabbed him at the Newark airport—the general never made it to the crap table. But Sergei, who stayed home, disappeared from sight. Now he was Zack's business partner.

"Who are you man?" Elvis repeats.

"Just a guy looking out for his family."

***

Elvis and Zack discuss terms. Zack doesn't ask where the money is coming from. The Indians may be primitive but they're not dumb; they've been dealing coca and weed for years. In Colombia over forty per-cent of the economy depends on the drug trade. He's not sure about Mexico.

He tells Elvis a front company will accept a wire payment through a bank in the Caribbean. "Except for my fee. I want it up front. In cash."

Elvis wavers. "How do I know you won't cut me loose?"

"You don't. But that's how I do business. My man at the port will want his cut too."

Elvis gazes around the room, as if considering Zack's terms. Finally he nods. They'll meet back at the cantina tomorrow.

Zack finds a relatively clean motel on the edge of town and boots up his laptop. He sends some e-mails and waits for the replies. He will drive Elvis to the port of Houston; he needs to make sure his team is in place. He leans back against the headrest. The sheets are cool, the pillows surprisingly soft. He has been on the road for a while.

A knock on his door wakes him. Through the blinds the late afternoon sun has turned heavy and red. He rolls out of bed, cracks open the door. Dora Anuncion steps in, sits down on the bed.

"So, can you do this?" she asks. Zack smiles. She digs into her cargo shorts, pulls out a scrap of paper. "Here is the wire information you'll need."

Zack takes the paper. "I'm thirsty. Let's get a drink."

"I should get back." She looks at her watch, one of those Dick Tracy numbers with the time, temperature, directions, maybe the whole Internet on it too. "He'll wonder where I am."

"Tell him I tried to put the moves on you." She smiles. They get in the Pontiac. "So who is this joker?" Zack keys the engine.

"Name's Duane Pollack. We're not sure where he's from. He showed up a few months ago."

"No one's checked him out?"

She turns her face toward him. "What do you think?"

Zack shrugs. They backtrack through the *colonias*, past squalid shacks, a rusted car, a child's tricycle upside-down at the edge of the road. Nearby is a dump overflowing with glass, fast-food wrappers, a dented bucket. The detritus of a desperate population.

"This looks like a refugee camp," Zack says.

"They have to live someplace," Dora says.

"Why do they keep coming?"

Her laugh is hollow. "Because the alternative is starving in Mexico." Her face gets a faraway look, as if she's dwelling on a painful memory. "These places have grown unsupervised for years. No electricity, running water, sewers. Two or three families sharing one home."

"The law looked the other way?"

"Until the developers showed up."

"Developers?"

Dora's lips curl. "They promised to provide electricity, running water. The infrastructure to turn these slums around. They lied. Never built anything. Just took the money."

Zack nods. It is an old story.

"Eventually it got embarrassing. So the legislature decided to outlaw new settlements. Made them illegal." Her voice tightens. "Which, of course, was worse than doing nothing. The developers moved on to their next prey. But the people – they have nowhere to go."

Zack grunts. "What will happen to them?"

She presses her lips together. "Maybe they'll ask for your services one day."

"How do you know so much about places like this?"

"I made it out. I was lucky."

They get a drink then drive back. She hops out of the Pontiac, leans her elbows on the open window. "I don't have to go." She smiles lazily.

Zack considers it. Dora is his type. All legs. But the time isn't right. He swallows. "Not yet."

She glides back to her car. He watches her hips sway. She wants him to know what he is passing up.

***

Zack hears from Sergei the next morning. The deal is on. A shipment will leave Odessa within sixty days. Once the cargo is offloaded, Elvis will truck it across the border.

Zack waits for Elvis and Dora at the cantina, but they are late. Finally the door swings open, and a young Latino hurries in. He waves his arms at the woman behind the bar. Even in Spanish, the words can't spill out of him fast enough. The woman tightens her lips. She looks over at Zack.

He approaches the bar. "Is there a problem?"

The boy looks at Zack, then at the woman. The woman stares at the floor, perhaps mulling over her options. Then she gestures to the boy.

"Di le que paso. Con la mujer."

Zack stiffens. "Tell me what about the woman?" He leans across the bar, splinters be damned.

The boy answers in unaccented English. "Your friend, the girl. She was here early this morning. I drove her to the airstrip."

"Airstrip?"

The boy explains there is a private airstrip a few miles from the cantina. Oilmen used it to visit their wells. Dora asked him to show it to her. "When we got there, she told me to stay in the car, but she got out. She hid behind a ridge."

"Go on," Zack says grimly.

"A few minutes later, I heard the sound of an airplane. I snuck a look. A private plane landed. A man wearing a suit got out. He had a briefcase in his hand. Then, I see the man who was here yesterday –"

"Elvis?"

The boy nods. "He just appears. From nowhere. And the woman is in front of him."

"He and the woman together?"

"They were walking toward the plane. Slowly. Close together. The man in the suit gave him the briefcase. And then –" Zack reads the fear in the boy's eyes.

"They pushed her, pulled her up the ladder. She disappeared inside. The man – Elvis – went down the steps. And then the plane took off."

Zack runs his tongue around his lips. "Describe the man in the suit."

"An Anglo. He looked rich."

"What about the plane?"

The boy hesitates. "One engine. White. Blue numbers and letters on the side."

He tells Zack the numbers he recalls. Zack feels the door open behind him. He raises a finger to his lips and turns around. It is Elvis, a briefcase in his hand. Alone. "Everything okay?" Zack asks.

Elvis smiles. "Couldn't be better, compadre."

Zack makes a show of looking behind Elvis. "Where's Dora?"

"I sent her back, man. She couldn't wait to get back to them Indians." He makes a sound that could be a laugh or a sneer. "This thing she's got for them, you know. She's like a goddammed saint. Gonna save them."

"From who?"

Elvis hesitates, a lopsided grin on his face. "You know, man. The bad guys."

***

The scenery changes as they drive northeast on Fifty-nine. Patches of irrigated desert give way to fields of bluebonnets and Indian paintbrush. Farther on, a mantle of green covers the prairie.

Despite the air conditioning, the close, humid air inside the car settles on Zack's forearms. He smells the tension on Elvis. After an hour, he pulls into a rest stop. While Elvis goes inside, Zack places a call to his intel analyst back east. Elvis comes out with a bag full of candy bars and soda. His face twitches. Zack wonders how much he put up his nose last night.

Outside Houston Zack loops south to the port, a huge facility that stretches twenty-five miles from the Gulf inland. He heads toward the mouth of Galveston Bay. Sergei will hide his shipment inside a cargo of steel rods and bars the Russians will dump on the U.S. market.

Zack flashes his ID and he and Elvis are admitted to the Barbours Cut terminal. As they make their way to the wharf, they maneuver around warehouses and sheds, forklifts, trucks, and cranes. Railroad tracks curl around the sides of the buildings. Zack wrinkles his nose, surprised by the briny tang in the air.

They head toward a small shed behind the pier where his port contact should be waiting. Everything looks normal to Zack. Too normal. No odd movement catches his eye. Something is wrong. Where is his back-up? They have almost reached the shed when Zack's cell phone rings.

"Yeah?"

"Zack, it's over. Let it walk." It is his contact agent.

"You know, I'm kind of tied up right now," Zack says into the phone. His eyes stay on Elvis. "I'll talk to you about those motorcycles later."

"It ain't gonna happen today, man. Let it walk."

"Got it." Zack snaps off the phone. He slows his breathing, forces himself to remain calm. Something has happened. Something bad.

"What's up, man?" Elvis tilts his head.

Zack shakes his head and opens the door to the warehouse. He doesn't like what's going down, but he follows orders. A beefy man with a tomato-red face and neck is waiting for them. Zack pushes up his sunglasses and pulls him aside. When they finish their business, Zack watches as the man and Elvis make their deal. But his mood progressively sours, and when Elvis hands over the cash, needles of rage edge up his spine. It wasn't supposed to end like this. He pulls his shades over his eyes.

***

Inside the hotel room three agents and the ASAC sit at a round table. All four, with their impassive Bureau faces, seem hewn from the same block of granite. Zack's anger has been building, twisting inside him all day. His icy calm has vanished; he feels as weak as a tuft of tumbleweed.

"What happened?" He swipes his forehead with his sleeve. The heat in the room is oppressive.

"We lost her," the case agent says.

"Dora?"

The agent nods. "She didn't report in."

"What happened?" Zack repeats, suspicion coating his words.

"We don't know. That's why we pulled you out."

"But she spent months putting it all together. And Elvis is a punk. Someone's behind him." Zack eyes his superiors. They don't disagree. "Let me find out who it is."

The ASAC shakes his head.

"Why not? You know as well as I do it's the only way."

"No," the ASAC says. "We lost a good agent. We can't afford to lose another. Go home and regroup, Mueller. It's over."

***

Back in his room Zack stares at the ceiling, a series of spongy panels peppered with tiny holes. He wants to leave this damp, deadly place where the green grass looks painted on and the pretense is as thick as air. He takes a swig of bourbon. As he swallows, his cell phone trills.

"Yeah?"

It's the analyst he called on the way to Houston. "That plane? I ran down the numbers."

"And?"

"It's a Cessna. Belongs to Maverick Oil."

Zack sits up straight. "Say again?"

"A Grand Caravan. Registered three years ago."

He thanks the analyst and disconnects. The plane belongs to Maverick Oil. A suit got off the plane and handed Elvis a briefcase full of money. Why would an oil company give money to a scumbag like Elvis? Unless he was working for the oil company. Unless they are the ones behind him.

Zack paces the room, thinking it through. It is crazy, but it fits. Maverick backs a spurious arms deal. Stage-manages an insurrection, knowing the Mexican government will come down on the rebels. Then with their cover in place, the oil company comes in and drills. Zack blinks. A corporate-sponsored war. With the indirect support of the Mexican government. It's crazy all right. Crazy like a fox.

He corners the room. No one at the Bureau has said a word about any of this. Not one of the people in the hotel room. Zack calls the analyst back. "What do you know about Maverick Oil?"

"I was wondering when you'd ask," the analyst says. "It's a small company, but they're expanding into Mexico and South America." There is a pause. "The CEO is an old college pal of Huntington's." Zack sucks in his breath. Gerald Huntington, the ASAC of the Houston office, has made known his desire to retire from government service. With six kids, his public sector salary just can't pay the bills. "They were frat buddies at Texas A&M."

"I see," Zack says.

Once again he hangs up. Images of rainforest people dance across the white wall. The Indians are caught in an intractable vise. If they rebel against the oil company, they will be overpowered. If they turn on their own soldiers, they will be killed.

But now it makes sense. Lured with the promise of wealth by his old buddy, Huntington sanctioned Maverick's plan. Allowed it to go down. Hell, he probably saw it as a slam-dunk. It was easy to rationalize: an economy based on oil is much preferable to a drug cartel.

There is only one problem. Dora's blood is on their hands. The Bureau's, Maverick's, even the Mexican government's. Dora, who came from nothing. Who was cheated out of the opportunity to make a difference. For Zack, it is an issue of loyalty. Huntington's. Dora's. His own. Again he paces the room.

Later that night he slips into Elvis's hotel room. The shower is on. Zack hears off-key singing from the bathroom. At length Elvis emerges, a towel around his waist. When he sees Zack's Sig Sauer aimed at his chest, his singing stops.

***

Houston, Texas (AP): The FBI today announced it is searching for Duane Pollack, a mercenary known to be active in the Mexican Rainforest. Pollack, aka Elvis, disappeared several weeks ago after two million dollars from Maverick Oil was reported missing. FBI sources fear the money will be used to finance an armed revolt in the Mexican rainforest, an area Maverick Oil hoped to explore. US ports are on alert for suspicious cargo. Meanwhile, Maverick Oil's plans to explore in the rainforest have been put on hold.

In related news, former Houston FBI chief Gerald Huntington says he's rejected an offer of employment at Maverick Oil, although there is some dispute at Maverick headquarters whether an offer was ever tendered.

Zack finishes his coffee and folds the newspaper under his arm. He tosses a few coins on the counter. Elvis won't be surfacing. He made sure of that. Neither will the cache of weapons. Sergei was happy to switch the port of entry back to Newark, especially after Zack warned him that the FBI might be on to him.

He opens the door of the restaurant. A cold clammy drizzle is falling, but he smiles. He is home, back East in Jersey, thousands of miles from Texas. The drilling has been blocked. The Indians are safe. And since his recent retirement, there is a healthy bank account, a commendation from the Bureau, and an arsenal of Russian weapons in a nearby warehouse. He whistles as he moves down the street. Dora would be proud.

THE END

HIGH YELLOW

I grew up in Washington, DC, and I always wanted to set a story there. For some reason, it never quite worked until now. HIGH YELLOW remains one of my favorites, not just because it triggered so many memories of my childhood, but for what it says about the culture of what was – until the Kennedy administration – essentially a southern city. It was written for and published in Megan Abbott's A HELL OF A WOMAN: An Anthology of Female Noir (Busted Flush Press, 2007).

Patricia Thomas' mama said everyone needed a fixer in their life, and from the moment she met Desmond McCauley, Patricia knew he would be hers.

She stepped down from the streetcar at Connecticut and Calvert into a wall of September heat so heavy and humid you could carve big chunks out of it and swallow them whole. Despite its pretensions, Washington D.C. in 1957 was a sleepy Southern town where summer didn't end until October. Even Congress had the sense not to come back until then.

She tried to keep an unhurried pace as she walked the three blocks to Oyster School. She didn't want to sweat on the first day of the new season. She'd dressed carefully in a crisp, black and white sleeveless outfit she snagged in Hecht's bargain basement. She'd ironed starch into it, but in this heat it wouldn't last. She was wearing black pumps, and carried a little black bag. Her thick, dark glossy hair, good hair, was held back with a wide red band.

As she rounded the corner, she nodded coolly at the Negro man who stepped to the side and doffed his hat. Afterwards she savored the little thrill that ran through her. Likewise when she stopped into People's Drugs for a comb, and the woman at the cash register with chocolate skin made sure their hands never touched when she dropped Patricia's change in her palm. She smiled. With her dark hair and eyes, pale skin, and delicate features, Patricia was passing. She looked like an exotic beauty -- maybe Oriental, maybe Italian – but definitely not colored. High yellow, they called it.

Patricia remembered asking her mama if the father she never knew had been white. She recalled how her mother's lips tightened as she shook her head. "He was just a light-skinned no-good nigger who ran out on us first chance he got." Her mama, a Southerner with skin like brown ochre, had spent years scrubbing floors, ironing shirts, and cooking meals for the Friedman's, a white family who lived near the school. They kept telling Patricia she and her mama were part of their family, but that was just white folks' talk, Mama said. An excuse to have Mama babysit their kids when they went to Mexico every winter to get away from it all.

Her mama would laugh at all Mister Friedman's jokes, put up with the Missus's mood swings, and never said anything about the empty booze bottles under her bed. Every year they would take the streetcar down to 9th and G to buy the Friedman's a box of Velati's caramels for Christmas. Good thing, too. Turned out Mrs. Friedman was her first fixer. It was through her influence that Patricia got her job teaching first grade.

Which was how Patricia came to believe in fixers. "Look at me, sweetie-pie," her mother had warned. "Don't end up like me. You got the right cards in your deck. Play 'em. Whatever it takes, you make life better fo' yourself." Once Mrs. Friedman intervened on her behalf, and Patricia bought her a few bottles of gin, she understood. She definitely wanted a better life, and she'd do anything to make it happen. Oyster School was just the beginning.

Now, as she mounted the steep steps to the school, she let out a hot breath. The first week would be the usual confusion of learning the children's names, assigning desks, and figuring out what they knew. Oyster School was in a white neighborhood inhabited by government officials, ambassadors, and long-time Washington residents. There was talk of expanding the school's boundaries to include the coloreds and poor whites who lived across the bridge, but the school board kept putting it off.

Still, Patricia loved her students. She patiently taught them how to sound out letters, and she would clap her hands when they figured out the words to "See Spot Run." She giggled when they correctly added 6 bananas to 4 apples, and told them they would have a fine fruit salad. Her students liked her, too. She wasn't elderly and frumpy like Miss Murray, who wore gloves every day because she was allergic to chalk. Nor was she like Miss Finkel, whose manner was so stern it sent chills through everyone, even the principal. She was Miss Thomas. Fresh, young, and lively. She was *their* fixer.

But when Desmond McCauley walked in, his shy little son clutching his hand, Patricia felt a jolt. Maybe it was his wide appealing face, his blond hair slicked back with Bryl Creem. Or maybe it was the way he politely greeted her and had his son, Franklin, do the same. Or maybe it was his wintry blue eyes so utterly lacking in deception.

Whatever it was, she wondered if he felt the same spark when they shook hands. She did sense a slight hesitation on his part. She thought his eyes widened just a little, and his expression took on a more observant cast, as if he was seeing her -- really seeing her. She looked into those eyes and let her hand rest in his just an instant too long. Then she squatted down to assure Franklin they would be great friends and that school would be loads of fun.

Once she was able to coax a shy smile out of the boy, she stood up slowly, and stretched to show Desmond her long legs and slim waist. Desmond smiled, a flush swimming up from his neck to his face. "I can't thank you enough. We just moved here, and Franklin doesn't have many friends."

"Where did you move from?"

"Cleveland, Ohio."

"Nice place, Cleveland," Patricia said, as if she'd just been there last year. "Now, don't you worry, Mr. McCauley.

I'll take good care of Franklin."

Desmond swallowed. "Thank you, Miss Thomas. Thank you."

***

A month later, a hot scrim of summer still hung in the air. Even so, Patricia could feel her anticipation build, like the knowledge that the season would eventually burn itself out and submit to autumn.

The day it finally happened had been routine. The children had spent the afternoon working on colors and writing down "blue", "red", and "yellow" next to dabs of paint. Patricia got ready to dismiss them for the day.

Usually Mrs. McCauley came to pick up Franklin. Like her husband, she was blond. No wonder Franklin was flaxen-haired. Today, though, both parents came to the school, Mrs. McCauley two steps ahead of her husband, as if she was embarrassed to be seen with him. Patricia watched as she corralled Franklin, who was playing with Henry Deutsch near the jungle gym. Franklin was settling in well. He was quiet, but methodical for a six-year-old. Mrs. McCauley retrieved Franklin's plaid book bag and hurried him across the playground.

"We'll see you after your meeting, then." Mrs. McCauley said to her husband, inclining her cheek for a kiss.

Desmond pecked her cheek, gave his son a hug, but made no effort to leave. "Aren't you coming?" His wife asked.

"I'll just grab a cab, dear. I want to talk to Miss Thomas. About Franklin." He added hastily.

His wife nodded and disappeared. Desmond hovered at the edge of the playground while other parents collected their children. As if by tacit agreement, they didn't speak until all the students were gone.

She turned around. "You're still here." She pronounced it as if she'd just become aware of it that minute.

He nodded and looked at the ground.

She crossed her arms. "So. You wanted to talk about -- Franklin?"

Desmond studied his hands, flipped them over, then back again. She thought of washing the children's hands before lunch. Drying them on those rough brown paper towels.

"Actually," he faltered. "I -- I was hoping – well – would you like to have a drink?"

Patricia stared at him. "A drink?"

His forehead, cheeks, even his ears turned crimson. Must be all that pale skin. "Well, perhaps a cup of tea?"

Patricia tilted her head. He was watching her. She smiled. "You know? A cocktail would be just fine."

As they crossed Calvert Street to the Shoreham Hotel, a fragrance she couldn't quite identify hung in the air. Good scents lingered in this part of town. The late afternoon sun gilded everything in hues of gold. There was no litter on the streets. Even the hum of traffic was muted.

***

They spent an hour in the hotel bar, drinking cocktails and listening to Eddie Fisher crooning through discreetly placed speakers. The Shoreham was one of the most elegant hotels in Washington with an outdoor swimming pool, an enormous high-ceilinged lobby, and the Blue Room, a night club that attracted the best entertainers in show business.

Desmond seemed just as shy as his son, and Patricia carried the conversation. During the first round of drinks, she amused him with stories about her students. During the second round she pumped him gently about his marriage. Lorraine was sturdy Midwest stock from Omaha, he said. They met at Ohio State and fell in love, but their marriage was more an accommodation these days, he admitted. Best friends who lived together. "You know what I mean?"

She's lost interest in him sexually, Patricia thought. Aloud, she replied, "More than you know."

By the third round, Patricia told him she was looking for a new job.

"I thought you loved teaching." Des wiped his forehead with a white handkerchief.

"Oh, I do. But – I want to do something bet – I think I'm capable of more."

"Like what?" Desmond asked, picking up his cue.

"A government job. Working with international issues. Better pay, lots of travel, more responsibility." She eyed him. "I want to make a difference. Do something for my country. You know what I mean?"

"Yes." A tiny smile played around his lips. "I see."

Patricia leaned forward. She noticed a sheen of sweat above his lip. "What do you see?"

Desmond swallowed. Patricia lifted her index finger to his lip and gently stroked the sweat away. Then she ran her finger over her own lips, opened her mouth, and inserted her finger.

He stammered and cleared his throat. "I – I might be able to help, you know."

"Is that so?" Patricia smiled lazily, although she already knew he could. She'd checked Franklin's file in the office one day during lunch. She knew exactly where Des worked and what he did. Even who his boss was.

"What do you do?" She took her finger out of her mouth and wrapped her hand around her drink.

Desmond's eyes followed the track of her finger. "I'm an – an Assistant Secretary in the Commerce Department's International Trade administration," he said. "I help protect U.S. businesses from unfair pricing by foreign companies and governments."

"Well now." Patricia feigned surprise. "That sounds right up my alley." She smiled coyly. "If the right opportunity ever pops up, I hope you'll think of me." She met his eyes with an appraising look.

"Yes. I might be able to do that."

She twirled the little umbrella that had come with her drink, then put it down and inched her hand across the table. Her long, slender fingers were topped by pink nail polish she'd applied last night. It didn't take long for Des to cover her hand with his own. She let him massage the back of her knuckles.

Ten minutes later, he took a room under the name of Richard Dudley. Patricia came up in a separate elevator. She had hardly walked through the door before he tore her clothes off and threw her down on the bed. She let him do what he wanted. He was like a man who'd been starved, and it was over quickly. Then she rolled over and taught him a thing or two.

***

Moths played around the hotel lamp as she rolled on her stockings two hours later. Des was lying on the bed, smoking a cigarette, looking spent but quite pleased with himself. His blond hair was tousled, but his pale skin glowed like girls in love were supposed to. She gazed at his chest, which was curiously hairless, and his torso, slim except for an ever-so-slight paunch. His was the body of a successful man, a man on the way up. She snapped her stockings to her garter belt, then twisted around to stroke him. He moaned, stubbed out the cigarette, and pulled her to him. She unsnapped her stockings again and sank back on the bed.

The hum of traffic down in Rock Creek Park drifted through the open window an hour later, bringing with it a welcome breeze. Des lit another cigarette, and set the ashtray down on his chest. She watched it rise and fall with his breath.

"I've never had a woman like you," he said softly.

She smiled, watching blue smoke curl up over their heads and disappear.

"You're magic. We're magic." He moved the ashtray and nuzzled her leg with his lips. "You've revived something in me I thought was gone forever. I thought – I thought – well -- it would never happen again."

Patricia felt a ripple as his lips slid down her shin. "Honey, I could see that from the first time we met."

"What about you?" He asked hesitantly. Was I – was it good for you?"

"You were the best, sugar. A giant of a man. Never had anyone better."

***

The Negro elevator operator eyed her but kept a respectful silence as Patricia descended to the lobby. She was used to people staring at her, but there was something telling, almost bold in his look. Was her dress unbuttoned? Did he know she'd just made love all evening? Or was it something else, the thing that some colored people picked up without being told? Was he a spotter? No, spotters were generally fair-skinned Negroes. Still, she felt like slapping his face for having the audacity to challenge her.

The breeze had disappeared by the time she caught the bus, and her legs stuck to the seat as she rode across the Calvert Street bridge. "Across the bridge" was a euphemism for the other side of the tracks. Most high yellows lived in Portal Estates off 16th Street, but Patricia lived across the bridge. During high school she'd gone on a few dates with a boy from Portal Estates – Clarence, his name was -- but after his mother met Patricia's brown-skinned mother and discovered where they lived, Clarence stopped calling. Patricia didn't care. Across the bridge was just temporary.

By the time she got off the bus, it was almost midnight. She walked the two blocks to her house on Lanier Place. As she unlocked the door, she heard her husband's voice.

"Where you been, baby?"

She went into the front room. She'd met James at Howard University. Her Mama had just died, and she was lonely. Patricia didn't have a lot of friends: the whites kept her at a distance, the colored girls hated her because she looked white. James had light skin that passed the brown bag test, but with his wooly black hair and distinctly Negroid features, he would never be high yellow. Still, he wanted to take care of her forever, and at the time, Patricia didn't have the strength to resist. He was a good man: honest and hard working. But he was boring, and even his job as manager at Hahn's Shoes wouldn't get them where Patricia wanted to go.

"I've been job hunting, Jimmy."

"From three in the afternoon till midnight?"

"I left your dinner in the oven."

"I don't want dinner. I want you."

"And I want us to have a better life." She spared a brief glance around the front room, with its shabby furniture and faded curtains. "So we can move out of here. Find a nicer place." She looked at him. "Don't you want that too, sweetie-pie?"

"I want us to have a baby, Patsy. Isn't that the best job in the world?" He grinned. "Come upstairs, baby doll. We need to practice."

She shot him a look.

He changed the subject. "So where you lookin' for that new job?"

***

The weather cooled, the leaves fell, and the gray of November descended. Patricia didn't notice. Her afternoons and evenings were full of Des. They met twice a week at the Shoreham, once in a while at the Sheraton Park. Between the passion and love-making, Patricia mentioned the new job as often as she could. Des said he was working on it.

Over time Des emerged from his shell. His smile grew broader, his step more assured. Between the sheets, too, he developed into a sensual, giving lover. It made him happy when Patricia climaxed, so she made sure she did. In fact, he was turning out to be the best lover she'd ever had, and

Patricia was half in love with him. She couldn't figure out why his wife didn't want him, but she was thankful she didn't.

One afternoon just before Thanksgiving, Patricia rushed from school to the Shoreham. A conference with an anxious parent had made her run late. She was just crossing Calvert Street, watching the wind whip leaves into tiny eddies above the ground, when she sensed someone following her. She stopped and turned around. No one was there. She shook it off and hurried to the hotel.

After their lovemaking, Des lit a Winston and cradled the ash tray on his chest. "I have something to tell you, Patricia."

" What's that, sweetie?" She snuggled in close and ran her fingers across his milky skin. That was another thing she liked about him. There was almost a delicacy to his body.

"We're going to Havana the week after Thanksgiving," he said. "For a conference."

"Havana, Cuba?"

When he nodded, a little thrill ran through her. It was finally happening! A new job, travel to an exotic location. A vision of casinos, men in tuxedos, and women in long gowns flashed through her mind. Her fixer had come through. She snuggled in closer. "Oh, baby. This is wonderful. When do we leave? I have so much to do. "

He pulled away and stubbed out his cigarette. "Patricia, I think you misunderstood. Lorraine is coming with me to Havana," he said softly.

"Lorraine?" He wasn't making sense.

"She – she wants us to spend time more together. She's noticed we've grown apart. She wants – she's talking about a second honeymoon."

Patricia froze. If she stayed absolutely still, the words he'd uttered wouldn't count, and they could start fresh. From the beginning. She didn't move a muscle, but nothing happened. Then Des looked at her with such a sad, wistful expression her stomach flipped over.

"What -- what about Franklin?" She managed to ask.

"Lorraine's mother is coming in from Nebraska to take care of him."

Patricia swallowed. "But Des, this isn't --"

A loud banging at the door cut her off.

They both sat up, startled. "What's that?" Des frowned.

"I don't know."

The banging persisted. Between the knocks were muffled thumps, as if someone was throwing themselves against the door. Patricia and Des exchanged anxious looks. Hotels had notoriously flimsy locks. Then a raw voice shouted. "You in there, baby? If you are, open this door."

Patricia felt her jaw drop.

Des didn't notice. "What the hell?" He reached for the phone. "I'll take care of this."

But Patricia stayed his hand. Wrapping the blanket around her, she jumped out of bed and stared at the door, as if she could see clear through it to the other side. "No, don't Des. Let me take care of it."

"Are you crazy, Patricia?" Des picked up the phone but didn't have the chance to call, because Patricia ran to the door and opened it wide. James stumbled into the room. He nearly lost his balance, but righted himself and looked around. Patricia wrapped the blanket more tightly around her. Her heart was pounding so fast and hard she could hear it in her ears.

James started toward her, rage spinning off his face. "What the hell…?"

Patricia backed away, terrified.

Des jumped out of bed. "You. Stop right there!" He shouted. "Before I call the police!"

James ignored Des and kept going toward Patricia.

"Did you hear me?" Des yelled.

James's response was to pull out a knife.

"No!" Patricia gasped. "Put that away!"

But James raised the knife in the air. The blade gleamed in the lamplight. Patricia recognized it – it was the kitchen knife she used to de-bone chicken and fish. As he closed in, she backed up until she hit the edge of the bed and fell across it. James kept advancing, brandishing the knife in the air.

Suddenly Des appeared in her field of vision. He jumped James from behind, caught his arm, and twisted it. James lost his balance and fell on Patricia. As he did, the knife slipped out of his hand and skittered across the carpet. Des bent down and scooped it up faster than Patricia would have thought possible. Lunging forward, Des plunged the knife in James' back.

James raised his head and looked at Patricia in surprise. Patricia was surprised, too. She wouldn't have thought Des had a chance in a match-up against James. Her husband had to be four inches taller and thirty pounds heavier. But there Des was, stabbing James again and again, like a madman, his face a frenzy of fury and hate. James gazed at Patricia. He looked like he wanted to say something but couldn't quite form the words. Then his eyes rolled up, and his head fell forward.

Finally, it was quiet. Patricia disentangled herself from her husband. Blood gushed through his jacket and pants, staining the bed sheets, the spread, the carpet.

Des stared at James, at Patricia, at the knife. "He was going to kill you," he whispered.

Patricia kept her mouth shut.

Des hesitated. Uncertainty flashed in his eyes. "You saw, right? He was going to kill you. Maybe me, too."

For one brief moment, Patricia didn't know what to do. She saw her life careening out of control, away from her government job, her job as a teacher, even her life with Des. She was terrified of the secrets that would be revealed, and maybe some that wouldn't. Then something occurred to her. She could fix this. All it would take was a little work. She sucked in a breath and fought back the fear.

"Yes. I saw, Des." She nodded her head. "I saw the whole thing."

"Well, then..." Des let his voice trail off. A violent shudder ran through him. He went to the phone and lifted the receiver.

Patricia ran over and snatched the phone away. "What are you doing?""

"I'm calling hotel security."

"No. You can't."

He reached for the receiver. "Of course I can. He was going to kill us. This was self defense."

"No. It's – he –" Des tried to grab the receiver, but Patricia kept it away from him. "Wait. Think about what you're doing, Des."

"What's to think about? The man is dead. We need to report it. He was –" Des stopped. "You opened the door. Why did you do that? What the hell was going through your mind?"

"I – I don't really know. I just wanted to stop the banging. I thought ---"

Des's face grew pinched with anger. "If you hadn't opened the door, this might never have happened." He squeezed his eyes shut. Another tremor shot through him. He seemed to be struggling for control. He opened his eyes. "It doesn't matter. Give me the phone."

"No, Des. Think what will happen when it comes out you were here in the hotel room. With me."

"That doesn't matter," He sounded stoic. "You don't play around with death."

"Are you prepared to lose your job?"

"My job?"

"If this gets out, it'll be all over the papers. There'll be lots of publicity. The Commerce Department won't be happy that one of its Assistant Secretaries is making news like this. They'll get rid of you, just like that." She snapped her fingers. "And what's Lorraine going to do when she finds out?" Des started to speak, but she cut him off. "She'll throw you out, Des. She probably won't ever let you see Franklin."

Des paled.

"I know what it's like to grow up without a father. Don't do this to your son."

"No, Patricia. You're wrong. It's not like --"

"Listen to me, Des." She held the receiver close to her heart. "We can fix this."

"No. We have to take responsibility."

She ignored him. "You registered under a fake name, right? Paid cash as usual?"

"You know I did."

"And I came up the back stairs." She nodded more to herself than to him. "This will work." She put the phone down, went over to James's body, and started rolling his pockets.

"What are you doing?"

"There's no one who can prove we were here."

"The desk clerk knows what I look like."

"Honey, you look like every other white man who ever checked into a hotel under an assumed name."

Des stared at her. But he didn't pick up the phone.

Patricia reached into James's pants pocket and pulled out his wallet. "It's okay, baby. I'm gonna fix everything." She extracted James's driver's license and glanced at it briefly.

"Who is he?" Des's voice cracked.

She looked at Des, then back at the license. "Why do you care?"

"I want to know his name."

"It's better if you don't. He's just a colored man."

Des frowned.

"Tell me something. How hard do you think the cops are gonna work to find the killer of an unidentified colored man?"

"I –I don't know."

"Well, I do." Patricia slid James's driver's license back into his wallet and dropped it into her purse. "Not hard at all."

Des swallowed.

"Des, you can never speak of this again. Never. Understand?"

He hesitated, then gave her a brief nod.

"That's good, honey. Now let's wash up and get out of here."

Patricia went into the bathroom and ran the hot water so long that it steamed over the mirror above the sink. She wiped a small circle in the middle and peered at her reflection. "Another thing, honey. I think you'd best postpone that trip to Havana."

***

Patricia checked the Post and the Star every day, but there was nothing about an unidentified colored man found dead at the Shoreham. When a week had passed, she put out the word that James had left her. She didn't know why, and she didn't know where he'd gone, she told her neighbors. She was disconsolate, of course, so miserable that she'd decided to move. There were too many painful memories here. She was going to give up teaching, too. Someone had kindly offered her a new job at the Commerce Department. In the International Trade administration. Patricia packed her things and said sorrowful goodbyes. She moved to an apartment in Cathedral Mansions off Connecticut Avenue on the "right" side of the bridge.

The first few months, Des was more dependent on her than ever. There was a primitive, almost violent quality to his lovemaking, as if killing James had somehow filled Des with her husband's life blood. He had never been more virile or passionate. Through it all, though, he was true to his word. He never spoke of James. In fact, he never spoke much at all.

To make up for his silence, Patricia began talking about their future, after he left Lorraine. She was careful never to overlook Franklin and always made him part of the tableau. "And then you and I and Franklin will drive to Luray Caverns.

We'll have to make sure Franklin brings a sweater. It gets cold down there."

It wasn't until winter dissolved into spring that things changed again. Des lost his ardor. Oh, he would come to the apartment and make love to her, but his passion had faded. What had once been spectacular sex became mechanical and rote. By the time the dogwoods were at their peak, Des told her it was over.

"I can't do this any more, Patricia."

"Do what, sweetie-pie?"

"Every time I'm with you, I see that dead colored man. I need to make a clean breast of it. I'm going to tell Lorraine and go to the police. I'm prepared to take responsibility. I was the one who killed him. I'll keep you out of it. I promise."

Patricia laughed harshly. "I don't think so."

"I figured you'd say that, but I've made up my mind."

"Have you told anyone yet?"

"No."

"That's good."

He inclined his head. "Why are you so opposed to doing the right thing?"

Patricia sat down daintily in the new Louis XVI chair she'd bought at the fifth floor furniture department at Hecht's. It was a far cry from the bargain basement. She took a breath.

"Because that wasn't just any dead man, sugar. That was my husband, James."

Des froze. "What?"

She repeated what she said.

Confusion spread across his face. "But he was a -- a Negro."

"That's exactly right. He was. And so am I. You ever heard of the phrase 'high yellow?'"

Des's mouth fell open. He stared at her for a long time. She saw him take in her dark hair. Dark eyes. Her pale skin. Saw comprehension dawn in his eyes. His face grew hard. "My god. I've been screwing a nigger."

"Yup. And you killed one too, honey. Two facts you'd best keep to yourself, don't you think?"

Des's eyes went dead, losing any flicker of emotion. His coldness was so unnerving Patricia went into her bathroom and quietly closed the door. The subsequent silence lasted so long that she flinched when her front door finally slammed.

***

Patricia dressed the next morning in a new red dress from Woodie's. Strolling to the bus stop, she was aware of eyes watching her from behind the shades of nearby homes. She lifted her chin. She was a good looking woman. No sense hiding it. As she rode the L-4 downtown, she started to map out her plan. Des's boss seemed like a nice man. She took out her compact with the tiny mirror and checked her make-up. He would do. After all, her mama always told her she needed a fixer in her life.

THE END

A BERLIN STORY

This story first appeared in the SHOW BUSINESS IS MURDER anthology, edited by the late, great Stuart Kaminsky (Berkley Prime Crime, 2004). The time of World War Two has always resonated with me – I can't think of another period of history that has been fraught with such bitter conflict, such a clear demarcation between good and evil, or such stunning examples of either heroism or cowardice. I still return there for inspiration. This story plumbs Berlin's cabaret culture of the early '30s: the desperate need to party, the hollowness of the frivolity, the sense of impending doom. To that end the story also pays homage to Christopher Isherwood, whose work captured that atmosphere perfectly.

Herr Hesse should never have stayed for the last number. Indeed, some expressed shock he was there at all. A physics professor at the University of Berlin. Well-dressed; a touch of gray in his hair. Why would Friedrich Hesse visit *Der Flammen*, a seedy cabaret tucked away on a side street?

It came out later that Ilse had asked him to stay. Ilse -- the star performer at *Der Flammen*. Ilse, with the sad brown eyes and short blonde hair and a black sequined costume that stopped at the top of her thighs.

He sat in the audience that night, a glass of Schnapps in his hand. Elbow to elbow with the riff raff, all of them vying to be decadent. The life of the genteel Prussian had vanished, replaced by the ennui of the jaded. No one pretended to innocence in the Berlin of 'Thirty-two; what counted most was scandal. It masked the pain and despair.

He suffered through buxom women in skimpy costumes and the men pretending to be. He turned away from the animal parade. But when the orchestra sounded a drum roll, he twisted back toward the stage. And when Ilse appeared in the wavering beam of the spotlight, he brightened like a man glimpsing salvation.

In her first number she flounced across stage as a mountain girl, long braids pinned to her head. She wore a leather vest laced tight across her breasts, but not much else. It wasn't until the shepherd boy unlaced it and forced her to ride the goat that Hesse looked away. Next she marched onstage in an Imperial Regimental jacket, a rifle slung over her chest. She sang and crawled and shot and saluted her superior officer, who relieved her of her jacket and threw it into the wings. The randy shouts of the audience drowned out the last verse of her song. Through it all, the professor politely sipped his Schnapps, as if Ilse were reciting poetry in a salon.

In the finale, she sang a sad ballad, wearing black sequins, fishnet stockings, and stiletto heels. A stray lock of hair fell across her face, throwing her profile in shadow.

As her final note hung in the smoky air, the professor rose, put on his hat, and walked out. Skirting the bank of snow on the street, he cut through a narrow alley and knocked at the stage door.

The janitor found his body the next morning, half-hidden in a corner at the back of the stage. A pool of blood, now congealed, had seeped across the floor. The police found entry wounds in his chest and bullet casings that had come from a Lugar.

***

Ilse slouched at the manager's desk wearing a silk robe with Oriental pretensions. The smoke from her cigarette floated above her head like a halo.

"When did you meet him?" The burly detective asked. His weary eyes said there was nothing that could shock him.

"Several months ago. At a café on the Kurfürstendamm." She smiled prettily. "We were both having tea."

"He was alone?"

"Not then. But he returned the next day. Alone."

The detective took off his coat and slipped it over a chair. He knew her type. Arrogant. Smug. Confident in her charms.

"What happened when he came into your dressing room?"

Crossing one leg over the other, she dangled her foot in front of him. "He paid me a visit."

"And what was the nature of this visit, Fraulein?"

"Must you be so indiscreet, Herr Inspektor?"

The detective shifted. The office wasn't much bigger than a closet. He felt too big for the room. "You knew, of course, that he was married?"

"Aren't they all?"

"What did he give you in return for your -- favors?"

"What I expect from all my lovers. Kindness. Passion. A gentle touch."

"And perhaps a few thousand marks, conveniently wrapped in a white linen handkerchief?"

She fluffed her hair. A whiff of cheap perfume drifted his way. "You presume, *mein lieber*."

"When did he leave?"

"When we were finished."

"And you made sure your friends were waiting for him, yes? Ready to roll him for his cash. What was your cut, Fraulein?"

"Inspektor. You are unkind."

"But he put up a fight, didn't he? Your friends didn't count on that. He struggled, and things spun out of control."

She drew herself up and tossed her hair. Even in the dim light of the office it gleamed.

"I do not know what happened when he left my room. I had nothing to do with his death."

***

Frau Hesse poured tea from a Chinese teapot on a cloisonné tray. A small, birdlike woman with brown hair swept back in a bun, she sat primly on a flowered sofa, flanked by two men whom she said were colleagues of her husband.

The detective sat on a silk covered chair, his bulk spilling over the seat. He would have preferred to question her alone, but she was the wife of an important man. Fumbling his teacup, he was loath to ask the key question, and was taken aback when she pre-empted him.

"I knew Friedrich was unfaithful," she said, her face bland and composed. "I've known for years. But you must understand. He was an excellent provider, and in these times, when inflation bleeds the value out of everything, I was grateful."

Hoping his face didn't reveal his surprise, the detective asked about Hesse's work.

"He was a professor at the Chemical Institute. He was experimenting with radioactive elements."

He frowned. "Radioactive elements?"

"Uranium."

His frown deepened. "It is what – this uranium?"

Frau Hesse and the men exchanged glances. "He studied neutrons, protons, and electrons." Frau Hesse said. "Subatomic particles."

He shrugged. He was a police officer. Not an educated man.

Patches of red flared on her cheeks. "They are tiny particles. The elements of all matter. Together they form atoms. My husband theorized that under bombardment by neutrons, an atom of uranium would split in half. Much of his time was spent stripping protons from neutrons in an attempt to verify his hypothesis."

"And did he?"

Again the wife and the men exchanged glances. "He was close," the wife said. She bowed her head.

The detective made another note. "You seem very knowledgeable about his work."

"We met at the University years ago. I am a scientist as well." A tiny shrug fanned her shoulders. "But there was only room for one in the family. I was content to be his wife and the mother of his children. He is – was -- a brilliant man."

He set his teacup down.

Clear blue eyes gazed at him. "Indeed, he *was* a man. With a man's flaws. Yet, he always came home to me. I loved him beyond description. " She looked away, then, and her jaw tightened, as if she were struggling to control her grief.

One of the men laid his arm around her delicate shoulders. "If that is all, Inspektor…"

"Of course." The detective took the names of the colleagues and rose from his chair. "*Auf Weidersehen*," he said with a slight bow.

As he stepped outside, he noted the *mezuzah* on the door frame.

***

Two days later the Inspector stamped his feet, shaking the snow off his boots. The manager of *Der Flammen* led him into the office. A little man with a sparse mustache, the sour smell of fear rose from his skin.

"She's gone," he moaned, wringing his hands. "She was due here an hour ago. I sent a boy around to her apartment near the *Nollendorfplatz*, but she was not there, and all of her things are gone. The show begins in thirty minutes. What shall I do?"

A bevy of women, their cheeks rouged, eyelids darkened with kohl, filed past the open door. "It would seem you have replacements," the detective said.

"*Nein*." The manager threw his hands in the air. "You do not understand. They demand her. If they do not see her, they will hold me responsible. They are not patient men."

"What men are these, Herr manager?"

"You know of whom I speak. They come in their brown shirts and boots. Almost every night, now."

"Were they here the night Hesse was killed?"

"I do not know."

The detective scratched his cheek. "Herr manager, I hear rumors about *Der Flammen*. Many rumors. I am sure you do not want trouble with your license."

"You would not. You could not."

The manager hesitated, then took a step back, seeming to shrivel against the wall. "Yes," he said reluctantly. His face grew pinched. "Yes. They were here that night."

***

It was not difficult to find her. A street urchin in need of a meal, a hundred marks exchanged; it was done. Entering a dark, shabby building, the detective mounted rickety steps. The stench of urine hung in the air. A yellow cat hissed.

On the third floor, a woman answered the door. Her eyes, suspicious and hard, widened when he showed her his badge. She was wearing Ilse's Oriental robe. "Ilse, you have a guest."

Ilse came to the door, dressed in a tattered robe and slippers. Her hair was lank, her face haggard.

He wasted few words. "Fraulein, did you know Professor Hesse was a Jew?"

Ilse looked at the floor.

"I do not hear you."

She looked up, her brown eyes rimmed in dark circles. "Yes, I knew."

"So that is why they killed him."

"Who?"

"The men who have been visiting you at *Der Flammen*. The ones in the brown shirts and boots."

"Why do you wince?" The detective went on. "You did your part. Lured the dirty Jew into a trap. Softened him up with your favors. Made him weak and defenseless. He was no match for them."

"No. You are wrong." Her hands flew to her face.

"How much did they give you to set him up?"

She turned away.

"How much Fraulein?"

She shook her head.

"You are aware that I can make your life most unpleasant. A charge of lewd behavior or accessory to murder will not sit well. Even in Berlin."

"You do not understand, Inspektor. If I tell you, I sign my death warrant."

"And if you do not, you go to jail." He circled a chair, letting the weight of his words sink in. "But you see, Ilse, you have another problem. You see, these men – these Brown Shirts – they will never believe you did not confess. So when you leave jail, as you eventually will, they will find you."

She stared at him, her eyes vacant and dull. "So I am *fickt*. No matter what I do."

He shrugged. She pulled her robe tight and started to pace. He waited. It wasn't long.

"They wanted to know what Friedrich was doing at the University."

"And what did you tell them?"

"The truth. I did not know. We did not talk about his work. We had – other matters to discuss."

He folded his arms.

"They didn't believe me either. They – they forced me to service them. One at a time. Like dogs in heat." She spat on the floor. "They said they would kill me if they found out I lied."

He studied her. Not just a whore. A pathetic, used up whore. "And so they killed him because he was a rich, powerful Jew."

"No. They did not like him, but they did not kill him."

"How do you know?"

Her sad eyes burned with a curious light. "They did not come until the night after he died."

"The night after?" The inspector stiffened. "You are lying, Fraulein. The manager said --"

She snorted. "He will say whatever you want him to."

"Perhaps you are mistaken. The stage lights are harsh and blinding. Perhaps they were there. But you didn't see them. They hid at the back of the theater until he left your room."

Her eyes tracked him up and down. "No. I told you. They came the night after. Demanding to know if he was the Jew who worked at the University."

The detective leaned his hands on the back of the chair.

"Please, Herr Inspektor. I beg you. Do not tell them I told you. They will surely kill me." She covered her face with her hands.

***

Ilse never came back to *Der Flammen*. For weeks the detective sifted through the reports of bodies that washed up from the river, or were found in the alleys, but none matched her description. He went back to the woman Ilse had stayed with, the cabaret manager, even the urchin he found on the street, but no one knew where she was.

He read up on uranium at the library, then, late one afternoon, met with a Berlin physicist. Afterwards, he took a walk. An icy wind slicing through him, he trudged down the *Nollendorfplatz*, ignoring an overture from a young boy with eyes as heavily kohled as a woman's. On the *Kurfürstendamm* he gazed at a church as if its gothic spires might tell him what to do. And on his wintry hike, he thought about the professor, his wife, his colleagues. The Brown Shirts and what they were doing. His own job, his family, his country. By morning he had come to a decision.

He arrested the Brown Shirts and prepared to bring them to trial. Of course, there were heated denials. Even some threats on his life. His case, nonetheless, was solid: he had the manager's story and Ilse's friend's. He also had the casings from the Lugar, which everyone knew was their weapon of choice. He ignored Ilse's claim that they came to *Der*

Flammen the night after. She was a whore; she had fled. Dead or alive, her word would be suspect at best.

By the time it came to trial a year later, though, everything had changed. Hitler was in power, and the Brown Shirts were acquitted. The next day the detective told his wife to pack. They would go to Switzerland or Holland. Perhaps, if they were lucky, New York.

***

A light dusting of snow coated the streets. Hobbling on a cane, the former detective let his grandchildren drag him towards the skating rink. It had opened in 'Thirty-Six, just after they came to New York. Now, twenty years later, it was a family tradition. Every December, he and his wife brought the children, and now the grandchildren, into the city to take in the tree, the glow of lights, the holiday glitter.

The children chattered excitedly, their cheeks red from the cold. They watched the skaters circle the ice, dipping and gliding to the music. His attention was drawn to a tall, graceful girl, whose helmet of bright hair gleamed as she twirled.

Shadows chased the sun away, and dusk settled over the rink. The skaters cut sharp silhouettes against the pale ice. But it wasn't until the lights snapped on that he noticed the group at the next table. A tiny woman wrapped in a fur coat, her hair pulled back in a bun, surrounded by children and two adults.

"*Oma.*" A little girl squealed in delight. "You must taste the chocolate. Like Lindt's, but hot."

"You taste it for me."

Steam rose from the cup. The little girl sipped and smacked her lips. Chocolate rimmed her mouth. The old woman brushed her hand across the girl's hair, her smile revealing a deeply lined face. Then, as if aware she was being watched, she turned toward the detective.

The old man blinked. He knew this small, birdlike woman. The steady gaze. The clear blue eyes that, after a moment's appraisal, deepened in recognition. But how? How did he know her?

"Herr Inspektor." Her voice was serene and pleasant. "How delightful to see you again."

His forehead wrinkled. "Madame, I apologize, but –"

"I am Frau Hesse, Herr Inspektor." She smiled. "Wife of Friedrich Hesse."

Her name burrowed into his memory, and the long ago case sprang into his mind. He rose and slowly made his way to her table.

"It is good to see you on this side of the ocean." Her smile made it seem she'd been expecting him.

"We came from Holland," he said.

She nodded. "I came after the trial. You remember."

Yes. He remembered. He leaned his hand on his cane.   "My one regret was that I did not bring them to justice, Frau Hesse. In failing them, I failed you. And your family."

She looked at him for a long moment. "No. You did everything you could." The thin smile on her face made him frown. This woman had the ability to surprise him, he remembered. Anticipate him. Say the unexpected.

"You see, Herr Inspektor, justice *was* served. The men who were tried, they were not guilty. They did not kill my husband."

He chose his words with care. "Madame, please. Do not spare my feelings. We are both too old for that."

She twisted around to the woman next to her. "Deanna, take the children. I will follow."

The young woman collected the children and walked them to the ice. Frau Hesse tapped the empty chair. The detective sank onto it.

"Do you remember what my husband was working on at the University?"

"Radiation, was it not?"

"Not quite," she said, the teacher correcting a student. "Radioactive elements. Subatomic elements that could be isolated in uranium." Her expression softened. "What neither I nor my colleagues told you was how far his work had taken him."

The detective held up his hand. "No Madame You are mistaken. It could not have been radioactive isotopes your husband was studying – uranium or otherwise. It was simple radiation."

She drew herself up. "Inspektor, do not presume to tell me about our work. I was a physicist too, if you recall."

"Yes, Frau Hesse. I remember all too well. That's why I know it was radiation. Not the other."

She frowned, the sides of her mouth tightening. "Perhaps you should tell me what it is you remember."

He cleared his throat. "What I remember is that your husband was set up by a prostitute in a cabaret. A group of Nazi thugs ambushed and killed him. Unfortunately, incidents like those were all too common back then."

She tapped her spoon against her cup. "But Inspektor, that was only part --"

He rode over her words. "No, Madame. I beg your pardon, but you are wrong. You see, if it were any other way, if it *had* been radioactive uranium your husband and his colleagues were experimenting with, I might have deduced something quite different."

She studied her tea cup.

"You see, if it had been radioactive uranium, I might have suspected they were trying to create nuclear fission."

She jerked her head up.

"Which would mean they would soon be able to build a nuclear bomb."

Her eyebrows arched. "Indeed."

"And then, I might also have suspected that word leaked out, as it always seems to in these matters, and that the Nazis demanded he turn over his work to them. Your husband would have refused, of course, but it would have only been a matter of time. They would have blackmailed him, exposed his "activities", perhaps even tortured him. And not just him. His colleagues. His wife. Perhaps even his children. Your Friedrich would have —"

She cut him off. "We couldn't allow that to happen," she said quietly. "You understand, don't you? In the end, we had no choice. We had to protect the work. Even at the expense of --" She drew in a long, shuddering breath. "It was decided I should bring the work here."

"Where you met with scientists who would later would form the Manhattan Project."

She nodded.

"And you were satisfied to let the Brown Shirts take the blame for his death."

"So we hoped." She shrugged her delicate shoulders. "We didn't know if it would go. It was all very fragile. Indeed, our biggest fear was you, Inspektor."

"Me?"

"We were certain you knew. Or would discover it soon enough. You made us hasten my departure. Later, we were surprised by your silence. We decided you were a friend." She paused. "And so you were." She leaned back in her chair. "But how? How did you figure it out?"

He hesitated. "His mistress confessed that the Brown Shirts came to the cabaret the night *after* he was killed. Not the night of his death. The rest was not difficult."

He stared at the skaters. The tall blonde was now partnered with a dark young man. Arms entwined, they skimmed the surface of the ice, skating in perfect synchrony. "But my dear Frau Hesse, I have a question for you. How – how could you let yourself – and your colleagues – how could you do this terrible thing?"

Swallowing, she stared at her teacup for so long he wondered if she would reply. Then, she looked up and waved a hand towards the children. "There is your answer, Inspector."

He twisted toward the children, his and hers. Their eager young faces sparkling as they followed the skaters. Bright new stars shooting across a cold, dark heaven. He looked back at Frau Hesse. Her eyes filled.

"You see?" Blinking hard, she smiled her tears away. The gentle smile of a friend. "Perhaps you will join me for a Schnapps, Herr Inspektor? It was my husband's favorite."

THE END

JOSEF'S ANGEL

This story begins during World War Two but jumps to Chicago in the 1970's. The plot and characters surprised me; I didn't know it would turn out the way it did. Happily, that's one of the joys of writing crime fiction. JOSEF'S ANGEL was originally published by Amazon Shorts and is online today.

Sunlight glinted off their black leather boots when they marched. Strutting, goose-stepping, even kicking if you happened to be in their path. Josef learned to scuttle to the other side of the compound when they came his way. At the same time, there was something perversely reassuring about the boots. Seeing them meant another night had passed, and he was still alive.

He'd kept his stuffed lamb with him from the day he'd come to this place. Just a dirty, scraggly lump of wool, it was the only thing he'd salvaged from his life before. One morning, though, while veering away from the boots, the lamb dropped in the dirt. He bent down to retrieve it, but the boots had already picked it up. Josef gazed past the polished black leather, the gray uniform, the shiny gold buttons, into a face with cold, measuring eyes.

"*Bitte.*" He held out his arms for his lamb. Please.

The face smiled and held out the lamb. Relief coursed through him. *Woolig* was coming back. Then the boots tossed the toy to a huge, snarling dog straining against its leash. The dog's jaws clamped down on *Woolig*, shook it from side to side, and tore it to pieces. Josef heard the boots laugh.

He was always hungry. Not the kind between breakfast and lunch when Mama gave him a biscuit to take away the empty feeling. Or the kind when he took tea early and ran back outside to play. This hunger scraped his belly so raw that he scrabbled in the dirt, eating roots, nuts, and objects

239

covered with sand just to dull the pain. All the while knowing he'd probably throw it up later.

He needed the hunger. The hunger meant he was still alive. It was only when your stomach started to bloat like some of the other children that you started to die. Listless, dull-eyed, aimlessly wandering the grounds. All of them smelling like pee. Like him, none of them looked up. But they didn't look down either, no longer bothering to scrounge for food. When that happened, Josef knew the boots would soon haul their bodies out of the sheds.

Josef hung on. His mother had promised to come back. Every day he peeked around trees, bent over wooden bunks, willing her to appear. She hadn't come yet, and he was afraid it was his fault. She'd told him not to lose the scrap of paper she stuffed into his coat the night they took her away.

"You'll never be lost," she'd whispered frantically. "It has your name written down. And where you live."

But it must have dropped out of his pocket when they brought him here, and now he couldn't remember his address. He barely remembered his name. He kept waiting until the hot summer day when he was lying behind the shed in a patch of shade. He was nodding off when a small green leaf gently fluttered across his face and settled on his shoulder like a kiss. His eyes grew wet, and his throat squeezed shut. After that, he stopped looking for his mother.

Soon after that, on another afternoon that mocked him with its beauty, Josef was trudging back from the latrine when he felt the hurry in the air. Boots marched crisply; a whine rumbled in the distance. Josef looked up. A long coil of trucks snaked into the camp. A man stomped across the compound. His uniform was gray like the others, but it was festooned with ribbons and badges, and his boots were the shiniest of all. An important man, the guards whispered. Close to the Fuhrer. He held a metal cone in his hand, which made his voice loud when he spoke into it.

Other boots herded everyone toward the gates. Children screamed, guards shouted. The officer lowered his cone and watched. His shoulders sagged, as if issuing the order had sapped all his strength.

Josef gazed at the trucks. The exhaust from their engines made waves in the air. Some of the children were already boarding. The boots were telling them they were going to see their mothers, but Josef knew it was a lie. He didn't have his scrap of paper anymore; how would they know where he lived?

Moving slowly so he wouldn't be noticed, he crept to the back of the crowd. Behind him and a few paces east was a sleeping shed. There were no boots between him and the shed. Slowly, quietly, he backed up and ducked inside.

The sun threw rosy shafts of light on the slab of wood they called a bunk. Josef threw himself underneath and started to count. If he made it to ten, he would be safe. He made it all the way to eight before a shadow fell across the threshold. He stopped counting.

Who was there? He debated whether to peek. Curiosity won, but when he inched his face to the edge of the bunk, he sucked in a breath. The form in the doorway was on fire! Flames shot out around it in a silent frenzy of light. But there were no screams of terror and no cries of pain coming from it. There was no sound at all, except the distant shouts of the boots.

Josef remembered his mother's stories about angels who swept down from heaven, adorned in heavenly light. How they visited Jacob, father of the patriarch for whom he was named. Josef's pulse thundered in his ears. Was this one of those angels?

The form in the doorway raised its arm and beckoned. Josef burrowed back under the bunk. It must be a trick. If it really were an angel, God would tell him what to do.

Then it spoke. "I will help you," the voice whispered. "But there isn't any time. You must run to the fence post on the side of the compound. Now!"

Josef rolled to the edge of the bunk. The angel glittered, blinding him with its flames. It beckoned again.

Afraid to move, afraid not to, Josef squeezed his eyes shut. When he opened them again, the angel was gone. Only the afternoon sun remained, streaming across the floor. He waited for the angel to return, but when he'd counted to ten, and nothing happened, he slithered out from under the bunk.

Trying to keep himself small, he stole to the door of the shed. Most of the children had boarded the trucks. Standing to one side so he was still hidden, he gazed at the fence. The angel said to run over there, but where? The fence circled the camp, no beginning and no end.

As his eyes swept across the yard, something glinted in the dirt beside a fence post. He stared at the object, then at the post. Something about the post was different. He studied it. It was crooked! Josef felt his eyes widen. He looked around for the boots, but they were still at the trucks. He sidestepped to the fence. On the other side of the fence was a wide meadow with tall grass, and beyond that was the forest.

Josef bent down and picked up the object. It was a shiny gold medallion, imprinted with the figure of a man astride a horse. The horse's front legs were curled as if it were leaping over a fence. Over a fence. Under a fence. Was that what he was supposed to do? Josef's fist clenched. He palmed the medallion, and tentatively pressed a hand against the fence post. The post moved.

At the same moment, the trucks revved their engines. Brakes squealed. The air was choked with fumes. The first of the trucks lurched forward. The children's screams rose to an anguished pitch. The sound of beating wings thumped. A flock of startled geese rose out of the meadow. Josef pushed against the fence post. It fell back at an angle, opening a space just wide enough for a small boy to wiggle through. With the fence's sharp edges pricking his skin, he wedged himself through. As he did, his shirt became stuck in the links.

Suddenly a shout went up. "Look. The boy. Stop him!"

Josef heard the stampede of boots, charging, running, closing in. He thrashed and twisted, wrestling the fence to get free. A spit of bullets whizzed by his head. Then, a voice close behind him shouted through the bullets.

"Achtung! What are you doing? Do you want to kill me?"

The bullets stopped. But Josef didn't. He struggled free of the fence to the other side. Staggering to his feet, he plunged into the tall grass and ran as fast as he could. Brambles scraped his skin, insects buzzed his head, but he kept running until he reached the edge of the forest. Only then did he realize the medallion had slipped from his hand.

Thirty Years Later

A blistering wind swirled dust in the vacant lots, and the sun-baked sidewalk scorched the souls of his shoes. Sweat soaked the back of his shirt. A faint babble from a television spilled from an open window: "I began by telling the president 'there's a cancer growing on your presidency.'"

Rabbi Joe carried his bag of groceries past the sanctuary and down the hall to the kitchen. Already, it was twenty degrees cooler inside the synagogue. A gift from *Hashem*. After transferring the bag's contents to the refrigerator, he took out a cold can of pop and rolled it over his forehead.

Beth-El was in Lawndale, a south side Chicago neighborhood that had been ground zero during the riots. Five years later, the wounds were still raw. Stores never reopened, windows remained boarded up, vagrants loitered in abandoned lots.

The *shul* had deteriorated too. To be honest, most of the congregants had deserted years before. The only ones left were the elderly, the sick, and the poor – the ones who had nowhere else to go. But it was his Joe's first pulpit since receiving *smicha*. He wondered if it would be his last.

He was bent over his desk, lost in the *parshah* for the coming week when the outside door slammed. Footsteps slapped down the hall, and a young black boy stuck his head into Joe's office. No older than nine or ten, the boy wore plastic thongs on his feet, shorts, and a shirt so old its red stripes had faded to pink. Edging up to the desk, the boy jabbed the air with his finger.

"You a honky. You de ohpressor."

Rabbi Joe moved his copy of *Rashi* to one side.

"You the devil." The boy went on.

"Nice to see you again, Clarence." The boy showed up regularly, especially now school was out. Always around lunchtime. "Who told you that?"

"My mamma." Clarence's chin rose defiantly.

The rabbi nodded. "What else does she say?"

"That the white man keep the black poor and beggin' so's he won't rise above."

"Your mamma is a Black Muslim, Clarence. Do you know what that is?"

"'Course." The boy glared.

Joe smiled and pushed himself up from his desk. "Good. Then you'll understand what I want to show you."

The boy hesitated.

Joe turned around and smiled. "Come on. It's okay."

They walked down the empty hall, past walls with peeling paint, a rack with frayed *tallit*, a shelf with a few scattered *Siddurim*. The boy seemed to register the shabby surroundings.

"Why you stay here, Rabbi Joe? You ain't got no prayerfuls."

Joe laughed. "Good question, son." Timely, too. Last month he'd been offered a teaching job at the *Yeshivah*, up north in Rogers Park. He hadn't turned it down. Yet.

"I ain't your son. I Abdal Hakim."

"Servant of the wise?"

"How you know?"

Smiling, the rabbi opened the door and they stepped inside. Though the rest of the *shul* was in disrepair, the sanctuary, with freshly painted walls and a gleaming oak *Aron Kodesh*, was airy and light. Near the top of the walls, on all four sides, were three stained glass windows that sent slashes of red, blue, and green light across the room.

Joe led the boy to one of the windows. The figure of a man stood over a slab of stone. A smaller figure bound with ropes lay on the slab. The man had his arms raised, holding a knife that glistened in the light. Clarence stared.

"Each of these windows tells a story, Clarence." The rabbi pointed to the window. "The man in this story is Abraham. He's an important man in my religion. But he's important in yours, too."

The boy squinted.

"You see, Abraham had a son named Isaac."

"'Dat him in the picture?"

"That's him. But Abraham had a second son, too, although he's not in this picture. Can you guess what his name was?"

The boy frowned.

"Ishmael. And Ishmael was the founder of your great religion."

"I know that." The boy pointed to the window. "What the daddy doin' to Izaak? He beatin' him?"

Joe shook his head. "Abraham thought God wanted him to sacrifice his son, and he loved God so much he was willing to do it. That's what you see in the picture. But at the last minute, God told Abraham not to. He saved Isaac. As a matter of fact, God saved Ishmael too. And made sure he grew up to be a famous man."

Joe waited as Clarence gazed at the window, neither of them in any hurry to leave. The windows soothed Joe, relieved his stress, reassured him of God's presence. Even now a sense of calm and well-being sifted through him.

Clarence moved to the next window. Three winged angels were walking down a block of steps. At the bottom of the steps lay the figure of a man. "In this story a man named Jacob, Isaac's son, by the way, had this dream about angels coming down from heaven on a ladder to talk to him." Joe rubbed his chin thoughtfully. "Do you believe in angels, Clarence?"

The boy looked at the window, then gave it his back. "No way, man."

Joe dropped his hand. "Why not?"

"'Cuz 'ifin there be angels, what they be doing 'round here?"

"Angels can go anywhere they want, you know. I've seen one."

Clarence's eyes narrowed.

"I wasn't much older than you," Joe said softly. "In fact, it's because of that angel that I'm alive today."

"Man, that's bogus."

"I'm serious. The angel I saw helped me escape from – well, he saved my life."

"For real?"

Joe nodded. "When I was a little boy, I was a prisoner. With a lot of other children. All the other children were taken away on trucks, but I hid myself away. That's when my angel found me. He spoke to me, like this one did to Jacob." The rabbi gestured towards the window. "He told me to go out and look for a sign. When I finally got the nerve to do it, I found a piece of gold on the ground. Near a fencepost."

Clarence's eyes grew round.

"The gold piece had the imprint of a horse and rider on it," Joe said. "And the horse's legs were up in the air, as if he was jumping. That was the sign, I realized. I was supposed to jump, too. I did, and I got through the fence and ran into the woods. To freedom."

"Dag.. you still holdin' onto that thang?"

"No. I lost it when I ran. But I really didn't need it. Somehow I knew I would make it." He flipped up his palms. "And, you see, I did. The angel did his job."

Clarence cocked his head.

"I think God had a plan for me, Clarence, and he sent that angel to make sure it happened."

"That why you a preacher?"

Joe laughed and guided the boy toward the door. "In a way." They left the sanctuary and went into the kitchen. Two fresh *challahs* lay on the kitchen counter. Clarence eyed the braided loaves. "You hungry?"

Averting his eyes, the boy shook his head.

"That's too bad," Joe said smoothly, "because Mrs. Gershon – you know -- the old lady with the cane around the corner? She brings them to me every week. But I can't eat them."

"You cain't?"

"I – I have this allergy to wheat, you know? But don't tell her. I don't want her to feel bad." Joe shrugged. "You'd be doing me a favor. Otherwise, I'll have to throw them away."

Clarence slipped the loaves under his arm and turned around. As he walked out, Joe noticed he was favoring one foot. The plastic thong on the boy's sandal had come apart from the base.

***

Joe stood on a ladder washing the windows inside the sanctuary, wondering how much time he had left. He couldn't pay the bills last month, and it wasn't going to get any better. It wouldn't be so bad at the *Yeshivah*, he reasoned. Maybe he'd even go to Israel on sabbatical.

When Clarence showed up, the boy was wearing new sneakers, and Joe thought the boy looked a little fuller around the middle. Clarence yanked his thumb at the angel window.

"Does an angel got to be white?"

"I don't think so," Joe said. "Why?"

The boy smiled. "'Cuz I think I done seen one."

"Is that so?" Joe climbed down the ladder.

The boy nodded. "I be pushing my bed over by the window the other night, it bein' hot n' all. I couldn't sleep. So I look-ed out the window and saw some kinda thang bendin' over the steps outside our building. All dressed in black. I couldn't see it good 'cuz it was late and it was real dark. There

247

wasn't no moon, neither. But I seen it lef' something on the steps. And then, well, this thang just wasn't there no more. I sneaked down the stairs – my momma tol' me 'boy, don't you never to open the door to strangers, hear' – but I open it anyways. And there was this big ol' basket of food. And new shoes, too! Just my size."

The rabbi smiled. "Sounds like an angel to me."

"They straight, too." The boy pirouetted in his new shoes, then looked at Joe. "Hey, preacher. You got any more windows to learn me?"

***

As he passed Seidman's pawnshop, something made Joe look up from the weeds poking through the sidewalk cracks. When he saw what was lying in the window, he crept closer. Disbelief sent a chill down his back.

He pulled open the door. The shop bulged with shelves of suitcases and leather goods, jewelry, art. A wizened old man with a bristly mustache leaned his elbows on the counter. He was watching a small black and white TV.

"You believe this?" The man straightened up as Joe came in. "A president secretly tapes his conversations for two years? An enemies' list? What kind of country are we living in?"

Rabbi Joe didn't answer.

"They're saying he had five microphones in his desk and two more in lamps by the fireplace. And that's just one room." The man shook his head. "Well, one thing's for sure. Sooner or later we'll know the truth." He looked Joe up and down. "So. I'm Seidman. What can I do for you?"

"I'd like to see one of those medallions in the window."

Seidman shuffled over and leaned in. "Which one?"

Joe pointed. He thought he saw disapproval in the pawnbroker's eyes as he retrieved it and handed it over. Joe studied the piece. It was dull and brown, and a big splotch of tarnish concealed most of the imprint, but if you looked closely, you could see the legs. A chill edged up his spine. It was the same medallion. He was sure of it.

"You a collector?" Seidman stood in front of him, arms folded.

"No."

"You never know these days. I get people –" He sniffed. "Well, I don't know why they bother. Monsters."

But Joe was back thirty years. A summer day. A piece of gold glinting on the ground. A fiery angel framing the door of the shed. It took a moment for the pawnbroker's words to register. "What did you say?"

"I said, why some people want to collect this *drek* is beyond me. But they tell me there's a market for it. And it's growing." He shrugged. "Like I said, what kind of a country--"

Joe cut him off. "What are you talking about?"

Seidman frowned. "That." He pointed to the medallion in Joe's hand. "Nazi Military memorabilia."

Joe stared at the pawnbroker, then the medallion.

"That there's a horseman's proficiency badge. See the man on the horse? Only Germans of stature got this badge. The elite. High ranking army officers."

"A German Army officer?"

"Maybe SS, but, come on, how many Nazi thugs could ride a horse?" Seidman said scornfully. "No, this belonged to a real German."

Joe clutched the medallion. A long-buried image swam past his eyes. The man with the ribbons and badges. Shouting orders through a metal tube. Retreating across the compound, his shoulders hunched. It was shortly after that Joe had seen his angel. Found the medallion. Heard someone shout, "Achtung. Do you want to kill me?"

He brushed a finger across the medal. The image of his angel had sustained him as he worked his way across Europe. The angel had kept him safe as he crossed the ocean. He'd promised to spend his life honoring the God who gave it to him. He'd become a rabbi because of it.

249

Sure, he might have entertained the notion, during a moment of quiet self-reflection, that his angel was actually a person. A human being. But that didn't make what happened less of a miracle. His *rebbis* had said so: *Hashem* had chosen him. He was proof the Nazis didn't win. That was all that mattered. And Joe believed them.

Now, he raised a weak hand to his temple. The medallion that had saved his life -- his medallion -- belonged to the enemy. Was this some cosmic joke? A dirty trick? Were the past thirty years a mistake? A quirk of fate? Did it all come down to a tarnished sportsman's badge in a pawnshop? A dull ache gathered in the center of his chest.

He was still staring at the medallion when he became aware that Seidman was watching him. Joe looked up. "What did you mean 'this belonged to a real German'?"

Seidman shrugged. "The German army and the Nazis… you're talking two different animals." He fingered his mustache. "Some of them – the soldiers -- were even decent men."

Joe looked out to the street. Two boys with dark skin and wooly hair sassed each other as they trudged past the shop. He watched them turn the corner, jabbing each other's shoulders as they disappeared from view.

A bit of trash, a foil wrapper, perhaps, swirled in their wake, glinting in the sun as it drifted down to the sidewalk. Joe watched it settle, dull and gray. He tipped his head to the side. As he did, a beam of light leapt up from the sidewalk. He canted his head the other way. The light disappeared. Joe realized he could reclaim the light at will just with a shift of his head. He could make the piece of trash shimmer and sparkle or stay flat and dull.

He turned around. Angry, self-righteous voices spilled out from the television. Joe only half-listened. The choice of faith was his. Not his rebbis'. Not Seidman's. Not even the men on television. In the end, it didn't matter who'd been the instrument of his salvation. A German soldier, a Nazi, an angel – it was divine intervention, regardless. He had survived.

Wasn't that the lesson of the windows in the *shul*? The lesson he was trying to teach Clarence?

He pulled out a handkerchief and started to buff the medallion. As he rubbed it with the soft white cloth, the surface of the metal gradually brightened, and the imprint of the horse grew more distinct.

Seidman cleared his throat.

Joe looked up. The man's arms were folded across his chest. "How much?" Joe asked.

Seidman's scowl reached up to his eyebrows. "For that?"

The rabbi nodded.

The man shrugged. "Twenty bucks."

Joe pulled out his wallet.

Five minutes later, Joe made his way down the street, the medallion safely tucked in his pocket. He couldn't remember feeling so light. Even the blistering heat seemed soft. In a world overrun by evil, a man had sought redemption -- by saving the life of a child. The cycle of hate had been broken. That man had been his angel.

Joe grinned. He knew another boy who could use the miracle of the medallion. A boy who might – with the right encouragement – reclaim his hope and faith. He couldn't wait for Clarence to show up at the *shul*. He had something to give him.

THE END

ALSO BY LIBBY FISCHER HELLMANN

THE GEORGIA DAVIS SERIES

Doubleback

Easy Innocence

THE ELLIE FOREMAN SERIES

A Shot to Die For

An Image of Death

A Picture of Guilt

An Eye for Murder

STAND-ALONE THRILLER

Set the Night on Fire

Chicago Blues (Editor)

ABOUT THE AUTHOR

Libby Fischer Hellmann, an award-winning crime
author, has published seven novels. Her most recent, SE
NIGHT ON FIRE, is a stand-alone thriller that goes l
part, to the late Sixties in Chicago. It was short-li
ForeWord Review Magazine as the Best Book of 201(
suspense/thriller category. She also writes two crime
series. The first, which includes the hard-boiled
INNOCENCE (2008) and DOUBLEBACK (2009,)
Chicago PI Georgia Davis. In addition there are four n
the Ellie Foreman series, which Libby describes as
between "Desperate Housewives" and "24." Libby h
edited the acclaimed crime fiction anthology, CH
BLUES. She has been nominated twice for the A
Award, and once for the Agatha. Originally from Was
DC, she has lived in Chicago for 30 years and claims
take her out of there feet first. More at her v
www.libbyhellmann.com

CPSIA information can be obtained at www.ICGtesting.com
Printed in the USA
LVOW081545210612

287115LV00002B/32/P